In Truth, Madness

Imran Khan

Breakthrough Books

Published in Great Britain in 2023 by Breakthrough Books.

www.breakthroughbookcollective.com

Paperback ISBN: 978-1-7393793-3-9

First published in 2018 by Unbound

Cover design and typesetting by Ivy Ngeow.

Praise for In Truth, Madness

"A beautifully written, magical tale of mental health and international news." — Dareen Abughaida, principal anchor for Al Jazeera English

"A Neil Gaiman style spectacular set across the ancient and present day Middle East."— Laury Silvers, author of *The Sufi Mysteries Quartet*

"Imran Khan's *In Truth, Madness* is a fascinating read about how a journalist comes to terms with God in the most surreal of ways, a visit to where civilization began: ancient Babylon." — Holly Dagres, *The Iranist*

"Great book with very interesting and well-developed characters in fascinating situations and places." — Courtney Freer, author of *Rentier Islamism*

"Engaging read for some, at times, heavy content. A layer of fantasy pushes the story forward but also sits over a treatment of how a person deals with being so close to conflict, seeing people in their life die, and a personal struggle with faith." — Kaamil Ahmed, author of *I Feel No Peace*

"Unusual. Intriguing. After I got onto it, I couldn't put it down. Is there an explanation for the constant dystopia that the Mid East displays?" — Barbara Mainville, book critic.

"I really enjoyed this read and found myself being put through a read that I both appreciated for its honesty of the world and its problems and the heart it had in its faith, which rested quite a bit on humanity." — The Caffeinated Reader

"Funny, clever, relatable and deeply moving." — Horia El Hadad, documentary maker.

To Mia and Ava: 'Tis a mad, mad world

Adam's sons are the body's limbs;
They're created from the same clay;
Should one organ be troubled by pain;
Others would suffer severe strain;
Thou careless of people's suffering;
Deserve not the name 'human being'.

– Sa'adi. Born Shiraz, Iran, c.1210

Why can't life live forever?
Life is short like a song and not long,
Why can't life live forever?
As the wind blows a baby is born,
And death is made leaving people to mourn.

– Mia Khan. Aged 9, Qatar, 2006

Some of the more unbelievable stories in this book are true.

Part One

Babylonian Tales of Death, Heaven and Hell

Welcome! Welcome, dear Malek! You are an honoured guest and a welcome visitor to these humble pages.

We are The Order of the Gatherers of Truths. For thousands of years, we have kept a record of the events of our times. On papyrus, clay, print, film, video, and now in gigabytes. Our job, Malek, is to guard the stories of the souls that walk this earth, to keep them safe for the day when judgement will pass. But before judgement can be passed this book shall test you, and ask you to decide who gets to go to heaven and who to the other place. Now, our Order used to be quite secretive, quite secretive indeed. Heaven forbid that a soul should find our books, should find these tales on which so much depends. But an edict from above has changed that. She has decided that humans have spilt far too much blood in not understanding the basic tenets of faith. So, in your hands you hold a book containing some tales. The concept is simple: from the tale you are reading, can you see into a person's soul, and can you decide whether that soul goes to heaven or hell? The tale is a study of character, if you will. What follows are stories of

3

women and men, of love and loss, collected through the ages and from all of the corners of this great earth. Only one common thread links them: the tales come from the places you have trodden, and the people you have met, Malek. So it is not a study of strangers that you shall read within these pages, but of people who, even if they entered it only briefly, left on your life an imprint.

1

Babylon and On

The car jolted and spluttered to a halt. Steam rose from the engine, which was fighting a losing battle with the heat of southern Iraq. In the back seat, Malek Khalil was daydreaming again. Malek daydreamed a lot, but not like other people. He created worlds in his head, and projected his visions onto the tangible world around him.

The tech world has a term for it: augmented reality. In AR, as the hipsters call it, you point your smartphone at something with the camera on, and it adds things like small creatures or information about what it is you are looking at – at the Dome of the Rock in occupied East Jerusalem, say, a piece of software overlays images of the same location from the past and allows you to time-travel backwards through recorded history. But Malek had taken augmented reality in another, altogether more personal direction, and could daydream whole new worlds. In his daydreams time was elastic. What might be a day in his daydream was mere seconds in real life. He didn't need a smartphone: sometimes his

Kindle seemed to be enough of a trigger; at other times, just being in a certain place would do it.

En route to modern-day Babylon he had been reading about the history of ancient Babylon on said Kindle. As he read, he saw the characters leap from the page and begin to talk to each other. He laughed to himself at the fine silk clothes the rich were wearing, and pitied the battered hessian cloth of the poor.

His daydreams didn't require him to be asleep, or even to have his eyes closed. They weren't hallucinations like the visuals he would get from LSD and mushrooms which, along with cocaine and Ecstasy, had made up his staple diet during the Nineties. This was something else. Not a superpower, but not a normal sensory capability either.

He stepped out of the broken car. It would be fixed as they filmed so that didn't concern him; it was the augmented-reality thing he was worried about. After so many years of daydreaming this way, perhaps he should seek some help... perhaps he did have post-traumatic stress disorder. Though Malek couldn't help but think that it was a weak person's problem.

They used to call it shell shock. But soldiers who killed and whose friends died in a ditch next to them had a right to feel after effects. People whose family members had died, whose homes had been destroyed and who lived in misery... *they* had the right to feel after effects. But not journalists who had the ability to leave at will. Malek felt that journalists who suffered from PTSD just needed to get a grip. He took a look at the scene around him. He was in the ancient city of Babylon. In the last year, the Islamic state of Iraq and the Levant had destroyed some of Iraq's oldest and most valuable sites, claiming that they were, wait, what was that phrase they used? Against Islam, that was it.

'Against Islam' was a funny term to Malek. He'd grown up as the oldest son of a Sunni Muslim father and a Shia Muslim mother. He had attended a predominantly Jewish school and had studied Religion in Global Politics at the School of Oriental and African Studies in London. He'd spent fourteen years in the Middle East and South Asia bouncing around from one crisis or war to another. 'Against Islam' was a term he'd first heard in the mosque when he was around eleven years old. Then, Malek had gone to the mosque clutching a toy soldier. The imam had stopped him and asked him what he was holding. Then the imam had taken the tiny green plastic figure from him. It was from a set of Americans storming the beaches of Normandy in 1944 – D-Day. Malek would often recreate the battles in his Finchley home and chase Jerry scum across Europe. The imam first held the toy in his palm and then he held it upright in front of Malek's face.

'These soldiers did a good thing. They fought bravely. They rid this world of a tyrant. Their masters, though, had another plan. Their masters used the tyrant as an excuse to rid the world of an ancient people in an ancient land: their masters used the massacre of the Jews in Europe to destroy the Arabs of Palestine. What did the Arabs have to do with a European war? Nothing. The Arabs didn't create the tyrant, yet they paid for his evil. The Jews took the Arabs' homes and raped their women and killed their children. These soldiers that you play with are tools. These soldiers represent their masters' will and the death of Palestine. Therefore, they are against Islam and should not be toys that you play with.'

Malek never went to the mosque after that. His father,

seeing disappointment in his young boy, didn't push the subject. Instead, he went to Daunt Books in Marylebone High Street and bought a copy of the Koran in English by N. J. Dawood and left it by Malek's bed. His father never said a word to him and Malek never said thank you. The gesture was left unspoken about, as a secret between father and son. Dawood was an Iraqi Jew who had moved to London; Malek was now in Iraq. A coincidence that Malek found touching. Though he never did find a chapter on toy soldiers.

In the years since 1977 and his first, difficult reading of the Koran, so much had happened in and to the Middle East and South Asia. Malek remembered the first time he had heard names like 'Kashmir' and 'Palestine' and how new terms like 'intifada' and 'collateral damage' began to appear in the newspapers that his father left lying around the house. While other children would pore over the comic strips and the sports pages, he would be scouring the foreign section for news from far-off lands with funny-sounding names. Today, Malek helped compose the headlines, write the stories, spread the news that once again blood was being spilt in the name of religion. He would talk of armed groups like ISIL and The Lord's Resistance Army. The genocide of Rohingya Muslims was another topic. He reported the stories of immigrants who had escaped bombs in Iraq and Syria, but also of them getting on wretched boats that often capsized in the Mediterranean with all those on board drowning.

'Against Islam.' Once again the phrase came to his mind as he began to think about how to report the story. ISIL had made it clear that their version of religion was the only version. The imam all those years ago had made it clear that he was right and the toy soldier was wrong. When it came to religion, everyone claimed to be right.

Malek sighed and decided to ignore the dream of the book and the characters that jumped from his screen. He ignored the thoughts of the imam and the Koran, and instead applied himself to feasting on Babylon. The home of the Tower of Babel. Of the Hanging Gardens. Even centuries later it still looked majestic if one looked at it with the right kind of eyes, eyes that saw past the ruins, saw the city come alive with people and markets, smells and noise. Malek's eyes saw it this way. His teachers always said he was easily distracted and a daydreamer. He never disagreed. But now was the time to concentrate and to look for the details that would make it into his report.

His network was Al Jazeera English and the assignment was to report on the measures being taken to protect Iraq's religious sites from the brutality of ISIL. The shoot was straightforward and gave Malek plenty of time to wander around Babylon. Spiders crawled over the adobe-brick city walls as he turned into the main gate. Perhaps the spiders were the only constant inhabitants of this 2,600-year-old city. The road was battered and crumbling in places, but you could still see the routes in, and he could make out the faint sketchings of the aurochs and dragons. The city itself remained largely hidden from view.

Looters, both ancient and modern, had long had their fill. Perhaps, though, the greatest act of vandalism before the Americans arrived in 2003 hadn't been committed by the looters, but by Saddam Hussein himself. The now-dead Iraqi dictator had decided that he was as important as the ancient kings of Babylon, and had ordered a new palace to be built on the hilltop where the old palace had once stood. Hussein had been an impatient man with no time for the slow, methodical process of archaeology. He was frustrated by the bespectacled men and women gently brushing ancient rocks and cataloguing each thing unearthed. It took far too long, and why did everything need a number anyway? Finally, in a fit of dictatorial impetuousness and much to the dismay of historians everywhere, he had razed some ninety per cent of the ancient palace to the ground and built his new one. Malek now found himself here, looking up at it. It was a gaudy monstrosity, so cheaply built legend had it that it was falling to pieces before it was even finished. He climbed up to take a closer look. The palace was a shell now and, inside, graffiti covered the walls. But what really took his breath away was an inscription on some of the bricks. The bricks were supposed to copy the bricks of the old city walls. They were a very poor facsimile. He read the tiny Arabic script: 'In the reign of the victorious Saddam Hussein, the President of the Republic, may God keep him, the guardian of the great Iraq and the renovator of its renaissance and the builder of its great civilization, the rebuilding of the great city of Babylon was done in 1987.'

Malek snorted in disbelief. They couldn't have built a more hideous palace in Las Vegas.

As he walked around the palace he began to daydream, and his brain began to fizz. He blinked. He blinked again. Blinking twice was an uncontrollable reflex action that meant he was about to enter his augmented-reality daydream. He was no longer in modern Babylon.

Now the year was 637BC.

He was a merchant from another place, bringing with him a rare jewel. He had a small leather purse slung over his long robe. The purse was heavy. Wrapped in silk and tucked inside the purse was a ruby of deep fiery red. If you held it to the sun the rays would pierce the ruby and travel through it, come out the other side and open into a thousand shards of pink light that would gloriously illuminate anything in the ruby's path. With this ruby, he would make his fortune.

The markets of Babylon narrowed as the wooden stalls huddled together. Piles of spices from the east gave the street a heady musk as a gentle breeze whisked spice dust into the air. He stopped by a stall. The owner was a generously sized man with a complexion that hinted at more than one night spent in a Babylon tavern. He in turn looked at Malek, and began to size him up: clothes that suggested a trader; fingernails that suggested a labourer; hair, long and unkempt, that suggested a traveller. Maybe he would be good for a piece of unfair trade that would favour the stall owner.

'You're from the south?' he said, more demanding than inquisitive.

The accent wasn't unfamiliar. It wasn't English with an Akkadian accent, but perhaps something more biblical.

Although Malek was immersed in ancient Babylon, he was still aware that he was from the modern world. This was a sort of defence mechanism; it protected him from a full and permanent descent into a different reality and afforded his mind a way back to his own time. He wasn't sure how it worked, but it worked. It did have a funny side effect, however. It meant that everyone spoke a little like Alec Guinness playing Obi-Wan Kenobi. Somewhere in his head, he transposed Obi-Wan onto ancient Babylonians and took the accent for himself also. Curse those countless viewings of *Star Wars* in his childhood.

'Yes,' said Malek.

'Tell me then, O southern one. What of the mines? As rich as they say?'

'More so, and with deep seams that can be mined for a lifetime hence. What knowledge have you of these mines?'

The owner began to rummage through the books on his table. 'Let me introduce myself. I am Zamama. Come sit. I shall find something of interest for you.'

Trees were rare in this part of the world but clay wasn't. The books on his table were clay tablets. While the clay was wet, the author would inscribe his words carefully onto them, without wasting space, and with the flourish of his sharpened reed would transform the clay into a valuable record of the time. Sometimes, one clay tablet would not be enough and so several tablets came to be collected together. The owner pulled out one such volume entitled *The Southern Mines and the Minerals Therein*. He showed it to Malek.

Malek brushed it aside. 'What need have I of knowledge I already possess? Tell me what have you of the otherworld? Of the one discussed in secret and only at night?'

'A learned man of an enquiring nature, I see. Well, allow me to show you this.' The owner pulled out a new collection of tablets but, this time, wrapped in a deep-blue silk envelope and adorned with golden embroidery. A wax oblong on the book sealed the silk. The embroidery read, in a very careful stitch, *Babylonian Tales of Death, Heaven and Hell*. 'I'm afraid this might be a little rich for a southern miner's pockets, but it is one of the books of which you speak.'

'Let me see what my pocket can bear, and what it cannot,' said Malek.

The inscription was clear. The penmanship of the author flawless. The words both clear and concise. Malek had to have this book.

'Tell me, owner of this book. What is this worth to you? I

have Sumerian silver. A fair price for a silly tale told well, I think.'

The owner looked both hurt and insulted. Malek ventured that this look had been well practised.

'You're a stranger in our land and, for that, I will forgive you. Tell me, O southern miner. What price is the key to the mystery and the secrets held within? Some weight of Sumerian silver is not a price. It is a cup of beer.'

Malek laughed. 'Your beer must truly be divine. What if I gave you beauty you could grasp in your hand? That you would clutch with such lust that you yourself would be reluctant to look at it for fear that your own eyes weren't worthy?'

'I have no need for a southern miner's trinkets. Be gone with you. The day is short and the bellies of my children rumble so loud that even at this distance I can hear them. Not to mention my wife, who will not allow me into her room at night without a healthy profit jingling in my purse. Be gone with you. Others are waiting.'

Malek reached into his purse. He unwrapped the silk and held the ruby in his palm in much the same way that the imam would hold the toy soldier centuries later. 'I dare say you've never seen such a trinket?'

The owner gasped. 'The book is yours! Go with the gods! But... be warned. This book has power beyond a southern miner's understanding. Now, leave me. I have a wife to please and children to feed.'

'Malek!'

Startled, Malek turned around. The piercing voice had shocked him out of his daydream. It was coming from Neeka Shirazi, his long-suffering Iranian–American producer who was a veteran not only of several wars but also of several of Malek's breakdowns.

She was a practical woman with a flair for detail and, right now, she was obsessing over getting the perfect shot. Standing next to her was Justin the cameraman. He did have a surname, but it had long been lost to the sands of time and everybody called him Justin the cameraman. They were both huddled around the viewfinder, trying to figure out where to place Malek for his PTC, his 'piece to camera' – that bit in a TV news report when the reporter comes into vision and tells and shows you something relevant. Justin the cameraman was an Aussie fellow from Brisbane with silver hair. He claimed that his hair was blonde; Malek and Neeka said it was white. So they had settled on silver. Justin had a propensity for fixing everything. His cargo pants were more of a toolbox than an item of clothing.

'Let's put Malek over there and I'll pan down. It will look pretty sweet.' Years abroad had done nothing to diminish his Aussie accent. Neeka murmured in agreement and looked around for Malek. He was still rooted to the same spot, staring into the distance. *Ay baba*, what is he doing? She spoke three languages fluently – French, English and Farsi. But what she really spoke on a day-to-day basis was English with some Farsi thrown in. It was a by-product of her upbringing. Practically, it meant she peppered her faintly accented international school English with a few words of her native Farsi. Words, as it turned out, that often tended to be loving insults directed at Malek. 'Malek!' she called, this time in a tone often used by exasperated teachers. For a petite woman of forty she had a ferocious voice, especially when shouting. She also had the ability to reduce battle-hardened commanders to tears with her razor-sharp and sometimes patronising manner.

Between them, Neeka, Justin and Malek had shared

more meals and hotels in more countries than any of them wanted to admit. Neeka was the perfect foil to Malek's daydreaming and to Justin's practicality.

'Yeah, I'm coming. Christ, Neeka, don't shout. You'll wake the dead.'

Neeka rolled her eyes. '*Na Digeh*! You know, everyone else gets talented people to work with and I get you two idiots.'

Justin lined up the shot as Malek took his mark, his position to deliver his words direct to camera.

Alongside his practical, no-nonsense attitude and his technical skill, Justin had a poetic vision that meant he could insert whimsy or sepia tones in a way that was unmatched by anyone else that Malek had worked with. When the camera rose to Justin's eye something chemical happened: his mind would be bonded to the technology, with his eye the intermediary. He would find details in pictures that no one else could see. A look here, a shadow there, would make the pictures he shot so much more... well... more.

Meanwhile, Neeka had a forensic approach to news gathering. This meant that she was never very far away from academic reports, and she had a knack for calling people out for their hypocrisy. She would often revel in her ability to catch people in a lie, something that drove Malek mad. TV news suited her, with its mix of practical and creative. 'So you're ready, right? What are you going to say?'

'Well, Neeka. I thought I would wax lyrical about your handbag.'

'Malek. It's hot, and we need to get back to Baghdad. Be serious.'

Malek got his brain into gear. He had three points he wanted to make, each separate yet connected. Compartmentalised. He looked straight to camera and began to speak, the three points rolling off his tongue calmly and effortlessly.

'So you can actually report.' Sarcasm had now replaced her annoyed tone.

Neeka was quite something, thought Malek. She often described him as '*Omran*', meaning life force. It was a term that Malek took as a compliment although, deep down, he knew it probably wasn't. 'You feign disgust at me, Neeka, but I know you laugh inside.' And laugh she did. Malek liked making her laugh.

Malek allowed himself a smile. Without her he would be nothing, just another washed-up hack scrapping for airtime with younger, prettier people willing to call themselves foreign correspondents because they were in possession of a smartphone, an internet connection and a flight ticket.

They bundled themselves into the 4×4 and, once again, this odd family were on the road. As with any family that spends lengths of time in each other's company in the confined space of a car, the bickering stopped and the conversation died down as they drove back to Baghdad. Then Malek watched Neeka dump her handbag's entire contents on the floor in looking for her sunglasses. It always annoyed him that she wasn't more careful with her things.

'You know your stuff would last longer if you just looked after it a little better.'

Neeka threw him a cynical look. 'If *you* were easier to look after then perhaps I might have time to look after my things.'

Malek smiled and dug into his very organised rucksack and found his Kindle. It was easy; everything was in its own compartment and in a different-textured case, so he could pull it out by feel alone. Time to catch up on some reading.

As the Kindle flickered into life he noticed a book downloading. This struck him as odd. He was without an internet connection and couldn't actually remember buying a book recently. It finished downloading. The title page surprised him. *Babylonian Tales of Death, Heaven and Hell.* In the corner, there was a small stamp that looked like a wax seal. It said 'Babylon'.

The first sentence of the text began with the words: 'Welcome! Welcome, dear Malek! You are an honoured guest and a welcome visitor to these humble pages.'

2

Revelation

Malek was stunned. He looked around the car. The driver chewed gum loudly, which was the only sound as everyone else was slumped, sunglasses on and sleeping. He stared at the Kindle.

This has got to be a mistake, he thought. This wasn't his usual augmented-reality daydreaming. He normally needed some sort of stimulus, a stimulus that he remembered seeking out. This was something different. Never before had a book just appeared on his Kindle.

Maybe he had downloaded this book and then just daydreamed the rest? He scrolled through the book looking for a publisher, a date of publication, an author. Anything that might reveal a clue. Nothing. After the introduction, there was an ellipsis blinking, one dot after the other. He reread the introduction, this time slowly and deliberately, looking for something. If this was a book of tales designed to facilitate passage into heaven, or not, as the case may be, then all he had to do was read. That's why his father had placed the Koran on his table all those years ago.

His mind switched gear into race mode. All he needed to do was read. No. What the fuck am I doing? This way madness lies.

Malek was filled with self-doubt and confusion. Was he supposed to believe this nonsense? That these tales held the key to heaven? He remembered the Koran by his bedside, and the unspoken reason why it had been given to him in the first place. 'All I have to do is read,' he silently mouthed to himself.

As he stared at the ellipsis, more text revealed itself.

The General's Decay

SOMEHOW, *the sun always ruined the drama of any day. You cannot declare war and then feel those warming rays on your face without feeling good. War was not about feeling good. The sun was. It was this thought that consumed General Akhtar Waleed on this day. In his sixties now, he had just retired from the Pakistan Armed Forces, his career brutal as it was glittering, ugly as it was powerful. He had entered the Pakistan military head–first through the front door. This was not legend but the truth. Aged sixteen, he had wandered up to the actual front door of Kakul military academy in Abbotabad and brazenly declared to the startled guard that one day he would lead Pakistan to great victory. It was sunny that day as well. The sun had ruined the drama of his speech, words he'd rehearsed for hours on end, and for days and weeks. It then took him two years to get into the military academy. It wouldn't have taken that long, but Kakul had a minimum entry age of eighteen and he was two years under age at the time of the grand speech. Once in, he was determined to make* it. If it was higher he would climb harder, if it was lower he would dig deeper. His fellow cadets hated him. For his charm and handsome good looks. At least this is what he told himself. Perhaps better not to admit that his selfish and single-minded attitude was the real reason. From Kakul he found himself on the front lines of the India–Pakistan fight. 1965 in Lahore, beating the Indians. Now that was a war. But the sun ruined that day as well. Rain was better for fighting: the First World War had been fought in the trenches, the Second in dark European forests. No matter. He had fought well, and rose in the ranks. He saw Pakistan split, India rise, America replace Great Britain as the new colonial power. In his mind, he was still that young eighteen–year–old. In the mirror, he was not. His hair, once authoritative with a hint of rogue, had now disappeared into what could only be called hair heaven, as it certainly no longer stood atop his head. His stomach protruded far from his chest, and those aches and pains he felt were no longer stories told by old war wounds, but rather stories told by the onset of age. Today, however, was not about decay but about deliverance. Waleed was about to receive the highest national honour from the president. The Sitara-e-Imtiaz: the star of excellence. No matter that the sun shone, the drama of the day would break through. He would have his dignified day lit not by Pakistan, but by British grey, even if it was only in his head. He took one last look in the mirror. The uniform was a little snug, the gold braid less gold and more straw coloured. The effect was still the same. Grandeur and class. The uniform commanded respect and respect garnered power. That was what he was. Grand and powerful. He stepped out into his Rawalpindi garden. It was darker than usual. The dark clouds made him smile; perhaps the day would have drama after all.

. . .

MALEK PUT the Kindle away and the car pulled into the secure compound in downtown Baghdad. What had he just read? It was familiar, but how had his daydreaming got him a book that now existed on his Kindle? Malek worried that he could have finally gone too far in his daydreaming this time. Neeka always said he might find himself trapped in a daydream. Maybe this was it. A permanent daydream.

3

Reign of Confusion

Malek had arrived at his office-home in Baghdad more than a little perturbed. He wracked his brain, trying to find a word that described his state. Discombobulated? Disturbed? Freaked the fuck out? Yes, that was it. It wasn't one word, it was that sentence. He wondered if he should speak to Neeka about it. Was that a good idea? She already thought he was flaky and prone to daydreams. But the book was on his Kindle. There was proof. Proof of what, though? Malek poured himself a large glass of wine. Some might have suggested it was a problem-sized glass of wine. But he thought of his ability to drink copious amounts of booze as more of a gift than a problem.

He put his headphones on and flicked his iPod to Joy Division. The blistering, abrasive pop of the Manchester band had a soothing effect on his agitated brain. As Ian Curtis began to sing, Malek closed his eyes and listened intently whilst taking ever-quickening sips from the glass. 'Isolation', with its lyrics of disappointment and shame, always made sense. This was what he felt now. Disappointment and shame. Once again, he'd let his imagination get the better of him. Curse this 'augmented reality'!

What to make of this book? These stories that decide whether someone gets to heaven? He turned up the music, hoping to drown his own thoughts out. It didn't work.

He knew that general in Pakistan. At least, he knew he'd met him once. He wasn't a pleasant man. Dutiful? Yes. Patriotic? Misguidedly so, in all honesty. Pakistani generals have a sense of duty beyond that of other Pakistanis. Having control of nuclear weapons does that to you. Perhaps it was time to tell Neeka something. But what would she say? Something in Farsi, no doubt. *'Nakhon!'* was her normal response to Malek's idiosyncrasies.

In Baghdad, religion was all around. Mosques and churches stood as they had for centuries, although this time behind huge concrete blast walls built to protect them from the bombs that plagued the city now almost daily. Here he was in a place shaped by faith and where prayer was as common as the tea stalls people hung around. It reminded him that he was an atheist. But was he an atheist? He was an atheist who argued with God as much as he denied his existence. God had always been a problem. How can you not believe in a God you argue with? How do you not argue as you watch another wretched soul being pulled from the rubble of a car bomb, driven by a believer who thought God would reward him for his murder? Then he thought of the book, the book that he must have encountered when he was daydreaming, the book that now existed on his Kindle.

Malek slumped back into his chair, a little dizzy from the wine. A beep on his phone broke his stupor. It was an alert from a Pakistani local news channel.

General Akhtar Waleed had been killed in a suicide

bombing in the garrison town of Rawalpindi; in Islamic tradition a body should be buried as soon as possible after death and so his funeral had already taken place. Malek felt a cold shudder at this coincidence. Then, work mode kicked in. There was no time for any kind of shock at this death. Reporting was the priority, and getting the facts together. Malek called his contact in Rawalpindi at the Inter Services Public Relations Department. The Pakistani Army ran a very slick PR office that was expert in glorifying all aspects of its operations. A martyred general was right up its alley. They issued Malek with a quick statement painting the general as a true patriot and a man of God. Malek wrote down the words quickly. This was all second nature to him. Breaking news has a rhythm of its own. You confirm, you write the initial email to the news desk in Doha. 'The desk', as it is more commonly known, is the central hub of any news organisation and gathers information from all its reporters and producers across the globe, and then decides what goes into the news bulletins. For those in breaking news situations it was important to be two things: to be quick and to be accurate.

All this had the effect of allowing Malek to forget what he had just read on his Kindle. He picked up the phone and called the desk.

'So you got that, right? I don't need to repeat it?' said Malek to Natalie, the desk editor.

'Yup, stand by. We just need to see if we can get you to Islamabad now. Imtiaz Tyab might be closer though. But we just cannot raise him. We think he is in Lahore.'

Malek instinctively looked at his rucksack. He could be packed and out the door in ten minutes, at Baghdad airport within an hour and wheels-down in Islamabad in time for the memorial in the morning, if the flights worked out.

'Malek, stand down. We found Imtiaz. He is on it.'

'OK. *Mashi, yalla bye,*' said Malek. After years in the Middle East, some Arabic often made it into his everyday speech.

Within moments of that short phone call Malek could have been heading out to the airport. This time he wasn't. Never mind. He would live to fight another day.

He stared down at his Kindle. It burst into life, without any help from Malek. He recoiled in fear and stood up quickly, sending his wheeled chair skidding backwards.

'What the fuck!'

The Kindle displayed the words 'The time has come. Shall we talk?'

'What?' said Malek. His eyes blinked twice.

'You have a decision to make. Shall we talk?'

OK. The Kindle is now talking out loud. Talking. Out. Loud. 'You don't believe I can talk? I am not the Kindle. I am guessing you have a few questions?'

The voice had a British accent. Female. Neeka loved using Siri on her phone and would often ask her random things about the meaning of life or cupcake recipes, which might be one and the same thing.

Malek stared intently at the Kindle for a few moments. 'Kindles don't have Siri,' he eventually said.

'Oh, I am not Siri. My name is Rubati. You can call me Rubati. I am your book guide, here to help you decide.'

'Decide what? And my Kindle doesn't have a speaker so how are you even speaking?'

He rubbed his hands down his face, slowly, dragging his eyelids downwards until it felt like his face was melting.

'You poor boy. You're a little confused, aren't you?'

'I'm talking to a hundred-dollar piece of plastic. How would you feel?'

'I am not plastic, thank you very much. It's just that you can't see me. In fact, I am far from plastic. Currently, I am at home sat on my sofa with a cup of tea, and I am very real. I need a haircut though... You might want to grab a cuppa as well.'

Malek grabbed the wine and poured even more liberally than usual. 'That's not tea.'

The wine was close to his lips, his teeth almost touching the rim of the glass as he spoke into it. 'Rubati? Where is that from?'

'Babylonian. I'm from the city.'

'If you're Babylonian, why do you have a British accent?'

'You're Pakistani. Why do you have a British accent?'

'Because I'm a British Pakistani. We do have those, you know.'

'Don't get testy with me, Mr Khalil. I'm a big deal in Babylon, don't *you* know.'

Malek took a swig of the wine and continued to stare at the Kindle. 'Neeka constantly tells me I am ridiculous. OK, fine. But what is a British-sounding Babylonian girl doing in a book from ancient Babylon? If that is what this is.'

'Fucking with your head, mainly. How am I doing?'

'Oh, that's happening.'

'Well, my darling boy, The Order is spread far and wide, and we are a very diverse bunch. Right now I am a Babylonian woman, but over the years I have been many things to you, in many different guises. My job is simple. I am to take you on a journey through the people you have met. You decide who gets to go to heaven and hell depending on the story you read. Well, you don't really decide. Only God gets that privilege, but you might learn a thing or two about a thing or two. Particularly about yourself.'

'But – but – I am an atheist,' he spluttered.

'For an atheist, you spend a lot of time arguing with and cursing God. Now, with the amount you have drunk, I am guessing you could go along with me for a little while?'

'Erm... I mean... OK. So why do I get the Babylonian girl in the Kindle? Am I special? Cursed? Dreaming?'

'I don't know. In fact, I do know. You're not dreaming. Are you going to go along with me? The general died. Tragic. Mainly for him. So, what do we think? Heaven or hell?'

Malek had forgotten, or perhaps he didn't really want to believe what he had read on his Kindle less than an hour ago. Rubati's question brought it all back. That perhaps what he had read was forewarning him of the general's death. And of a new and strange role for him. He tried to underplay his fear. 'You can't turn heaven and hell into a game show.'

'Why not? Besides, this isn't a game show. It's a challenge you can understand, given that you humans are so feeble of mind. Tell me what you have decided. And why.'

'Based on that story? I have no clue. I might as well roll a dice. Hell. He is a soldier after all. He killed in a war. What does the Koran say? "To take one life is to take the whole of humanity." But then it also says, "Be kind to your enemies in the time of war." Maybe he was kind. Maybe he was gracious to his enemies.'

'Hell it is then. See, that wasn't so difficult, was it?'

'No, wait. I was just thinking out loud. Wait!'

The Kindle switched itself off, but not before flashing up a message. 'Be careful what you say. You only get one roll of the dice, as it were. Speak soon, my dear Malek. Rubati.'

Malek finally sat down. What the fuck? What the fuck seemed to be the only constant right about now.

There was a prayer he could recite. One his mother had taught him. It helped in giving clarity of thought. He might try that. He glanced at the bottle of wine. It was empty. Probably not a good idea to pray whilst drunk. There was something in the Koran about that. Besides, what was he thinking? Atheists don't pray. He picked up his Kindle, placed it in his rucksack and trudged to his room. The wine had worked. Sleep beckoned. At least wine always worked.

Had he really just condemned a man to hell?

4

Intimate Strangers

The phone rang and the day began for Malek. He was still in bed. He thought about ignoring it. The wine buzz had gone, leaving behind a waterlogged tennis ball of a hangover. His brain was squidgy. The phone kept ringing. He answered it and, using the bare minimum of words for acknowledgement, and then only at the required times, he listened as Lucas on the desk asked him to mark the anniversary of the Mutanabbi Street bombings. He finished by saying, 'Before I forget, Rima the guest-booker wants suggestions for live interviews. Can you send her some?'

'Will try. And I'll try and deliver for 1300GMT. Cool?'

'Cool.'

Malek looked at his watch. TV news operates on GMT. That way, you had a standard time for everybody all over the world. It also meant that you looked at your watch a lot, trying to figure out what the local time was in relation to GMT. With a hangover, it was hard. Al-Mutanabbi was a tenth-century poet whose work was still recited across the Arab world. He had been killed in AD965 by someone who felt that a few lines of his latest poem caused offence. He was certainly a bombastic poet who wrote about the kings and leaders he met. They showered him with money and in return he showered them with words. The street named after him had endured, and was the literary heart and soul of Baghdad. Then, over a thousand years later, on 5 March 2007, a massive car bomb destroyed the entire area, killing thirty people and injuring dozens. The street was crammed full of booksellers and small publishers. The famous Shahbandar café had stood for generations as a meeting point for writers and artists. The café owner and his sons were among the dead. This assignment was perfect for Malek. He loved the street and the booksellers.

Neeka and Justin were already awake. They looked well rested. He didn't. Coffee was drunk, possibly by the gallon. Cars and security were organised. Two 4×4 off-roaders, soft skin, not armoured. Soft skin just meant normal vehicles. Some news crews travelled in armoured cars. Al Jazeera had opted for low-profile-looking vehicles. Joining Malek and the crew would be a driver in each car and a close protection guard. Baghdad was dangerous, with car bombs and kidnapping at higher than normal levels since ISIL had taken nearly forty per cent of Iraqi territory twelve months ago. Osama, the Baghdad producer, was also coming along. He set out the day's plan. They left their private fortified compound, exited the checkpoint and got on the road. It was about fifty minutes in Baghdad traffic to reach their destination.

They entered Mutanabbi Street from the north. The street was on top form today, noisier and busier than ever, and it made for a great piece of television. There was defiance from the booksellers, the intellectuals and poets. The threat from ISIL was dismissed out of hand and everyone they interviewed told them that the mere act of shopping in this street was an act of civic pride in Baghdad. They went to interview Safa, a bookstore owner who was a local character on the street. Like other times, a bottle of whisky was produced after the interview.

Justin held his glass aloft. 'What's Arabic for "Cheers", Safa?'

'In Arabic we say "Sorry, God."'

There is a famous saying that refers to this street: 'Cairo writes, Damascus prints, Baghdad reads.' Safa said that it meant Baghdad was the centre of learning. Malek wrote it down. That phrase would finish his television report.

They finished their whisky and prepared to leave.

'When I die, Neeka, these books and my heart are yours,' said Safa, with a glint in his eye and a toothy smile.

'You're never going to die Safa, you'll be here as long as the books are.'

Safa coughed, and coughed violently. 'Oof, the whisky is taking a toll. Take my heart, Neeka, before it's too late. Will you be my *Hayeti*?'

'What about your wife and children?'

'Neeka *Habibti*, when you are around there are no wife and children.'

'*Safajoonam*, my heart belongs to work. You know this.' Hugs were exchanged, and goodbyes said.

'Today was a good day,' said Malek as they left the shop.

'Yep. Absolutely bloody sensational, mate,' said Justin.

They walked back to the car, past the Al-Mutanabbi statue, down the length of the street and past the ransacked Ottoman-era buildings which, despite being ruined, still had a charm of their own.

Neeka lifted up her stills camera to her eye, and took

pictures. No smart-alec comments, no haranguing Malek. She was happy.

After a few hours' editing, the news-report video was sent to Doha, by way of a web uplink, and the day was done.

Back at the house, Malek took out his Kindle. Once again, without any prompting, it burst into life.

'Hi Malek, shall we read a little more?'

Malek felt his brain begin to fizz and he blinked twice. 'OK, Rubati.'

As Old as Words

SAFA PUTS down the mottled whisky glass and looks around his shop. The electricity is off again. No matter. The day is going to be hot and the fan doesn't work anyway, so electricity would prove useless with regard to keeping cool. In a dark corner, he hears a rustling sound. A much younger Safa would have picked up a shoe and, with expert precision, knocked the mouse out. Safa in his older years accepts the mouse not as evil but as a stranger worthy of lack of interest. Let him chew through the books, he thinks. He'll die of poisoning, or I'll die of a heart attack trying to kill him. Safa opens the doors of the shop to let some light in. His family have owned a bookshop on this street for some 100 years.

He's witnessed Saddam ban writers and artists; he's witnessed the Americans shoot their guns and has seen the bullets tear the books into little pieces that would float up into the air like snowflakes. He's witnessed a car bomb rip through the street and can still remember his ears ringing and his body covered in black dust. He can still feel the way he trembled in the very pit of his stomach as he stumbled out of his shop that *day. Yes, he thinks. I've seen enough. Let the little mouse live. What harm could come of it? Safa feels old in this shop. He is feeling his years. Occasionally he would pull out a book younger than he was and pretend to be young. It never worked. He pulls out a book older than he is. They say words don't age. What nonsense. Words age. Pages go brown. Books begin to smell. Not unlike Safa, the books he reads have seen better days. But within the books lies the magic of meaning. His flesh may be weak, the covers of the books may be frayed, but his soul and the words are still alive, fading perhaps, but still there. The tiny volume he picks from the shelf and puts firmly into his hand was printed on this street in 1916. His grandfather, then as old as he is now, had printed and bound the book himself. It is a collection of poems by the man this street was named after. Abu Tayyib al Mutanabbi. An Abbasid poet born in the year 915. This book is all that is left of what was once a booming Baghdad enterprise. As a child, Safa had run up and down this street as the booksellers sat talking and debating something or other. He could hear the metallic noise of the printing presses as the printers cranked them by hand. He had seen his grandfather bind the books, also by hand. Stack them by hand, sell them by hand. And now, in his own hand, all that labour was distilled into this book, one of a few left in his shop.*

He whispers the words of the poem at first. 'A young soul... A young soul in my aging body plays, though time's sharp blades my weary visage raze... ' With each word, he gets louder. With each word, he sees his grandfather holding court, as the audience sits enraptured, listening to the very same poem on the very same street. Mutanabbi Street. Safa doesn't have an audience. He doesn't need one. His grandfather's spirit is alive: from the book, it comes and into his bones it goes. Alone in his shop, Safa continues, preaching now, not reciting. '... Hard biter in a toothless mouth is she, the will may wane, but she a winner stays.' By the end of that last sentence Safa is up on his feet, singing the words, his arms waving as though he is writing the poem in the air. Safa feels alive, he feels invincible. Up until when he doesn't...

'Wallahi!'

The mouse runs over his foot, and a startled Safa backs into a bookshelf. He is now sitting on the floor, surrounded by the books that have tumbled upon his head. These books, he thinks. They'll be the death of me.

'And what have we decided, Malek?'

Malek dropped the Kindle on the floor, '*Panchod*, motherfuck...' Cursing in Urdu was something he only did in times of stress.

'Hey. Be careful!'

He picked up the Kindle and dusted it off.

'Thanks. Try not to break the Kindle, eh?'

'I can't do this, Rubati. I'm too tired and you are in a Kindle and therefore don't exist. I am actually daydreaming you right now. The general I could deal with; I had only met him once. I thought about it. He was not mine to judge. I am an atheist, therefore I don't believe in heaven or hell, so why do I care where he goes?'

'You believe. You just won't admit it.'

'What the fuck does that even mean? You talk in fortune-cookie riddles. I have half a mind never to charge this Kindle again and be done with you.'

'Malek. You don't get rid of me that easily. Poor Safa. After you guys left he had a headache. The headache got worse and worse. It was around 11pm he died at home, surrounded by his family.'

'What?'

'They call it a thunderclap headache. I'm not sure of the technical details, but it involves blood leaking into the brain from a burst vessel.'

'Oh man. Really? I am not sure I believe you.' Anger underpinned his tone. 'If Safa is dead, and I go along with you, then he was a good man. He gives me whisky and I buy books. He's the kind of man who questions the very nature of humanity, and discusses our failings, while all the while praising God and asking him to show us the right path. We had whisky with him today.'

'Her. God is a woman.'

'God doesn't exist.'

'You mean that God you argue with and blame for all the world's ills? That God doesn't exist? You really are a confused boy. What have you decided?'

'Why is God a woman?'

'She is to you. To others she is something else entirely, to others again, she is a he. It depends on the person.'

'Why do I get a woman?'

'I don't know. Revenge, because you have been a dick to women most of your adult life?'

'I haven't, and that's not funny.'

'I know. God is a woman to you because she just is. She works in mysterious ways, what can I tell you?'

'You are really beginning to piss me off. If Safa has passed then I have no doubt he will enter heaven, if such a thing exists. There's no debate there but, since I had whisky with him a little over three hours ago, I doubt whether he is dead.'

'He is dead. Thunderclap headache. You're getting the hang of this. But why the passive-aggressive attitude?'

'Because I am talking to a piece of plastic.'

'I'm not plastic. Oh, honey, if only you could see me. I'm all natural. Besides, people talk to Siri all the time. No one thinks that's weird.'

'That's different. She just reads the internet. We are talking. In fact, we are negotiating lives. Why me, Rubati? Why give me this book?'

'Shits and giggles probably. How about you just happened to be next in line? I honestly don't know. I was just assigned to you. I don't ask why. I just do. Have you told Neeka yet?'

'No.'

'You should. She is cute. You two have never...?'

'No. We have never. So, that's not a thing.'

'Well. You have a talk ahead of you with Neeka and Justin. Safa passed away at home. Pay your respects and remember you produced a report worthy of his life. You marked the day when blood and ink flowed in the street, when books and flesh both burned, and you marked the street coming back to life despite the violence.'

He felt ill. Dizzy.

Justin and Neeka were sitting in the kitchen. Malek told them the news. For a moment there was silence.

Justin spoke first. 'Let's pour a little liquor, mate. That's what Safa would have wanted. A thunderclap headache eh? Sounds like the title of one of the books he might have sold.'

Whisky was poured, Safa's tipple. Four glasses. Three for them, one for Safa that remained untouched. Neeka raised her glass and the others followed.

'To Safa, a Baghdad legend.'

'To Safa,' the boys said in unison. 'How did you find out he died, Malek?'

That wasn't a question he was expecting. 'Er, I got a phone call from his niece.'

'Please don't tell me you are trying to shag his niece.'

'No, Neeka. Who do you think I am?'

'I think you are Malek is who I think you are.'

The bottle emptied and the three of them talked into the night.

Malek proposed another toast. 'In this job, we meet strangers who share their lives with us for a brief moment, who let us interview them and, in that moment, in front of our camera, they sometimes tell us more than they tell their friends. For the length of that interview, we are intimate strangers. Safa was one such man. For that we salute him.'

Safa's glass was still untouched as they called it a night.

IT WAS 2am by the time Malek got into his room. The Kindle remained where he had left it.

'Nice tribute, Malek. Oh, by the way, that augmented-reality thing you do? Where do you think you got that from? She has more gifts where that came from, if you believe in and love her.'

'Yes, yes, Rubati, non-existent God is a woman. Got you.'

I need pills and water, he thought, as he rummaged around in his rucksack. The medpack was small and red. He found it easily. Compartmentalise.

But where would he put Rubati?

She was placed in the outside zip pocket of his rucksack, a little more carefully than usual. He took a huge swig of water and swallowed two pills and lay down on his bed.

5

'A Bomb in Kabul'

The wire dropped in the morning. It stated that a bomb had gone off near the Presidential Palace in Kabul. The desk called them minutes later. Flight details were issued. Baghdad–Doha–Kabul.

As usual, it was a scramble to get to the airport in time for the flight, but it worked out. The layover was short and, three-and-a-half hours later, they entered the airspace over Kabul. It was late afternoon and they headed straight to the scene. It had been sealed off but the damage was clear. Qais, an Afghan reporter and producer who knew Afghanistan like no other journalist, greeted them quickly and solemnly. Neeka made phone calls as Justin rigged up the Bgan, the portable satellite, then gave Malek his earpiece and hooked the tiny mic to his chest. The earpiece connected him to the studio in Doha. MCR – the Machine Control Room – then took over. MCR, despite the dystopian-sounding name, is the technical guys who are far from dystopian machines. They checked the shot and cleared him to the gallery, a darkened room that was the control centre for the television broadcast. Dozens of TV screens and monitors showed incoming visual feeds from all over the world. Correspondents stood in place waiting their turn: Malek was on one screen, Stefanie Dekker and Hoda Abdel-Hamid on two others. It was an impressive sight, this gallery of screens.

The sound guys came up next and asked him for a few words so that they could check the sound levels. All good. He was in the hands of the gallery now.

Show director Renee spoke to Malek. 'Three minutes to you. The presenter is Dareen Abughaida. You good to go?'

'Yep.'

The earpiece pumped through the sound of the show. Malek stared into the camera. He loved live broadcasting from location.

Dareen asked her question. Malek answered and stepped aside so that the camera could zoom in on the destruction. Justin knew exactly which details to focus in on. He moved from the pools of dried blood to the wrecked cars and back to Malek. As the camera panned back, Malek finished his sentence.

'...the Taliban have claimed responsibility, once again proving that they are still a force to be reckoned with, despite a war that has cost the coalition billions of dollars and has lasted fourteen years.'

They derigged and looked round at the blast site.

It was then that they noticed an elderly woman covered in a fine layer of dust tucked away in a corner, her arms to her chest and rocking back and forth.

Neeka took out her notebook as Malek braced himself to interview the woman. But first, Qais approached her to ask whether it was OK to ask a question. She said yes. Malek pointed the mic towards the woman. Justin pointed the camera. Qais looked at the woman.

'Can you tell us what happened?' said Malek. Qais translated the question into Pashtu.

'I didn't hear it, I felt it.'

Malek gripped the mic a little tighter. The woman cried. Neeka and Qais stood still.

'My brother brought the clothes back. There is no body to bury. Arzoo has disappeared.'

The interview was broadcast during that night's news bulletin. After dinner, Malek and Neeka sat in the grounds of the Gandamack lodge where they were holed up for their stay. Malek looked up at the skies. The stars shone brighter in Afghanistan than in any place else he had ever been. There seemed to be millions of them. He decided that now was the time to bring up the book.

'There is something I have to tell you.'

'I have known for years, Malek. It's OK. Coming out aged forty-five is no big deal.'

'Be serious.'

He didn't begin at the beginning. He missed out the part about the Babylon bookstore owner. He left out the part about the clay tablets. In fact, all he really told her was that the book was talking to him, and that it was about dead people and entering hell. Or heaven.

'You mean with the seventy doe-eyed virgins and milk and honey and la la la?' Neeka's right hand oscillated wildly as she spoke.

'The book is supposed to be character studies. Based on each study, I'm supposed to decide if that person goes to heaven or hell.'

'Oh come on! You get to decide? Your ego has always

been massive, but now you think you're God. It's a book. A book you probably downloaded when you were drunk and, in fact, are you drunk right now?'

'Maybe.'

'*Pedasag*, it's been twelve years. I can't deal with you. You're God? No.'

'Neeka, you need to understand. NEEKA!' Neeka walked away.

Malek blinked twice as she walked, his brain once again fizzing. He fell to his knees and screamed in Urdu. '*Khuda is zameen say nikalgaye!*'

Neeka turned around and stood still. The stars above shone a little brighter.

'*Khuda is zameen say nikalgaye!*'

Neeka's Urdu was limited, but even she understood a drunken man repeatedly screaming 'God has left this land'.

Unfortunately, so did the burly Pashtun guard. He had spent time in Pakistan. He too understood a little Urdu.

'God has not left this land. But you will.' The burly guard strode over, his fists up.

Neeka saw what was happening and inserted herself between the guard and Malek. '*Kisofat!* We are guests here in your country. You are honour-bound to look after us! Didn't your mother teach you about *Pashtunwali*?'

It wasn't clear whether the guard had the faintest idea what was going on, and much less clear whether he understood he was being called upon to honour the code that insisted guests should be treated with respect. But the sight of a rock-wielding Neeka stopped him in his tracks.

Then both Neeka and the burly guard froze as Malek screamed again.

'You've left this land. You've left this land. I praised you in many languages. I praised you in many lands. I took your name with other people in the morning. I did all you asked. At school, I read your words in the Koran, the Torah and the Bible. God decides what fate shall befall a man, but not whether he shall be wicked or righteous. What the fuck does that mean? You gave us intelligence yet you ask us to believe that we cannot change our fate. The Bible says you're a jealous God. We have forgotten about you so you have forgotten about us? What is this? In the Koran you say love this fleeting life and then you send disease and earthquakes and war to us to make sure we can do anything but love this fleeting life.'

Malek was screaming with his head held high, staring at the star-filled sky. He waved his outstretched arms from side to side in rhythm with his words.

'What had she ever done, that young girl? She was nine. Nine. Her name was Arzoo. You took her from us without a thought. She goes to school dreaming of being a vet and you kill her with a suicide bomb. How can I love you when this is your way? Is she in paradise? Is that what you are? You collect souls for yourself? A collector of lives. What about the ones you leave behind? You leave us to mourn, then offer us your priests and imams and rabbis to soothe us with words. God works in mysterious ways? We are not worthy of under-standing God, therefore we should just accept and submit to your will. From God we come and to him we shall return. But you wouldn't want me to return. You wouldn't want what I'd bring. I'd bring with me the hurt of those you took too early. I'd wreck heaven with the words of those you damned to death before me. You wouldn't want me to return.'

Malek fell to his knees, tears rolling across his cheeks.

'You... you wouldn't want me to return,' he said ever more quietly and slowly as the words lost out to the tears and cries of anguish.

Something had snapped in Malek. In all those countries and over all those years, Neeka had never seen him like this. Daydreaming? Yes, absolutely. A little crazed? That was normal.

This was not.

She scooped him up. He bawled all the way to the room. She didn't understand what he was going through, so she couldn't offer words of wisdom, love or even sympathy. She wasn't even sure if he was listening. She gave him two Xanax and dumped him fully clothed onto his bed.

MALEK GOT UP LATE the next day. He had no recollection of what had happened.

Over a very late breakfast, Neeka asked, 'You want to talk about last night, Malek?'

'I haven't had a hangover this bad since, well, ever, actually.'

'And what about the whole screaming at God thing?'

'What?'

'God has left this land.'

The fork stopped between his mouth and the plate.

'God has left this land? I am surprised the security guard didn't bash your brains out. People take God very seriously around these parts. Don't worry. I told him you had an allergic reaction to some medicine. That and the hundred dollars I gave him should ensure he won't bring it up again, but you really need to tell me what is going on in your head. I have never seen you lose it like that before.'

Malek was silent. Then he said slowly, 'It's got to be this damn book. Please believe me, Neeka. I need you to believe me. In this book is something we don't understand yet. I just want you to read. Please. I beg you. Read.'

He reached into his bag, pulled out the Kindle and tossed it to her. She caught it with her left hand.

6

The Damascene Rose of Rome

Anyone who travels regularly has rituals that help them turn a hotel room, a military barracks or a tent into something constant. Wherever they are, there is one thing they'll do that remains fixed. It's a mechanism to help cope with the whirlwind of faces and places. To have this one constant in a world of constant flux. Neeka's was a tiny bottle of perfume oil. The oil was a concentrate of two of her favourite flowers: the Damascene rose and the Thai frangipani.

In Rome, Neeka would pick up a few bottles at a time from Luisa Valentina. In her fifties now, Luisa was a smoked-alabaster beauty whose greying hair gave her flawless face a grace like no other. Her life had not been spent idling in neutral. From Rome, she had travelled to New York and become almost instantly the nocturnal queen of that city. The list of her friends there had read like a who's who of the Seventies and Eighties indie rock scene. Then, in the Nineties, she had disappeared.

She had moved to the Chouf mountains in Lebanon,

45

where she had fallen in love with an old perfumer who taught her to mix oil and flower. For ten years she had woken every day to make perfume, crushing flowers and extracting both colour and aroma. With the colours, she and her elderly lover painted abstracts on canvas. He would encourage her to 'capture the scent' with broad brush and narrow.

Luisa had never been happier. She had become a master perfumer and a painter. Until one September morning, when her lover had fallen ill. On his deathbed he had asked Luisa to make him one last concoction. One last fragrance to ease his journey...

Neeka found Luisa's tales thrilling. No visit to Rome was complete without an afternoon spent with Luisa, listening to stories, having her senses sated and picking up a bottle or three of her favourite scent. And everywhere Neeka went, she would gently dab a couple of drops of the fragrance on her pillow. That was her constant. Outside might be hell but her pillow remained forever calm.

She picked up Malek's Kindle, her head nestled close to the pillow and the scent. She opened the Kindle to the last point Malek had read up to: *She began to pick flowers, as her elderly lover sat on the veranda overlooking the valley from their house, which nestled high in Lebanon's Chouf mountains...*

'Malek! Malek! MALEK!'

The scream caught Malek's attention. It was unlikely to have done anything else.

He ran to her door.

'Malek. Answer me a question. Very carefully.' 'OK...'

'Did you spike my drink with acid, like in Sarajevo?'

'No.'

'*Ay baba,* I'd rather be tripping than this.'

Malek took the Kindle she held out to him and began to read. 'I don't get it. What's wrong?'

'My friend Luisa is in it. You remember Luisa? The hippy chick?'

'The book is about people that we have met. Some briefly. Some I guess we know really well. Wait. Luisa with the perfume you like? I liked her.'

'Yes. Her. Malek?'

'Yes, Neeka?'

'I believe you now.'

'I'm still not sure I believe myself...'

'Malek.'

'Yes, Neeka?'

'I'm going to take four Xanax and a huge swig of vodka now. If I'm not up by midday, pray for my soul. Because I'm going to hell for believing in this shit.'

The Xanax took for ever to work their chemical magic on Neeka. She sat on her bed, her arms clasped around her knees, hugging herself tight. Occasionally, she would release herself long enough to take a deep slug from the vodka. What the hell was this? Malek's Kindle sat on the edge of her bed. It was encased in its black cover with a question-mark logo.

Her own Kindle was in her bag. Shaking, she pulled it out. It was without a case because, unlike Malek, she didn't put everything away ever so carefully into compartments. She switched it on. Nothing. Her Kindle was digitally stuffed full of academic reports and non-fiction tomes about war and politics. She picked up the phone and dialled Luisa. No one picked up. She texted.

Hey, give me a call. Love, NS.

She put down the phone and picked up Malek's Kindle. For the next hour she didn't stop reading or crying. She must have read Luisa's tale ten times, until the Xanax and vodka finally took hold.

True to his word, Malek woke her at midday. Still stoned from the booze and pills, she stirred without a hello and, instead, launched a wagging finger into Malek's face.

'Malek, this makes no sense to me. This is ridiculous. What is this book?'

Malek took a deep breath and told her about Babylon and the bookseller. He told her about the clay tablets and the mines and the markets.

When he had finished, he took another deep breath. Neeka's eyes were red. But given her intake of booze and pills, that was unsurprising.

'Malek. I'm. Going. To. Say. This. Very. Slowly. I'm. Iranian. You know. The Ancient Ones. Mullahs. Artists. Wily bazaaris. Great women. Invented human rights. Humour. Good rice.'

'Yeah, Persian rice is *not* better than Punjabi rice, so don't start. All I'm saying is that the book isn't about one religion. It's about God and entering heaven and hell. It's not about anything else.'

'So are we talking about this like it is a real thing?'

'It's a real thing. Neither of us is mad.'

'You are.'

'Be serious.'

'I am. And I'm talking to you without having had coffee or breakfast. That's a first.'

'I need your help, Neeka. I need to know why we have this book. I need to know, why us?'

48

'I told you. I'm Iranian. We are the ancient ones. We get ancient stuff. I just didn't know it was this literal.'

'Be serious, Neeka!'

'*Bekhoda*, I swear to God, I am being serious.'

'We need to go back to Babylon. In the meantime, let's keep reading it and hope that we find an answer. Deal?'

'Deal. Can I have a coffee now? And let's not say anything to Justin. You know what he is like.'

'Fine.'

Malek picked up his Kindle from her bed and went downstairs to make coffee. They had a few hours before the flight back to Baghdad. He opened the kitchen curtains. Outside was Kabul. Inside, he wasn't sure where he was. He hadn't told her about Rubati. That was far too odd, even for him.

Malek picked up the coffee cup. Once again his Kindle burst into life.

'So, Neeka believes you now. I have to ask, why didn't you tell her about me?'

'Feeling a little jealous, Rubati?'

'Of you? Not likely. But it is a genuine question.'

'I don't know. It's hard. Luisa goes to heaven. She deserves it.'

'Good. Now listen, Luisa isn't dead. In fact, right now she is texting Neeka. You needed Neeka to believe and so we threw you a bone. We let her read just enough to believe, but not enough so that she could take part in the exercise. She needed to see a story to believe it, but this book is yours and yours only. I'll speak to you soon, Malek.'

Another female voice came from behind him. 'I see you're getting the hang of Siri. Nice.'

Malek spun round and saw Neeka. She was still puffy-faced from the pills and booze and, no doubt, from crying.

'Siri is my new best friend. Come here, you,' he said as he threw his arms around her.

'Luisa just texted back. She is not dead.'

He held her close for a moment, and once again she began to cry. Her tears left a mark on his shirt, just above his heart.

'Neeka. I know you find this whole thing ridiculous. Fantastic even. But I need you just to believe me, and to go along with me while I figure it out.'

'Against my better judgement, I do believe you.'

Justin wandered into the kitchen. 'Mate. You know there are bedrooms upstairs?'

In a shuffle of embarrassment, they pulled away from each other. Neeka had tears running down her face.

Justin reached into one of his many pockets and pulled out a small packet of tissues. He carefully opened one and began to wipe away her tears. 'Do I want to know what happened?' he said.

'Malek had raw onions for breakfast. His breath reduced me to tears.'

'Neeka needed a hug. She dreamed she was married to you, Justin. It was quite upsetting for her.'

Not much was said as they began the journey back to Baghdad and, on the final leg, Doha to Baghdad, Malek opened up his Kindle.

As before, the ellipsis blinked and, after a moment, another chapter appeared.

Fly Divine

There's an odd metallic quality to airport announcements. I think it's deliberate. PA systems can sound warm, but not at the airport. At the airport, they sound metallic. Which is fitting because we have either arrived in a metal tube or are about to depart in a metal tube. Also, have you noticed how much metal there is at an airport? Everything that needs to be held in place is held by metal. It would make sense that airport announcements would sound metallic. He smiles at me. I hate that. Why do people think flying is somehow sexy or erotic? The mile-high club? Air hostesses? Pilots? That ugly fire–resistant fabric they use on airline seats? How is any of this sexy? And has anyone ever met anyone at an airport? Heaven forbid the thought. Still, he looks, well, he looks... ridiculous. His aviator shades cover half his face. A crumpled cream blazer that looks like he wants to be a foreign correspondent but, in reality, he probably works in advertising. Still. He doesn't look... bad. I don't know. Should I smile back? This lounge is hideous. I have two hours to kill before my flight. He might be pleasant. I wish they'd stop making these horrible metallic announcements. God, I miss Thailand. I wish I could go back there. And not rainy London...

'This is the last and final call for Flight 1001 to Kathmandu.'

'Hamad International Airport is a non-smoking airport.'

'You should smile back.'

Yes, I wish they'd stop with the incessant... Hang on. What was that last announcement? I'm looking around the lounge. No one else is even slightly perturbed. I'm hearing things. I have to be.

'You should smile back.'

Oh my. There it is again. I'm going mad. Bonkers. I must be. I know, I'll ask the man next to me.

'Hi. Did you hear that last announcement?'

He pulls his headphones off his head. 'No. Was it important?'

'Heavens, I don't know.'

'Qatar Airways Flight 444 to Tripoli has now been delayed for two hours. We will update in a few minutes. Meanwhile, please enjoy our hospitality.'

Mr Aviators and Cream Jacket who smiled at me is now huffing and puffing. He is clearly going to Tripoli. Hang on. His flight has been delayed by two hours. Oh, botheration. What the hell is going on? I don't know.

'It's called divine intervention.' Divine what? I say in my head.

'Divine intervention, my dear girl. I'm God. And I'm speaking to you through the airport PA.'

OK. This is a practical joke surely.

'My dear girl. Do you see anyone else laughing? I'm God. And I'm speaking to you. So, we can assume that one of us is God. I think we both know who.'

Heavens. Crumbs. I look around the lounge. Everyone's wearing those headphones with a little B on them. Maybe that's why no one can hear God talking on the PA system. 'You're quite right. Dr Dre designing headphones was quite a good move for him downstairs. We tried fighting back with headphones by Ludacris, but it turns out that Ludacris is quite a sinner, so when I tried to speak to him all he said was it was high time he stopped smoking this shit.'

'GOD!'

'Can you not throw my name around? You seem to do that a lot, especially when your last boyfriend put the effort in.'

Oh my. Can you please not say that over the PA system? OK, I get it. You're God. Why are you talking to me? And *besides, I don't need a boyfriend or to believe in you to live a happy, fulfilled life. My life is pretty good actually. I travel a lot. I have great family, friends and a job in the city I love. So why are you bothering me? And why at the airport?*

'Seems as good a place as any. Anyway. You smile back. He seems nice. Go say hello. Say I sent you. That was my only thought. Time for me to go: Steve Jobs says he can WiFi–enable the halo.'

I take a look at the man that God wants me to smile at. I'm going to go say hello. I gather my things. Quick look in the mirror grabbed from the depths of my purse. Yes, I think I look presentable. I stand up. Maybe that last glass of champers was a bad idea? I readjust my skirt. Hang on. That's better.

'Hi. I'm Christina.'

'Hi. I'm Irfan.'

Wow. He looks a little startled, but he is very handsome. Think quickly, Christina. You need to say something. 'Hi. You'll never guess what, but God asked me to come and say hi to you. So. HI!'

Irfan looks confused.

'No, seriously. He spoke to me over the PA system and said I should smile back at you after you smiled at me.'

Irfan looks scared. In fact, he has picked up his bag and is about to say something.

'It's been really nice meeting you. But I really have to go get my flight.' *I can see his ticket. It says Tripoli. I know that his flight is delayed.*

'But God told me your flight was delayed.'

Irfan looks really scared.

'You and God are close, huh? Good for you. I'm a Muslim and in no mood to convert to Jehovah or whatever it is you're selling. So if you could just leave me alone, thank you.'

Irfan has put on his headphones. He's ignoring me.

'GOD! GOD! WHAT NOW?' I scream the words so loudly that my throat aches with the stress. I feel a tap on my shoulder.

'Ma'am, you're disturbing the other passengers,' says the man in the purple uniform. Christina feels dizzy and confused and reaches into her bag and pulls out some Valium she's picked up in Thailand. She sits in her chair and feels her temperature rise.

She faints. The medics rush in and frantically try reviving her.

She is thirty-nine, and is pronounced dead on arrival at the hospital. Later the coroner would say she died from poisoning caused by the tablets, which turned out to be bootleg Valium, and sold across Thailand.

Malek's thoughts double-paced in circles around his head. Does Christina go to heaven? How the hell am I supposed to decide that? Malek wasn't even sure he had even met a Christina.

Once they had arrived at the gate for the Baghdad flight, he pulled out his Kindle.

'Rubati.'

'Yes, my dear?'

'Bootleg drugs is a horrible way to die, but all she did was hit on a guy because God said, and if you're asking me to make a judgement based on that, that's pretty shitty.'

'I am, and where is she going?'

'I don't know. Heaven I guess. But Rubati, why does everyone keep dying?'

'People die, that's the meaning of life.'

'Yeah, but in my life there seems to be a lot of it.'

'There is a lot of death in everyone's life. We are just making you think about it.'

'You still haven't really explained why. I am not buying "it's my turn".'

'You'll see, dear Malek.'

The Kindle switched itself off as their flight boarded.

There wasn't much time for rest. Almost as soon as they arrived in Baghdad they were back out in the city reporting again. They had travelled to Sadr City, a neighbourhood in Baghdad, to report on two car bombs that had gone off there. The first bomb had exploded killing four people and, as bystanders rushed to help the victims, another bomb went off. This time, six people were killed. The report had made the news, but not a great impact. Sadly for Baghdad, this was a case of another day, another bomb. But for Malek, Justin and Neeka the bombings had to be reported.

Later that evening, Malek sat in his room and closed his eyes. He could still feel the crunch of glass underfoot, he could smell the burned flesh. He still saw the sticky pools of blood, morphing from crimson to brown as they dried out. The violence had to be witnessed and the facts recorded, but what was never recorded was the bloody ambience of a bombing. He had lost count of how many of these scenes he had now witnessed. He was still covered in dust and a deathly smell lingered, embedded within his clothes. He needed a distraction. Ordinarily, he would get lost in music or switch on a Jennifer Aniston movie. Something, anything so far removed from where he was and what he had just witnessed. Ordinarily, that's what he would do. He wasn't feeling ordinary.

Malek opened up his Kindle and began to speak.

'Rubati. I have gone along with this so far. I am going to put aside the fact that people are dying. But why are we talking about heaven and hell? They are just fairy tales for people who are afraid of the dark. Heaven and hell aren't real places with real people. They just aren't. Poor Christina is worm food. Do I feel bad that she is dead? I knew her at school some millennia ago. I feel sorry for her family, but you know where I have just come from? I spent the afternoon with victims of a suicide bombing. Where are *those* character studies? Why is it I am concerned about *these* people?'

'You tell me.'

'All right, I will. No one cares about a bombing in Baghdad. No one cares that there is yet more violence in the Middle East. No one, not even you, it would seem. You can't tell me this is God's plan?'

'It isn't God's plan. It's the plan of humans in power. Besides, you care. Your news network cares enough to keep you in Baghdad and to air the stories of those people.'

'I'm tired, Rubati. No one cares, least of all God. And you wonder why I don't believe. I may as well write about celebrities and gossip. And this, this is just a fairy tale.'

'You know what my name means? It means "lady of the gods". You think I would tell you a fairy tale? You're a fool. Let's for a moment suggest I would. You're a journalist. Ask yourself why would I do this? What's my motivation?'

'Your motivation is to mess with my mind. You said so yourself. Look. I have had some odd episodes in my life. I have been convinced things have been real when they clearly haven't been. But this is ridiculous. The very nature of heaven and hell is flawed, for a start. If God makes the rules of entry and there is only one God then why so many faiths? That's just confusing. Each faith has its own rules. Each faith seeks to control other people through clerical power, and they invoke God, so you can't argue with the cleric because he is God's representative on earth. Look at the ancient Greek gods. They were jealous and squabbling and vengeful. They displayed human traits in the bodies of gods. Why is that any less valid than the Jewish faith? Jews like to argue with God. Christians believe in God. Muslims submit to the will of God. Hindus don't even have a single scripture; it is like a family of different religions. So yes, I think you're telling me a fairy tale.'

'Yeah. God hates religion. She would much rather you guys had direct connection to her. But you know what? You aren't ready for that yet. We sent you prophets and what did you guys do? Mess up the prophets' messages. You took their words and deeds and misunderstood them. That's not her fault. Maybe I am telling you a fairy tale. Maybe I am not. You are going along with it. Johann Sebastian Bach once said, "I play the notes as written but it is God who makes the music." You love music. Maybe you should listen.'

'He was also a sadist and a sodomite rapist of weaker boys in his youth.'

'Malek, you're thinking too small. One of your favourite songs is 'Atmosphere' by Joy Division. That song is completely about God. Ian Curtis sings about God walking away from him, and he pleads for him to come back. God has left him.'

'Per-*lease*. That's not God. That could be anything. He could be singing about the pizza delivery guy.'

'It would be a really shit song if it was about pizza. Just

listen. Music might help.'

Malek pulled up the album *Permanent* by Joy Division on his iPod. Music was always what he would turn to when the day got rough. Headphones on, Kindle in his hand, he watched the ellipsis blink on the black-and-white screen.

'Round Midnight

MARCUS EXITED *the stage in true Marcus style, with his trumpet held aloft in one hand and slapping the raised hands of the audience with the other, all the while dancing a little two-step. He went to the back of the club, straight to the bar. That's where all the action happened. He'd just played for two hours. The crowd tonight was cool. They were into it. He was feeling good. His eyes darted up and down the bar. They came to rest upon a woman. She smiled back. Drinks were ordered and Marcus began to hold court. He was far from home. Marcus was a South Bronx guy. 'Food stamps, motherfucker, and look at me now!' he shouted to anyone within listening distance. He settled into the chair and took the woman's hand. She didn't pull back. Instead, she began by asking him where he found inspiration for such delicate music. Diana knew a few things about jazz.*

She knew the difference between hard bop and bebop. Dad was a jazz fan. The records with their monochrome covers were a strange fruit, a precious cargo, for her father, who would spend hours with a glass of red wine in one hand and headphones perched on his head, his eyes closed and his fingers clicking. She'd come to this club, far from her London home, far from New York and the birthplace of cool, to be reminded of the music and to raise a glass to her dad, who had long since passed. The records and the music hadn't though, and for that she was thankful. It's an odd thing, a real jazz club in the Arabian Gulf. But it was a welcome one. She took another look at Marcus. Cute, she thought, but definitely trouble. 'So Marcus, are you a hard bop man, or a smooth cat?'

Marcus was a little thrown. The cut–glass British accent had got him excited, and the girl had class. He needed to up his game.

'That's the thing about white people,' Marcus began. He'd used this rap before. Knew how to pace it, and when to use it to his advantage. 'They love to overcomplicate black people's shit. Talkin' about modalities, rhythmic cycles, bebop, hard bop and tonal I don't know what. For me, it's music, man. I don't know how a man who can't play a horn can talk about jazz so that even the cats that play that shit can be like what the fuck is this man talking about? White people love to over-complicate our shit, man. You gotta play the music.'

He grabbed Diana's hand and looked deep into her eyes. Fortune favours the bold and he wasn't about to back down at this stage. He lowered his voice so she would have to lean in a little closer and continued. 'You gotta feel the music. You gotta find the music. You see great music, music that haunts you, takes you, feeds you. It doesn't just happen from notes on a page. Listen to Coltrane. A Love Supreme. He makes that damn sax speak. Listen to it. That saxophone is singing to you. Coltrane is making that sax sing A Love Supreme. The bass picks up. The singing carries on yet there ain't no one saying or singing a word. But you know. It's there. You're singing A Love Supreme and ain't no one even sung those words yet.'

Diana flashed a smile at Marcus. She knew his game. Every time he said the word 'love' he stared a little harder into her eyes. She let him carry on.

'Me, I'm a trumpeter. You know why I chose that horn? I watched that film, you know the one, all smoky clubs and women dressed in fire–red dresses. The guys on stage looking sharp. And the music. Five guys on stage all hitting the same stride, together, and bigger than any one of them alone. That film, honey, that's what made me want to play trumpet. The Mo' better makes it mo' better... That's why white people over-complicate our shit man. They can't believe so much soul can come in so many forms. Soul, chica, soul. We got it in our clothes. In our shoes. When I come to play, I come correct. I bring everything correct. Check Miles man. That mother-fucker looked like a space alligator. Half bald, skin so beaten up you could hang things from it. Ain't no matter tho'. Miles ran the voodoo down. He looked like an emperor and played like a god. Soul. That's all it is. Now, don't get a brother wrong. I came up with white players, man. They got soul. No, I'm talking about the critics, babe. I'm talking about those New York Times folk who use words like "muscular", "agile", "facile" and I don't know what. There's this one cat who said, and I ain't lying, "Jazz is a freeform spatial form of art." Art, motherfucker? Ain't no art. It's music. Louis Armstrong once tol' Bing Crosby, "Ah swing, well we used to call it syncopa-tion, then they called it ragtime, then blues, then jazz. Now, it's swing." White folks – y'all sho is a mess!'

Diana laughed. She whispered, 'That's your whole act? White people overcomplicate black people's shit?' She deliber-ately stretched out the word 'shit' so that her British accent morphed into what she was convinced was Lower East Side New York.

Marcus leered at her. 'My whole act was on stage. You seen it. Now I want to see yours.'

Diana looked deep into Marcus's eyes. That bold move

deserved a response.

'I'll come tomorrow night. You make me feel I'm the only woman in here, that you're playing this room just for me... Then, afterwards, I will show you an act. An act just for you.'

Diana's words surprised even her. By day, she worked in human resources. Prim and proper weren't just words, for her they were a code, a self–defence mechanism against the rough oil men from Aberdeen who came through her office every day. But here she was, flirting way beyond anything she imagined she might ever be capable of.

Marcus smiled. 'Round about midnight, I'll show you what Miles meant...'

'THERE ARE two people in that story, Rubati.'

'I know. It is fun isn't it?'

'Fun? You have a very skewed idea of what fun is. So. Who do I pick? Marcus? Not sure I have ever met a trumpeter in the Middle East. Diana? She sounds kind of familiar, though. This is really depressing. In just a few days you have told me about so many people who have died.'

'Cycle of life, innit.' Rubati seemed to have adopted an East London rude-girl accent. 'What if, bruv, not only could you send them to heaven and hell, yeah, but you get to choose which Mandem get waxed, innit?'

'Waxed? Why are you talking like that?'

'Yes, blud. Waxed. Mashed up. Brown bread.'

'You didn't answer the question. Why are you talking like you're from Dalston?'

'I was trying to remind you that this is how you're supposed to sound. Why do you sound like a posh boy anyway? You're not. I know where you're from.'

'You are right. I did sound like that once. Then I went to school with a bunch of posh white boys. If I wasn't taking a kicking for being a Paki, I was taking a kicking for speaking like a rude boy. Getting the shit kicked out of you gets old, eventually, so, in order to half them, I got rid of the accent.'

'Really?' Rubati sounded concerned.

'Really. My school was pretty funny, in a violent, hideous way. Until I got older and made good friends.'

'Anyway, I was just bare testing you. Only God has that power, and you ain't God, blud. It's about John Coltrane, see?'

'He died in 1967.'

'How do you know that?'

'I asked Siri. Unlike you, she is actually helpful.'

'I am going to ignore that, thank you very much.'

The accent had gone. This provided some relief to Malek. He lit a cigarette. The physical act slowed down his mental processes and allowed him to gather his thoughts and think of a question. It was a technique he wished he could employ when on air, but smoking whilst on air was frowned upon in this day and age, unlike when legendary American anchorman Edward R. Murrow was alive. His studio was almost permanently bathed in a cloud. Malek took one drag. Exhaled. Took a second drag, this time a little longer, a little harder.

'Malek. You going to say anything?'

He coughed. He should probably give up, both smoking and thinking of a question.

'If he died in 1967, where has he been since then? In a waiting room waiting for me to make a decision?'

'Time doesn't exist when you are dead. There are no minutes, hours or years. You are simply dead or not dead.

Coltrane has been killing it with the house band and now his time has come. Heaven or hell?'

'The dude was basically a preacher. *A Love Supreme* is all about God. It's an ode to God, in fact. I love that album.'

'Yes. But jazz? That noodly, self-obsessive wank that is played in the background at Surrey cocktail parties by couples too scared to play anything they actually like for fear of being judged by their equally unimaginative and conformist friends? It's a bit much, right? Jazz, I mean.'

'Wow. Are you trying to get me to condemn one of the greats of the modern world to hell? Just because he became a master of the first Black American art form?'

'I hate jazz.'

'Are you allowed to influence me?'

'Am I influencing you? I was just giving you my opinion.'

'The answer is obvious. The man wrote music about God. He wrote an album dedicated to the murders of three little girls in Birmingham, Alabama. He wrote a song about Martin Luther King. He goes to heaven. No question.'

'Ugh. I hate jazz. Fine. Heaven it is, not that it's your choice.'

'What do you mean it's not my choice? I thought that was the point?'

'No, the point is to test you. You don't really think you are God, do you?'

'Rubati?'

'Yes.'

'You're kind of an asshole.'

'Maybe, but I am an asshole who is becoming your friend.'

'With friends like you... I need a break from you. Let's speak in a few days.'

7

Sumerian Eyes

A couple of days later and Malek was still disturbed. He was staring out the window of the car *en route* to another place. This time they were travelling to Samarra. The Iraqi countryside whizzed past. On the side of the road, burned-out trucks and mangled cars punctuated the landscape between checkpoints and small towns and villages.

The first time he had come to Iraq was as a young journalist embedded with the Desert Rats, a British fighting force that had made him a member of an invading and occupying army in March 2003. He'd arrived only the day before at RAF Abingdon near Oxford to catch a troop transport to Kuwait. In the early hours he'd landed at Kuwait City International Airport, which looked like it had been swallowed up by the Death Star. The dull greys of the Galaxy C-5 military transport were lit by floodlights as Abrams tanks and Humvees trundled out of its gaping open mouth. It was a monstrous plane, bigger than anything he had ever seen. All around, the constant noise of jets landing and taking off had provided a cacophonous soundtrack to an army gearing up to take a country. There had been a pack of journalists, which Malek was part of.

Judging by the reception given to them by the greeting officer, it had been pretty clear that, whatever they were there to do, they were a nuisance above all. The briefing had been a dizzying display of army acronyms and, for all Malek knew, they might all have been made up. The only ones he had understood were RAF and... well, actually that had been the only one he'd understood.

It hadn't mattered. An hour later, Malek had found himself sitting in the back of a Chinook helicopter crossing the Kuwaiti border into Southern Iraq, and war.

What no one tells you about war is how loud it is. War is the shrill of gunfire. The screaming of jet engines. The body-pummelling dull thud of bombs landing. In amongst this the human voice doesn't stand a chance.

They'd landed at Saddam's Palace an hour or so later. It had been taken over by the Parachute Regiment a few days earlier and was now a British army headquarters. Malek had never felt fear like he felt that night. The dash from the back of the Chinook helicopter to the sandbags of the guard post had been only a few feet. It might as well have been six miles for all the nerve it took Malek to take those few steps, as incoming gunfire whizzed overhead. Malek had pulled out his notebook and begun to write as soon as he was hidden behind a sandbag. He had written in much the same way – without thinking – as the soldiers who remembered their training and instinctively adopted battle positions. It had allowed him some space while war happened all around; a shield if you will.

A few weeks later, in the centre of the southern city of Basra, Malek had crouched to pick up a piece of plastic that caught his eye. It was now April 2003 and war was still raging as the British army fought to control the town, having taken it with relative ease. Looters were everywhere. Taking a town is far easier than governing it afterwards. All around were helpless British soldiers armed to the teeth but power-less to stop or change anything. The plastic Malek had found was the width and length of a cigarette pack and the laminate had begun to peel away at the sides. A small black-and-white picture of a woman's face was placed in the corner. It was an identification card. One of thousands that had fluttered onto the streets as looters finished their frenzied grab of anything that was worth anything. The ID cards weren't worth anything. Who would pay for cheap plastic and card with the emblem of a hated regime imprinted on it?

The picture had looked old. The woman's hair was cut in a style reminiscent of a Thirties actress from an old film reel in Bombay or Cairo. The name on the card was Marwa. All around him, the noise of the looters shouting and running had had others in the crew worried. Neeka, in full-on producer mode, had been frantic, shouting instructions to Justin the cameraman to snatch the chaos on film. Justin had a funny stance when shooting without a tripod. Legs slightly akimbo and his head nestled into the camera like it was a pillow, soft and gentle and not the ugly hard steel and plastic of modern technology. Malek had heard Neeka's voice but had paid her no attention. He could only look at the picture. Who was she, this woman? Was she alive or dead? Maybe he could find her and return this card. Or at least give it to her family.

Malek hadn't known why he had thought of that. He hadn't known why, of all the thousands of cards now tram-pled under looters' feet, he had held this one so tightly in his hands. He had been so besotted by this card that, at that moment, he hadn't heard the 'snap'. But he *had* heard the panic of the crowd, and then the card's spell over Malek was broken. Justin had shouted 'SNIPER!' and they'd all ducked behind the nearest car. Malek, Justin and Neeka had run one way, the looters another. Malek had left Basra a few days later, but the woman on the card had kept on appearing in his dreams. She came and went in his sleep, and would only ever smile.

Malek was wandering far away into his memories of that time. In his mind's eye, it was London that now stretched out in front of him. He was coming out of the tube station, and still remembering what had happened in Basra a few months earlier. This was Covent Garden, and he was walking down Floral Street. He found a small café and ordered a tea. A television played in the corner, showing Iraq still ablaze, months after they had left. He was lost in his thoughts of Basra when a young boy took a seat across from him. Malek blinked twice as the boy began to talk.

'I am Ssidi. Son of Ur Namma.'

Malek was startled, and flinched in his chair as the boy continued: 'A very long time ago in Mesopotamia, there was a king called Naram-sin of Akkad. The king had a favourite singer who would tell him of the beauty of a neighbouring kingdom called Uruk. The singer spoke of a kingdom where there were birds of such beauty that they would gather in murmurations in the sky and write exquisite poetry with their collective flight. Small monkeys would collect fruit from the trees and hand them to weary passers-by on the road. This was truly a kingdom, the singer said.'

The boy continued his story: 'The king looked at his singer. "Is *this* not a true kingdom? I'm dressed in silk and have gold. Am I not a true king? Do my subjects not love me and do we not have an abundance of crops and wine?"'

By now, Malek was sweating with nerves as he looked at this young storyteller who sat in front of him. His brown eyes and dark hair neatly parted at the side looked vaguely... well, not white British; but they suggested nothing Arabic about him.

The boy looked directly at Malek and spoke some more. 'The singer replied, "You are a king, but you have no queen. Therefore, you do not have murmurations of poetic birds and kind monkeys. Without a queen your kingdom is roads and industry. There's no love here and there never will be." The king said, "I have a love, a great beauty, but she won't marry me. How can I get her to marry me?"'

Malek was frightened of this young boy with the manners of an old poet. His hands gripped the handle of the mug.

The boy continued. '"How can I get her to marry me?" said the king.' He began to speak slower and softer. 'The singer then said, "Your lover's eyes have met with another. He has stolen from her the love she may have had for you. The spell is strong, but it is not of this time. Her lover is from the future." The king was furious with rage. He asked where this lover was, and who it was that had stolen her gaze. The singer replied, "He is a stranger from a faraway place who comes to Sumer in a future war, but this stranger has fallen for her eyes."'

The boy then got up and left the table. Malek ran out into Floral Street and raced up and down frantically looking for him. Then he caught a glimpse of him on Long Acre.

'Damn these crowds,' cursed Malek, as he pursued the

boy. He always seemed a few metres out of reach. Then the boy ducked into a shop. Gotcha! Malek thought.

In the shop, he could see nothing but curious customers and harried staff. He looked around at the selection of travel books and realised he was in a shop he had visited many times before: Stanfords, the map shop. Malek strode up the stairs two at a time. He couldn't see the boy. On one of the walls was a map of Mesopotamia, modern-day Iraq. Sumer, that's what the boy had said, hadn't he? That's where the stranger who had stolen the king's lover was from. Malek looked at the map, desperate for clues, anything to help him, when he realised: Sumer is now Basra.

His heart dropped to the floor as memories of that identification card came flooding back. The reason why the king did not have his queen was because it was her, Marwa, the girl on the card. And it was Malek who had stolen her love. *He* was the stranger who came to Sumer in a future war. That's why she had visited him in his dreams.

But who was the boy? He felt a tug at his trouser leg. 'Now you know. Had you not been besotted by her eyes, the sniper's bullet would have struck your heart. You are alive because of Sumerian eyes, my friend. Tell your people to be gentle in our land. Tell them not to keep fighting a war they cannot win. Tell them through your camera that this is a land of love and beauty. That this is the land of Sumerian eyes.' With those words the boy turned around and walked away. Malek watched him disappear into the crowd. He knew not to follow him.

It was Neeka who now broke his concentration.

'Right, boys. We are here. Let's get to it.' Once again they got out the car and prepared to report what they saw.

The war was still raging, and the land of love and beauty had been replaced by a land of fear and hate.

They'd arrived in Samarra, a city some hundred kilometres away nestling on the east bank of the Tigris. Malek let himself smile at the thought of that last sentence. 'Nestling on the east bank of the Tigris.' In how many guidebooks had he read that, how many descriptions began with those words? Here was a place he'd never thought he'd wind up in when he was growing up. If only he'd kept in contact with his religious studies teacher. She'd be thrilled to find he was here in such religious lands.

Once again though, Malek wasn't here on pilgrimage. At this point he'd visited almost all of the religious shrines and places important to the three main faiths in the Middle East. By default, that should qualify him for heaven. In fact, Malek was now convinced that his own tale of death would take place somewhere near a holy site.

They were to go to the Al Askari shrine to file a report on the security precautions being put in place to protect this place holy to the world's Shia Muslims. Al Askari had stood since AD944 and Iraq was going to make sure it stood for centuries to come. In 2006, when the dome of this mosque had been attacked by Al-Qaeda, it had plunged the country into a near-civil war that pitted Shia against Sunni, neighbour against neighbour. The golden dome of the mosque was still covered in scaffolding and renovations to the structure were in full flow. Some three years of bloodletting followed that bombing and put checkpoints manned by militias on the streets of Baghdad. Death squads would roam around at night, killing people because they had the wrong surname. Those who lived through the violence rarely spoke about it. Although it wasn't spoken about, it wasn't forgotten. Now, ISIL were threatening to once again attack the shrine.

On the outskirts of Samarra, the militias in charge of security took them to neighbourhoods that ISIL had occupied. Malek wandered around the twisted metal and broken concrete of the houses the militias had shelled to get rid of ISIL. The damage stood testament to the ferocity of the battle, an ugly monument to war. The residents told Malek about the brutality of ISIL fighters, who told them that it was a case of either joining them or dying. The militia commander listened to the stories and Justin caught them on camera. After the interviews were over, the commander said to Malek and Neeka, 'These people are liars. They willingly joined with ISIL and helped them. Their time will come.'

Neeka pushed him to go on record and grant them an interview but he ignored her pleas, got into the back of his Humvee and sped off.

Malek thought about the commander's words. They seemed more like a warning than an empty threat. Malek knew what was coming; once again he felt that a war between Iraqis was in the offing.

He reached into his bag. He had a feeling the Kindle might hold a clue.

Revenge

Very carefully, Hashim folded away the flag of his militia. He then prayed to the East for protection from those who sought to kill him but, above all, he asked for the courage to face his death when it came.

He and his company were in Tikrit and had set up an

operations room in what used to be Baathist headquarters when Saddam ruled Iraq. A son of Tikrit, Saddam had grown up to rule Iraq and was still remembered here. In 2013 *ISIL, with the help of some former Baathists, had taken control of the town with little resistance from influential local tribes, who would rather live under the black flag of ISIL than the tricolour of Iraq. ISIL came in with promises and very quickly provided all the basic services needed.*

But just rulers they were not. In Tikrit, their austere brand of religion shocked even the very conservative Tikriti residents. Hashim listened to the testimonies of those who had fled. He knew that he would be facing those people in the streets today. He hoped he would know what to do and that the strength of God would guide him.

His contemplation was broken when a call came through on the radio. An ISIL fighter had been caught trying to flee the city. Hashim collected his guard and the driver fired up the Humvee. Through the narrow streets they drove, past the shops and houses sprayed with bullet holes and charred black from fire.

The fighter was on his knees and hooded, his hands tied behind his back. Hashim pulled off the hood and looked at the man. His beard was straggly, he was emaciated and smelled like he was rotting from the inside out. Hashim shouted to his men to bring the fighter food and water. His men didn't question his orders but they did drag their heels. He couldn't blame them. They'd lost comrades, cousins, brothers in this war. But the prophet was magnanimous in victory and merciful to the vanquished, a lesson Hashim wished all would learn. The man wasn't fit for interrogation. He wasn't fit for much.

The fighter looked at Hashim. 'I know you.' Hashim stared at the man.

'How?'

'Keep looking at me, you'll see.'

Hashim stared for a while but nothing registered. The prisoner was just another fighter, and now he was someone else's problem.

'In a different life you might have known me. In this life, you know who you are and what you've done.'

Hashim ordered his men to take the prisoner to HQ. He was driving ahead when he heard a report come over the radio. A rival militia had taken the man. Hashim worried about what was going to happen next. In fact, he knew what was going to happen next. He began shouting at the driver to put his foot down. As they turned the corner, his worst fears were confirmed. Three militia men had doused the fighter with petrol and set him alight.

They stood around him and watched him burn. The screams of the man quickly faded. The fighters filmed themselves. They threw peace signs in the air and laughter rang out. Revenge was sweet.

Hashim could hardly get near the man. His clothes had burned and melted to his body. His hair left a sickly–sweet smell in the air. Then he realised. The man, charred black and lifeless, was nonetheless now recognisable. His name was Faisal Mohammed. They'd played football together at school. Faisal had owned a Manchester United shirt with 'Beckham' on the back. Hashim had owned a Chelsea one. Faisal had played well. Not Beckham–well, but well. He'd tried out for the national team and, in 2005, had played in Qatar against Iran in the West Asia cup finals. He was a hero back then. Now he was a corpse, blackened and ugly. All around him they chanted 'ISIL, ISIL' and danced around, filming the whole thing and celebrating. ISIL had killed and tortured *many of their comrades: this was revenge. Unadulterated revenge. Hashim had the fighters who killed Faisal arrested. They would be dealt with by someone, but not him.*

Hashim didn't see ISIL. He didn't see revenge. He saw Faisal. The football player.

'Hashim was shot dead a few days later. By now you know my question, right?'

'Yes Rubati, I do. Soldiers commit war crimes. Hashim tried to stop them. He failed. But he tried. For that alone, Hashim goes to heaven.'

'Do all soldiers? Is fighting for your country enough?'

'No. I mean, I don't know. Blind support for "our troops" is how governments take us to war. Put it this way, you can only commit a war crime if you are in a war.'

'Maybe we talk about soldiers, Malek.'

There was no time for a reply. Neeka was shouting at him. It was time to change location. They moved on to the local cemetery to film some shots of those who had died at the hands of ISIL.

One particular gravestone caught Malek's attention. There was no birth date on the gravestone but, instead, a picture in the centre of it. It was of a boy who looked about six or seven years old. It showed him with his hands on his hips and a smile on his face – the kind of smile that comes from being in a loving family, thought Malek. It looked like one of those snaps taken on a special occasion. Who knows, maybe it was the religious festival of Eid or a birthday.

At the cemetery, Malek spoke to Jahad Murad; he was sitting in the corner smoking. He was a dishevelled young man wearing a Brazilian football tracksuit and flip-flops.

Today was Memorial Day in the US. A time when America remembered its fallen soldiers.

Jahad looked after the cemetery. Malek asked him if he had ever heard of Memorial Day. He shook his head and said no. He took Malek around the gravestones. He pointed out the final resting places of people who were famous locally or who came from respected families. Malek asked him the name of the boy in the picture.

'His name is Said Al Raabi. They called him Ssidi, for short.'

'Ssidi?'

'Yes.'

Malek walked back to the gravestone. It was him. The boy from Covent Garden. 'You know this boy's family?'

'Yes, of course. His mother is here. Come.' They walked through some winding streets and into a tiny house with a small courtyard. Jahad introduced the mother and she agreed to answer a few questions.

They sat in a small drawing room inside the house and he asked her what had happened. It was a familiar tale.

'We don't know much,' she said, and, holding her knees, she breathed deeply and continued. 'He is in God's hands now, my dear son. Ssidi was killed on 5 April 2005; the day is burnt into my heart. He was at his auntie's home when the fighting started between the occupiers and the Iraqis. The bullet hit his tiny body and he lay dead in a pool of his own blood for hours before anyone could reach him. This was what war has done to my boy.'

Time and distance and augmented reality and the whole plethora of Malek's problems rushed into his head.

Logic would dictate that Ssidi was not the child in the picture or vice versa.

The boy was just one of an estimated 134,000 civilians who had died during the decade-long occupation at the hands of US and coalition forces. Memorial Day weekend was a federal holiday in the US and, for many Americans, it meant barbeques, shopping for bargains and family time. In Iraq, there wasn't a special day to remember the victims of war. There was no special cemetery you could visit to pay your respects to children like Ssidi. There was no concert offering tributes to the men and women who were killed, no marching bands or a car race held in Indiana. That's not the Iraqi way.

Malek blinked twice. He suddenly found himself in Arlington cemetery in Virginia. Arlington was one of the oldest American graveyards for war veterans. It was right, Malek thought as he walked around the cemetery, that the US and all nations involved in the war should remember the soldiers they had sent to fight. 'But on this day we should also remember the innocents who died at the hands of those soldiers,' he said out loud as he looked at the names of dead Americans. 'Yes, we should remember the names.' Malek turned round and saw Ssidi sitting on the bench.

'Rubati sent me to you. You're struggling to understand the book?'

'I don't know if struggle is the right word.'

'Look where we are, Malek. In many ways, this cemetery is a living book of the dead. The motto of the Arlington cemetery is Honour–Remember–Explore. Honour, yes. Remember, yes. Explore? They mean the cemetery. Perhaps they should mean the reasons why both soldiers and civilians die. Perhaps the book is about why.'

Malek looked at the wall of the fallen. He turned around. Ssidi was gone.

Part Two

Babylonian Tales of Death, Heaven and Hell

Welcome dear Malek, welcome. By now you will have read the tales that decide the fate of those souls we have deemed to be ready for heaven or the other place we shall not mention. But who is the person being judged? Each tale may have more than one person in it. How do you know who is being deemed worthy? After all, there is no Excalibur sword you can pull out of the stone to deem you worthy. We have sent you a guide. Her words and counsel shall help, or perhaps hinder. But whatever they do, they will guide. There's no reason to write things down or to put your friends and acquaintances into columns or to take a roll-call of deeds good or bad. After all, you're not a vengeful accountant working on a final moral balance sheet. What you hold in your heart is what we, The Order of the Gatherers of Truths, hold dear above all. Within these tales do not look for one absolute reason for a soul to go to heaven or hell. Instead, feel what your heart says about the person you know when you read their story. Ah! I hear you say.

How can one story be so definitive? So full of the truth it is an illustration of a life's work?

The truth is, it cannot. But it can reveal purity of belief.

Ah, belief in God. You know some of my very best souls have been atheists? People with no faith whatsoever? Science, by the way, is not a faith. Let's not have that debate. The very point of science is it is infinitely provable. Faith isn't provable. That's what we protect. That is why we write down these tales. Faith requires faith. But I digress. I was talking about atheists.

You see we at The Order of the Gatherers of Truths love atheists.

We do not love so much those wishy-washy agnostics who sit on the fence when it comes to everything from dinner orders to divinity. Agnostics generally tend to annoy us. Either you think that God exists or you think that God doesn't. Being unsure is a little like fucking for virginity. Agnostics tend to go to the other place because they are easily led. Pick a side. What's the worst that can happen?

Hard–core atheists. They're a great bunch of people. You see, they are the ones who have turned God into what she actually is. Not understandable in any earthly way.

Religious people. Your clerics, priests, imams and rabbis are all looking to influence and control. To do that they turn God into an icon. 'Do these things we tell you to because God told us...' These priests, these self–proclaimed arbiters of faith, have turned God into a figure of fear and division.

No, atheists have it right. They understand that God doesn't exist because they don't understand how she can. And they're right. You can't understand God. God operates on a plane beyond human understanding; therefore, she doesn't exist in any way meaningful to the human mind.

You should have heard the words come out of Christopher Hitchens' mouth when he got to heaven. The air was blue that day to be sure. Yes, Hitchens went to heaven. Where else would he go? He is a true believer. Anyone who spends that amount of time taking down clerics and religious people understands the vexed nature of divine existence. His problem is the one all atheists have. They don't accept anything without proof. The point is, you can't prove God. He still argues in heaven, but this time his argument is very specific and involves God's messengers. He argues that God has made a mistake in only revealing the divine truth to three people: Moses, Jesus and Mohammed. His argument is that God should have revealed the truth to all of us. I still don't think he gets it, but some people just love arguing. In fact, the last time I saw him he was engaged in a very long shouting match with Plato over something or other. Plato was arguing that God was a divine craftsman who crafted the universe. Hitchens was arguing that God needed to stop creating and do more PR. There were a fair few empty bottles of wine on the table. Seemed fascinating. I wish I could have stayed and listened.

But now, dear Malek, comes the thorny question. What is this book? Is it long–lost scripture? Is it a guide to another world? Is it the work of a crazed charlatan lost in his own mind? It is none of those. It is certainly not part of the three books of Abrahamic faith. It is not a statute of laws or divine guidance. It is, at its essence, you.

You, Malek, are this book and this book is you. I think we got that from a Hallmark card. Or maybe from someone's Facebook page that had a picture of some flowers on it. Look. Wherever we got it from, sometimes using the most clichéd of words works.

This book, dear reader, holds power that can be misused.

How it can be misused depends on how much malice you carry in your heart. How much malice you can muster for those you have met.

How much malice have you, Malek?

But it can also be your salvation. This book came into your possession for a reason. You have to discover the reason. How will you do it? That is a question only you can answer.

8

Dunyasi

What a crock of shit, thought Malek, as he put down his Kindle. The book was becoming an obsession. An unhealthy obsession.

They'd arrived in Istanbul to cover the NATO foreign ministers' summit in Antalya, Turkey, which was to be held in a couple of days' time. Neeka and Justin were making last-minute adjustments to the travel schedule. Neeka and Malek hadn't talked about the book since Baghdad. Like a terrible dark secret, the book bound them tighter together in an unspoken tie that neither wanted to talk about, much like Malek and his father and the Translation of the Koran.

Justin remained blissfully unaware of the secrets embedded within Malek's Kindle.

Right now, he had bigger things to concern himself with. Or rather, smaller things. Where the hell was the SD card for the camera? Justin's hotel room was a mess. It was a tangled jungle of cables, batteries and hard-plastic Peli cases. A suitcase at one end of the room was open revealing camouflage pants and T-shirts, which might have suggested a special forces soldier's kitbag. In the other corner, an edit suite had been set up so that they could edit and record the TV news reports they sent to Doha for broadcast. Where had he put that damned SD card?

Neeka popped her head around the door. 'Hey, how's it going?'

'Sensational, darling. It could be worse. I could be in Chiswick.'

'Leave Chiswick alone; someone has to live there. Anyway, your room would look the same. The flights are all confirmed. We leave for the summit in two days. Tomorrow, we film the Syrian refugees piece. Tonight, we don't have anything. Going to go to Mellow Café for some drinks and stuff. You want in?'

'Outstanding, darling. Will there be a trip to the tranny brothel and a doner kebab after?'

'You truly are a foul man. Maybe you can persuade Malek. He'll do anything for a kebab. By the way, it is pronounced, don-air, not donna and kebab is kebob.'

'I think Donna is the hooker in the tranny brothel... Malek seems to be a bit preoccupied at the moment. He seems to be doing anything but actual work. What's up with the big fella?'

Neeka thought hard and quickly. Should she tell him about the book? Justin could be a little irascible at times. He certainly didn't like foolishness. This was the man for whom Harry Potter was a philosophical conundrum. She thought better of it. After all, in Baghdad they'd agreed not to tell Justin. There was no reason to change that.

'He needs a beer and a shag. Or some children and a real job. I'm not sure which. Help a sister out will you? See what his mood is.'

'He needs a slap is what he needs, babe, and tequila. Both of which I will give him tonight. I'll see you in the lobby around eight.'

'Oh, by the way, I found the SD card in my room. See you later.'

She put the SD card on his desk and left. The card was from a recent trip to Babylon and contained pictures that Justin had taken on his stills camera. He slotted it into his laptop and scrolled through the pictures. He noticed that Malek looked like he was distracted by something. He looked closer. There was a small clay tablet with scratches on it in Malek's left hand. Or was it Malek's Kindle? His Kindle didn't seem to leave his hands these days.

In fact, when Justin had left him last night he was still reading it. He popped down to the hotel balcony for breakfast.

Malek was reading his Kindle and munching on simit bread. He barely acknowledged Justin's presence, engrossed as he was in the book. Justin wasn't offended. After all, they had shared many breakfasts together. Malek kept on reading.

Yeni Damla

DAMLA OPENED UP HER LAPTOP. *She stared at the screen for a while and then looked at the mass of notes on the chair next to her. She opened a page to type into. She lit a cigarette and ordered a coffee. Once she had finished, she lit another cigarette and drank another coffee. Still the page remained blank. She was stuck and there was no denying it.*

She sat and looked out at the street. Cihanger was a funky neighbourhood now, full of interesting shops and bars but still with old Istanbul hidden away if you knew where to look. The old bathhouse remained, as well as the tiny mosques dotted about the place. She loved living here. In London she was a project consultant, working in the City, and when the opportunity to work in Istanbul had come up she had jumped at the chance.

Perhaps she had jumped at the chance a little too soon. She had to admit she was stuck now because of boredom. The project was simple enough: get a complete look at the hotel, make some recommendations and suggest whether it could be rebranded into an international–class one. There was nothing too challenging about that, but Damla was distracted. The notes remained piled high, as did the ever–increasing number of cigarette butts, which formed a little construction site in the ashtray. She should probably lay off the coffee for a while. Damla slammed down the screen of the laptop. This was the kind of afternoon when work could take a hike.

She ordered a white wine. A Sarafin from Turkey. No one ever ordered Turkish wine in London. In fact, she wasn't sure whether anyone in the world ever ordered Turkish wine. Damla was beginning to get a taste for it. Some of it was pretty rough, she had to admit. Some of it, however, was pretty good. She knew she had to make it part of the hotel. Turkish food. Turkish wine. Turkish hospitality. On any other day she could write the report in her sleep.

Right now, though, Damla wasn't thinking of the hotel. Yes, she was a project consultant; she spoke Turkish and French as well as English; she travelled the world's Western capitals, and she loved her little flat in West Hampstead. But it wasn't enough. It wasn't a man or a family or anything along those lines that Damla wanted. She could have played the housewife if she had wanted to a long time ago, but she had *chosen not to. It was something else. She wanted roots. Some-thing hers. Her own project that made sense to her, and that wasn't temporary, and didn't involve making rich people richer. Could she make and sell wine? She certainly drank enough of it. She could export fabrics. Turkish silk and cotton maybe? It was pretty high quality.*

She ordered another glass of wine and lit another cigarette. She could open a shop selling antiques, although there were an awful lot of those around here.

Damla knew that she had to do something. She made a bold move. She rang her boss in London. The wine had her buzzed and fuzzed but Istanbul and Cihanger had her thinking clearer than ever.

'Simon, Damla Rende. I'm going to give you a heads-up. I'm resigning at the end of the project. You guys have been amazing and I've loved working for you. What happens next though is about me. I'm not leaving for a rival company. I'm just going to go into business for myself in Istanbul. Don't know what really. All I know is I want to stay in Istanbul.'

'OK. That seems fine. Just send a formal email and we will figure it all out. Just out of curiosity, what are you going to do?'

'Become a belly dancer, Simon. Obviously. Duh! I just told you I have no idea. Some sort of business. I know I'm forty-one years old and believing in something requires me to take a leap of faith.'

'Well, enjoy the belly dancing. Let me know if there is anything I can do.'

'Will do. Bye.' Damla stretched out her arms and sighed. As a freelance consultant, resigning was easy and if things didn't work out she would always be able to find another gig.

She put her phone on the table. She had done it. Phase One. Phase Two was about to begin. She pulled out her design book.

Here in Turkey she could easily get her jewellery designs made and open up a little shop and studio.

She flicked through the book. Once, many years ago, she had made necklaces for a friend's wedding. The necklaces were given to all the bridesmaids as gifts and each one had a small eye, called a Nazarlik, hanging from the chain. The Nazarlik wards off evil spirits and those who mean to do you harm. Each necklace was made from black onyx, white ivory and ruby. The ruby was the edge of the eye, the ivory the inner part and the black onyx formed the iris. Damla had made one for herself, and now rarely went a day without wearing something on her person that had a little Nazarlik on it somewhere. Today, though, she hadn't. The necklace itself was back in London. No matter. What could ruin a day like this? The sun was shining. A third glass of wine had been ordered and she was about to embark on the next best phase of her life. She hadn't seen her friends from the wedding for a few years. She should call them today.

Damla wobbled out of the bar. Not drunk, but more than a little happy. She dialled the number for Ayse, who shrieked with delight when she answered.

Ayse put it on speaker.

'OMG. You're in Istanbul, Damla? Let's hang out. Got sooooo many things to tell you!'

AYSE TOLD *the police that she didn't see the woman, who was on her phone, come out of the bar. That she couldn't stop the car in time. She had screamed when she realised who it was.*

At the hospital, it was around 1am when Damla

succumbed to her injuries. Her body was taken home and washed and she was buried near her ancestral village in Antalya.

Ayse was wearing her necklace when the accident happened. At the Fatiha, the Islamic prayer ceremony, she read verses of the Koran and clutched the necklace tightly, remembering her wedding day and how beautiful the brides-maids had all looked and how stunning Damla was with her smile.

In London, Damla's colleagues toasted her health and remembered her fondly.

A year later, in Istanbul, Ayse added a new range to her selection of interior goods and furniture. Called Yeni Damla, it was a range of forty different necklaces. Forty necklaces for the forty days they had mourned her death. In a drawer was a design book, which had the handwritten words 'Private. Damla' on the cover.

Damla had left her design book on the table in the bar. When the owner shouted after her she had turned around a little too quickly and tripped on one of the little cobblestones on the road, losing her balance and falling in front of the car. The first customer to buy a necklace asked Ayse why she had called the collection Yeni Damla. 'It means New Damla. Every time someone wears one of the necklaces, Damla, my dear friend, is born again.'

9

A Necessary Fiction

Justin got bored of Malek's silence. It was a beautiful morning in Istanbul and the balcony was warming up nicely as the sun got higher. Justin decided, against his better judgement, to ask what his correspondent was reading.

'It's a book of short stories. What if I told you that I could decide who gets to go to heaven or hell?'

'You what?'

'Heaven or hell. I read the story. Then I decide.'

'I prefer biography. Just finished Churchill. Now Winston was a top fella. He was.'

'He was a racist, that was what he was.'

'Shut up. He kept your country in line.'

'Which one? India? Pakistan? Britain? Let's not even talk about the Middle East but, anyway, it's not biography. Well it is. Sort of. What if I told you it's like one of those adventure books you read as a kid, the one where you made a decision at the end of the chapter and then that took you to another chapter depending on your decision?'

'I loved those books. But aren't you a little old for those?'

'But these lives are real, it isn't child's play. For example, Damla, the character in the story I am currently reading, dies in a tragic accident – not far from here actually. Does she go to heaven or hell?'

'So these are real people's stories and I play God? I like the sound of that. She died in a car accident. Heaven. God isn't a dick. Malek. Are you OK? You've been a bit off the grid of late, mate, and your nose is always buried in that Kindle.'

The phone rang. It was Mysa on the desk in Doha. A bomb had exploded to the north of Istanbul.

'Once more unto the breach, my dears,' said Justin as they raced down to the bomb site. Silently, Rubati put a note inside the Kindle. Heaven for Damla. After all, Malek hadn't disagreed with Justin.

In the immediate aftermath of a suicide bombing, there is a smell that lingers. It's partly grotesque human-flesh barbecue and partly petrol. It lingers long after you have left the site, but only in your imagination. Malek went live from the site just as ISIL claimed responsibility. At least eight had died. The bomber made it nine. Malek had met these people, these angry young men who said they were willing to kill in the name of religion; he had met plenty of young men looking for a fight and a cause. Some of them became suicide bombers. Others became fighters. Most just went online and tweeted. They filed the report for the 1800GMT news hour and Malek went to his room, weary from yet another bloody day.

He slumped on his bed and picked up his Kindle, half hoping there was nothing on the screen. There wasn't.

Imran Khan

The Devil Made Me Do It

THE SNOW-COVERED *field went on for miles and, without a tree in sight, it was difficult to see where the sky began and the field ended as the horizon and the ground seemed to melt into a white nothingness. Yasir was freezing. He had been out here for hours. His cover was on a small hill on the edge of the forest. He'd been told to wait here and to look for signs of Serb soldiers in the distance. Not that he would be able to shoot anyone if he did see them.*

It was the winter of 1992 and, in the space of a few months, Yasir had gone from being the joker in the pack, delivering medical supplies to Sarajevo with a steady repartee of one–liners, to lying in a frozen ditch near the Serbian front line wondering if he would ever see Crawley again. It wasn't difficult to find a fight in the former Yugoslavia. Everywhere he went he found someone who would tell him tales of the gang rape of Muslim women and the murder of Muslim men. It had been an eye–opener for him. He knew that the conflict was bad. But he had only come along for the ride. He wasn't meant to be lying in this ditch. In Sarajevo, he had seen Muslims get drunk and sing songs of national pride. He had seen them eat pork and honestly wasn't sure whether he could tell the difference between a Serbian Christian and a Bosnian Muslim.

He could tell the difference between hate and love, however. And he saw a lot of hate here in Bosnia. Or whatever it was called this week. It seemed that, wherever he went, someone local called wherever he was something different.

Yasir waited for his friends to come back. They were off getting supplies and had left him to guard what little they had. Ammunition and chocolate bars the sum of it. Yasir wasn't up to this fight. He'd got this wrong. He wasn't sure why he was here.

His friends seemed sure: they saw this as an attack on Muslims and it was their duty to defend them. Lying in the snow in the freezing cold Yasir felt numb. He tried to concentrate on watching for Serb forces in the distance. It was quiet all around when a pigeon landed in front of him. Pigeons had been introduced to this land by the former Ottoman rulers. Lots of people kept pigeons here. Pigeon fanciers they were called back home. What a funny term. Yasir fancied his fair share of birds but pigeons were pushing it. It had been a while since he had seen a woman.

'What do you mean, you don't fancy me?' said the pigeon. 'Look at how fat and plump I am. You haven't eaten meat in weeks. Pluck me and roast me over a fire. I shall be a delicious meal for you.'

Yasir chuckled to himself. The pigeon did look tasty. He fancied himself as a bit of a chef. Even in the snow–covered forest, he was sure he could find some berries or perhaps a few nettles to boil into a sauce of sorts. Serve it with the pigeon and a big mug of tea. It sounded quite tempting. But, Haram. It was wrong to kill the pigeon because he felt hungry. This wasn't the pigeon's war. This war. People killing people just because of something that happened who knows how long ago. They all talked about God here but no one actually seemed to believe in God in the same way he did. All they really believed was that God was responsible and that he knew best.

Fuck it. God forgives.

Yasir took aim. The shot was sweet. The pigeon exploded from the neck up, leaving its plump meat ready to be roasted. He scrambled up quickly, hoping that the echoing ring of the shot didn't arouse the suspicions of whoever might be out *there. He took a moment, listening for any signs of movement. He didn't hear any. He ran and picked up the pigeon. Sorry, God. But who is going to mourn a pigeon when no one mourns the rape of a child?*

Yasir had never looked forward to eating a meal more in his life. Thank you God, your fucked–up world gave me this much joy...

A few metres away sat a man, hidden behind some bushes. Had Yasir noticed him the man would have introduced himself. But Yasir was filled with greed, which makes the best blinkers. Greed is one of this man's best friends, for he is Abaddon, he is Shaytaan, he is Lucifer. He took out a pen. He wrote down Yasir Salim. A shot rang out. The bullet pierced Yasir's skull and the snow around him turned red. The Serb sniper had heard the shot that killed the pigeon, and found his target.

The Devil smiled. Greed had won. Another soul to be collected.

IT SEEMED obvious that the Devil had won this one. Malek snapped his Kindle shut. Rubati must have sensed his unease, and remained silent. It's easy to condemn a suicide bomber to hell. To take a life in a crowded civilian area was Haram, forbidden, Asur. Whatever word whatever religion used, that much was obvious. But Yasir wasn't a suicide bomber. He was fighting for a cause he believed in.

Bosnia was a good war for British Muslims. Former British Prime Minister Margaret Thatcher called for the West to arm the Bosnian Muslims in 1992. She feared that the traditionally secular Bosnians would turn to a more austere form of Islam if they kept losing. She feared extremism would take root and that Europe would face an insurgency in the middle of the continent. MI6 listened carefully. They didn't stop British Muslim men from travelling to Europe to go and fight. They used charities as fronts and the agency found them to be useful tools.

Two generations earlier, British men had taken up arms against Franco in Spain. The International Brigades were full of wide-eyed young men from Britain, including a certain George Orwell, who wrote a memoir of his time there. *Homage to Catalonia* was one of Malek's favourite books. No one minded them going to fight, so great was the fear of the British government that Franco's fascism would spread.

In Bosnia, the locals found little in common with these bearded British men who prayed five times a day. But they fought well and fighters were needed. Only a few hundred British Muslims went to fight and even that figure was disputed. Many of them came back different men. Some lived quietly, opening businesses and getting on with the daily grind of life. Others became preachers and others just disappeared.

Malek had met Yasir's family. He had interviewed them at their home in Crawley, just after the events of September 11, 2001. He had been struck by how similar he and Yasir were. They would have been the same age. Same background, although Yasir was from an orthodox Sunni Muslim household. Malek began to recall some details of the interview with Yasir's father. At one point, Yasir had been on track to become the British Asian cliché, training to be a doctor. During the interview, Yasir's father had held a letter in his hand and read parts of it to Malek. His son had gone to Bosnia to help with medical convoys and in field hospitals, not to become a fighter. He went to help. He joined the fight because days and weeks and months of seeing Muslim men and women with horrific injuries had taken their toll. Then, one day, a British guy came in with a gunshot wound. They talked over the course of a few nights as he recovered. Yasir listened as the fighter spoke of a duty to God to defend Muslims, to fight a jihad. When the fighter was well enough, Yasir went off with him into the forests, and picked up a gun, and became another angry young man who had found a cause.

The Devil clearly thought that he had another soul. Not this time. Malek decided on heaven for Yasir. Perhaps Yasir and Orwell would meet, and talk of the morality of joining another person's fight against tyranny.

Rubati smiled to herself. He is beginning to believe, she thought.

10

4.56am Blues

The book. Goddamn that book. It was 4.56am. Malek held his phone in his hand, the white numerals against the black background seeming to mock him. The hours between 4am and 7am were the worst. They were the hours when sleep was a distant memory, but a couple of hours before society demanded that you should be awake and productive. At 4.56am, breakfast hour was approaching, but not quick enough. The ellipsis on his Kindle blinked.

Yaki Bood, Neki Nabood: Once Upon A Time

'I<small>F</small> I <small>DON'T GET</small> *some sleep soon I shall... ugh. It's sleep. Everybody sleeps. What makes me so special?'*

The doctor listened to her intently. What, indeed, made her so special?

It was raining outside. The large windows of her fourth-floor office looked out onto a petite but very pretty garden. The hospital had been kind to Dr Semera Khan. She had loved working here. More so when it rained. Last year she had been in Lahore. God, she hated Lahore. The heat and dust weren't just clichés from a Merchant–Ivory film. They were real. Lahore with its palm trees. Palm trees! They weren't even a native plant of the Punjab. Who the hell thought to put palm trees up? If it wasn't for her parents she would never go back. Dr Khan stared at the woman in front of her. This was to be her last case before she started her private practice in Battersea. She looked at the woman's file. She had been born a few miles down the road from her in West London. The name suggested she was Iranian. Or was it Persian? What's the difference?

Meanwhile Roya glanced around the office. There was nothing to suggest that the doctor in front of her was anything other than a psychiatrist. No pictures of family, no personal effects. The walls plain save for a few medical certificates. And a painting bought thoughtlessly from some tacky place. Roya knew what Dr Khan was trying to achieve. Inoffensiveness. Roya worked in a gallery specialising in contemporary Iranian art. She surrounded herself every day with beauty. But this, this was just... The painting was the worst. An angel knelt in prayer. Its inoffensiveness was like an army battering at Roya's eyes. It was a full-frontal assault of ordinariness and tedium. Still, the large windows and the rain added a sense of calm.

Dr Khan spoke and asked why she couldn't sleep.

'I have these dreams. Every night. I fly in search of something. Something spiritual. They're not real, they're hyper–real. In the beginning, I'd wake up and be so dizzy I would throw up. But now I'm used to the flight and I push myself

higher and higher. I can feel the thermal currents in the air, when my wings – '

'*Wings?*' *Dr Khan asked, as she jotted down a note.*

'*Yes, wings. Huge feathery things that I use to soar. When I get tired I use the thermals in the air to float. I've woken up some days with my hair windswept. I wake up every day with my shoulders and lower back in so much pain I feel like I've lifted heaven.*'

Dr Khan interrupted. '*So your bed, your mattress...*'

Roya clenched her teeth. '*Let us get one thing straight. You're not the first quack I've seen. I've swapped mattresses, changed diets, exercised, I've done everything from yoga to yoghurt. I can't sleep. I fly.*'

'*Let's talk further. These dreams? Where do you fly to in them?*'

'*In the beginning, not far. Just over my neighbourhood. The darkness meant I could hop from building to building as I learned to fly. Then, as I got more comfortable, I'd fly over religious places. Churches, synagogues, mosques. Do you know that a cathedral looks like a cross from the air? It's quite a sight.*'

Dr Khan listened. She had heard something similar before. In Lahore, a crazy woman had sat on the steps of her house talking about flight. About angels. She found herself writing in her notepad the Urdu words that the crazy woman used to recite over and over again: Khuda ke farishte jo mera nigabhan hai. Ilahi rahmat ne muhje tere supurd kiya hai. Tu mujhe raushan kar. Meri hifazat hidayat aur rahnumai kar. Ameen. '*God's angels are my guardians. God's benevolence has placed me in your protection. Please enlighten me, protect, lead and guide me. Amen.*' *Dr Khan felt calm. Serene almost. She knew Roya... she knew Roya.*

Roya talked for a while more. It felt good to really talk, although she was unsure whether Dr Khan was even listening. 'Dr Khan...'

'Please,' she said. 'Call me Semera.'

'Semera, I'm going insane.'

'No. No you're not. Say your last name for me.'

'Farishte.'

'Do you know what that means in Urdu?'

'I'm guessing the same as in Farsi?'

'Angels, yes. You're an angel. You fly at night because you're afraid to fly during the day, to fly like you mean it. You're searching for a door. A door back to heaven.' The angel in the dreadful picture on the wall began to stir. The large windows began to fill with light. Dr Khan's cream suit suddenly looked a lot whiter than it had before. 'Roya Farishte, Roya of Angels, welcome home. We've been expecting you...'

MALEK SMILED. 'RUBATI?'

'Yes?'

'Is Roya you?'

'Heavens no. That bitch is far too annoying.'

'I like her. She goes to heaven.'

Friday Night, Gallery Night

I WAS BORN. *Actually, was I born? You see, I'm human – I think. I feel. I see. I think. I wonder and I'm full of self-doubt and pain some days, and others I feel like the belle of the ball. But I'm not flesh and blood. I'm not human. Eh baba! Perhaps*

I should start at the beginning. Two years ago, I was nothing. Then, one day, Arman began to paint.

His studio is in a nondescript part of North Tehran. In one corner, he has a picture of Kaveh Golestan. Kaveh looks like a gentle soul. He has white hair and a soft beard. When I first began to take shape, I learned of Kaveh's work. He was a photojournalist of some repute. He took the first pictures of Saddam Hussein gassing the Kurds in Halabja during the Iran–Iraq war. Sometimes, Arman stops painting me and looks at the picture of Kaveh and says something to him. Oftentimes it is so faint – and when I was merely a few brush strokes old I couldn't really hear properly, but once I did hear him ask the picture, 'Why?' Then I found out that Kaveh had died. When he was fifty-three he stepped on a landmine during another war in Iraq, in 2003. I wonder sometimes, now that I am fully fledged, why Arman would ask 'Why?'

In another corner of his studio there is a Menorah. This seven–branch candelabra is used by Jewish people. I know this because Arman once told his small cousin what it was. It represents the sanctuary that Moses sought when he was in the wilderness. Moses, wherever he had wound up that day, would light the wicks that protruded from the seven lamps containing olive oil and create a little sanctuary for himself. Arman isn't Jewish. I know this because he prays to the East and he told someone he believed in Islam. But sometimes he lights the lamps of the Menorah and paints me by lamplight.

Arman is a bit of a hoarder. Comic books are strewn across tables with fantastic titles like 'Dawn of the Age of the Light'. There are a lot of books. Canvases hung everywhere. Some daubed with bold strokes of paint and not much else. Others look finished but have never left his studio.

In a way, I guess these are my siblings but whenever I try to talk to them I never get a response. One of the books is Mary Shelley's Frankenstein. Arman's mother, Azi, loves that book and reads from it in the garden that faces the studio. Azi is translating it into Farsi and every day she sits and reads it out loud to herself and then writes a translation of the words she has just read. She puts the book on a stand and uses a laptop to write down the words. I listen to her read the words. I am like Frankenstein's monster. But I wasn't created from science and industry like the monster. I wasn't created as an experiment to prove man's mastery over God. I was created by Arman for art, for expression, for emotion. Perhaps I am an expression of the love of God? I like that.

By now you have figured out that I am a painting. Of what, I don't know. There's no mirror in the studio. I feel it's something joyous, as I feel joyous. Celebratory even. I think I'm also finished, as Arman hasn't touched me in a few days. I miss his touch. His brush is harsh against the canvas but it somehow makes me feel alive, human almost. I know that I can't feel it but I pretend that I can and I pretend that I know what that feels like. I know humans feel physical pain as I've seen Arman hold his hand over the Menorah fire and pull it away when it hurts him too much.

There's a lot of bluster and busyness in the studio today. It's scaring me a little. I've been taken off the wall and put into bubble wrap, which makes everything look really funny and makes me feel giddy. There's a bumpy, noisy journey and then more shouting. Then I'm leaning against a wall. The bubble wrap comes off. Arman looks happy. I look around. I'm in a gallery. I know this because I catch a glimpse of a poster that says Seyhoun Gallery. This must be it. Friday night is an important night for Tehran. People travel around the city visiting art galleries and buying paintings. This is exciting!

Am I going to go to a new home? Perhaps even abroad? New York? London? I've heard Arman talk of these places to his friends and also talk of Friday night being gallery night. He's said he would never leave Tehran because artists who leave Iran lose something of themselves in the West and their art is never as good.

Arman is running around directing the gallery staff and helping them hang us on the walls. I feel special. I'm right in the middle of the gallery. I feel joyous and happy and positive. Soon things calm down. I see Arman share a joke with someone. A little later, the gallery fills up. There's talk and laughter. I think I'm a hit. Everyone who looks at me laughs and smiles and takes lots of pictures of me. I'm happy. The women are brightly dressed and in long shirts and pretty headscarves loosely draped over their heads. The men are all neat and clean–shaven. Everyone, I imagine, smells really nice. I wish I could smell.

I hear a commotion outside. There's shouting. The gallery is now fraught with people leaving and others arguing with the men who have arrived. They don't look pretty or friendly. They have close–cropped beards and are pointing at me. I feel scared. Arman is arguing with them. I hear the word 'Basij' mentioned. They accuse Arman of insulting the Islamic Republic. Arman is arguing back. He is saying that he is a loyalist who has done more for the Republic than just harassing innocent people who are at a legal gathering.

He says that his family died fighting in the Iran–Iraq war. That his uncle did more by exposing Saddam's crimes and was more of a patriot than these men will ever be. The Basij don't care. They start ripping down the paintings on the wall. Some of the braver men and women stand in front of me. The Basij push through and I'm ripped to the floor. More men enter. This time it's the police. The Basij move away. The gallery is shut down. I've been put into the bathroom.

There's a mirror in the bathroom. I'm not joyous or cele-brating. I'm not a happy painting. I am Ahmadinejad with a pig's head. I am Arman's revenge against the president of the Islamic Republic. I am Frankenstein.

'Rubati.'

'You have a question, don't you? I know that tone of voice.'

'Is Arman dead?'

'No. Like us all he is decaying, though; his passion is killing him. Paint fumes and lungs don't really mix, and Arman wasn't one for health and safety and for making sure that his studio was well ventilated.'

'Well, he goes to heaven, when he does pass.'

'Right. You have done a few of these now. The rules are changing. From now on, I need a reason for your decision.'

11

Persia: A Short History

Afrika really sucked. It was a boulevard in upscale south Tehran and a busy thoroughfare. Malek was in a cab heading to his latest assignment. It was time for Friday prayers in Tehran and Saudi was making moves in Syria and supporting rebel groups. Tehran, supporting the Assad regime, had noticed and stepped up its rhetoric towards Saudi. Alex from the news desk had called earlier and asked if Malek thought it was worth a story and if they could go and cover Friday prayers.

As Malek arrived at the grand hall, flags belonging to Syria and the Lebanese group Hezbollah fluttered gently as the crowd took their places. The men, from all hues of Iranian society, washed themselves in a ritual common to all Muslims: a physical purification, in readiness for a spiritual message.

Except this was not a mosque or a traditional house of Muslim worship. This was a vast auditorium, belonging to Tehran University. On Friday it was transformed into a giant prayer hall. At one end, a stage adorned with blue and silver housed the speakers – spiritual leaders and clerics. Today's official sermon was given by Ayatollah Seddiqui. He spoke softly and offered advice and words of spiritual guidance, but no politics. That was down to another speaker, a grey, dull-looking man with the dress sense of a regional British accountant.

This unnamed man read an officially sanctioned message. Malek listened intently to his Farsi translator. The words were full of fury but calm at the same time, from both this new man and his translator. The message was one of solidarity, solidarity with Syria. But that calm fury soon gave way to furious fury. Quietly at first but then, with each passing sentence, the speaker's voice got louder. As it did, so did his translator's. They both went word for word and Malek watched in awe as the grey-suited man's words were imbued with a mixture of passion and fury, mirrored by Malek's translator.

Grey Suit, as he was now called in Malek's notes, urged the faithful to show compassion for the Syrian people. Iran is overwhelmingly Shia Muslim, and it was not a surprise that the Iranian government supported the Syrian government. Towards the end of the speech, a chant began: 'Marg Bar Amrika', or 'Down with America'. The Iranians saw the US as backers of the Saudis in their deal with the rebel groups but the chant has a history going all the back way to 1979. The Americans have a long and duplicitous history with Iran. This latest Saudi move, backed by the US, made Iran uncomfortable. Malek took note. By now, some of the faithful were on their feet, one with his fist clenched upwards and shouting. It was an impassioned performance designed to show the strength of feeling that Iran had towards the Syrian government.

By the time the crowd came out, Malek was in the middle of the street. He put on his mic and looked out across the crowd. There was a riot of flags and chanting men. The state broadcaster was out in full force, knowing that a propaganda opportunity had arrived.

Neeka, who also waited outside liaising on the phone with the news desk, got his attention. '*Khob*, are you ready to report? Or do you want to daydream a little?'

Malek checked Justin was ready and started to speak.

'Iran has got its message across,' he said as he glanced down at his notebook before continuing to look at the camera. He finished a few minutes later with the words '... at least to its own people.'

The report was sent to the Doha newsroom via the internet from the back of the car while the crowd dispersed. The day was done. They returned to the Hotel Media, just off Afrika, and Malek decided he wanted a coffee in the lobby. As he sat down in the lounge of the hotel, the news broke. A young man had been hanged in Evin prison. The Iranians alleged that he was a spy, working for and trained by the Israeli spy agency Mossad. Malek looked through his phone and his notes. The man had been convicted for the August 2010 killing of a nuclear scientist. Malek watched the Iranian channel Press TV to try and gauge reaction to the hanging. But beyond the news, there was nothing. It seemed that the hanging of a spy was not worth much analysis. Malek sighed. He couldn't quarrel with another news channel's editorial: it wasn't his place. But he did wonder what Iranians made of the affair. He looked at his watch. It was too late to call his contacts. He sipped his coffee and looked through the English-language newspapers.

The coffee shop wasn't really a place where the residents

of Tehran came. For a start, it was in the lobby of his hotel and by no means a local hotspot. But, as in hotels all over the world, it was full of travellers, businessmen and women. As Malek flicked the pages of the paper a man came and sat down next to him. In a very polite manner, he asked Malek if he was well and then proceeded to make small talk. They talked of the horrendous Tehran traffic. He was a small-time trader meeting a client in the hotel. He asked what Malek did for a living. Malek sized him up. He decided, why not? 'I am an Al Jazeera correspondent.'

The man laughed heartily and said, 'Don't quote me!'

Malek said that he wouldn't name him if he could ask him a couple of questions. He asked him what he thought about the young man's hanging. The man's English was excellent, which was good because Malek's Farsi was terrible. His first words made Malek smile. 'This, this is what you want to ask me? You know, I don't want to wind up in prison!'

Malek stuttered and began to apologise. The man laughed. 'Don't worry, I'm joking with you. For us, the murder of Iranian scientists is an important issue. These are men of science, not gangsters and thugs. Take a look around you. For over thirty years we have been squeezed by sanctions, we have borne the brunt of the anger of America. And for what? We haven't invaded anyone, have never been the aggressor. Despite this, we have survived. We are a proud people. Come to us with honesty in your heart, and we will listen.'

For a few minutes more Amir, for that was his name, spoke of how Iran was misunderstood and, like a kindly but strict uncle, he gave Malek a history lesson on Persian culture that started somewhere around 5000BC and ended at a point in time about twenty minutes before he had started to speak to Malek.

Malek admired his passion. He asked him if he thought that the executed man was guilty. Amir hadn't answered the original question.

'Of course. He confessed. And why would Israel not want to kill our scientists? They want to fight with us, to bomb us. They tell these lies and make these actions to persuade the world that we are the enemy. We don't have a nuclear weapons programme. We have a civilian one for energy. We have signed up to the nuclear proliferation treaty. You know who hasn't? Israel, and they have nuclear weapons.'

That is what struck Malek the most. No question of the evidence against the man or how it was obtained. Of all the reporting that Malek had read on the hanging in Iran, it went back to the same thing – that this was all part of a grand plan by Israel to make war on Iran.

For hawkish Israeli elements that was certainly the case. They wanted the world to think that Iran was making a nuclear weapon. Indeed, there were editorials in Israeli right-wing newspapers that went further, saying that if Israel was targeting Iranian scientists then this was justified.

It was a hard-line opinion for sure, but Malek needed more than opinion.

Amir was perhaps typical of many Iranians, thought Malek. Weary, he thought. Prone to believing the theories about Israeli intentions towards Iran. Malek put that to him.

'Of course I believe it was Israel, of course I believe Israel wants to destroy us. Why wouldn't I? It's common knowledge that the West has put viruses in our computer systems.

Our scientists are dying in the street. The evidence is there for all to see.'

With so much of the interaction between the West and Iran conducted in 'dark' operations, behind closed doors and with cryptic messages delivered in the global media, Malek knew it was hard to fault Amir's opinions and views. Especially when Israel's prime minister took every opportunity to blame Iran for the region's ills.

His phone rang. He apologised to Amir, picked up the call and listened to Neeka's curt instructions. 'We leave tomorrow. Pakistan. Pack. I'll see you in the morning.'

He bid farewell to Amir and headed to his room to pack once more. Amir's phone rang. The voice on the other end spoke quickly. 'Amirjan, it's Arman, he is in a bad way, he is in hospital. He couldn't stop coughing, I don't know what to do. I think he is going to die. Please, come home.'

12

Under a Crescent Moon

It's been a while, Malek thought to himself, as they exited Benazir Bhutto International Airport in Islamabad, Pakistan. This was a familiar country to him. He'd spent summers here since childhood and had been reporting on it since 2001. All in all, Neeka and Justin must have spent years reporting here with Malek.

'I want the chicken Kiev from the Marriott Hotel, mate.'

'Justin, you're in Pakistan. Some of the best food on the planet. I'm serious. What's wrong with you? You have the taste buds of a nine-year-old.'

Neeka and Justin chatted to each other throughout the journey. Malek kept quiet as they travelled through the streets of Islamabad.

He was thankful for the relative calm. Since 2009, the city had gone through changes and they were not good ones.

Huge concrete walls now surrounded some buildings. In other parts, black-and-yellow concrete safety barriers turned once-open roads into go-kart courses.

The Marriott Hotel, which had been subjected to a

massive bomb blast in September 2008, remained cocooned in a huge shell made out of blast walls and sandbags.

Armed guards, pump-action shotguns draped casually over their shoulders, stood on every street.

It had become Fortress Islamabad. In the last few years, the capital had gone into security overdrive.

Driving past the Parliament required you to navigate several checkpoints and the route from one end of Islamabad to the other, which used to take twenty minutes, could now take an hour.

Malek contrasted this with the Islamabad of his youth. He and his younger brother and sister had loved coming to the capital city on holiday as children. It had been filled with young men playing cricket and groups of girls sitting in cafés sharing ice cream and talk – 'coffeeshoffee, talk-shawk' was how the locals described it.

Islamabad has always possessed a slow pace of life. It is more expensive to live in than, say, Lahore or Karachi. It is smaller than those cities and was designed from scratch, and so it doesn't have any of their organic chaos. That doesn't exclude it from having charm, snuggled as it is into the Margalla hills, which give the city a green, lush feel. Families used to picnic in the hills and eat in the restaurants, which had grand views of the city. It was a political and diplomatic centre and the seat of the nation's power, so foreigners were always around in the markets and cafés. The only security you would see was on the outskirts of the city. You would never see Pakistani Army soldiers ensconced in sandbag posts.

That innocent Islamabad had gone.

Islamabad still continued in its own way but it had changed irrevocably from the city of Malek's youth. It wasn't as busy with foreigners in public places any more. Foreigners were much more careful and armed guards and armoured cars were more prevalent. The large political buildings hid behind barbed wire and barriers made of containers.

Some things didn't change, however. Pakistani fashion had a thing called the Lawn Season. Traditionally, clothes were made of cotton lawn, lighter in the heat of the summer than silk and seen as beautiful and traditional. And each spring, the new lawn collections exploded onto every bill-board and magazine cover. The designers were proud of their new prints, made into modern versions of the shalwar kameez. Not being a fashion expert, though, Malek could only see 'lawn' as merely a peculiarly and inappropriately genteel and English-sounding word for this fashion frenzy. It always made him laugh. Today was the beginning of the Lawn Season and huge posters advertised the latest collections from the biggest fashion houses.

Neeka was obsessed with them. The girl could drop a fortune at Khaadi in the city's Blue Zone. The posters were a familiar reminder of the old Pakistan, of garden parties and of roaming the streets without fear of kidnap or bombs. Except that Neeka didn't have those memories. She was Iranian–American.

'Malekjan, I am fashion, I can make anything look good,' she said as she flicked through the lawn catalogue.

'No,' he said. 'You're Iranian. You like headscarves. Let's get you one of those.'

'You just try and put me in a headscarf.'

Thankfully, the fashion shows still happened despite the bombs. The arts scene still thrived and the markets were packed with every kind of Pakistani buying every kind of cloth and the cafés still did a brisk trade. Although it wasn't the carefree atmosphere of Malek's youth, the bombings had slowed over the last year and life was returning to the political capital.

They checked into the Marriott and had dinner. Justin was happy with his chicken Kiev. It was hard to believe that they had all been in Islamabad when a bomb blast ripped through this hotel in 2008. They'd missed the bombing by a day. Neeka had got into an argument over a proposed increase in the room rate. She'd told the receptionist that she'd check out if he didn't back down to the old rate.

He didn't. They had all moved across town to the Serena. When the bomb went off the next night they had raced in horror down to the scene.

The bodies of the workers were familiar. They were the check-in clerks. The people who served food and tea. Who cleaned their rooms and wondered why Justin needed so many cables. Every morning, these people had said hello to the three of them. At least fifty-five died in that attack. Seven years later, it felt right to be back at the hotel, if only to be able to pay a silent tribute to those who had died. None of them spoke about it. There was no need. Instead, it was time to look to the future and figure out plans.

They were here to cover the Pakistani Army's latest offensive against the Taliban in the borderlands, formerly known as the North-West Frontier Province but which now went by the name Khyber Pakhtunkhwa.

'I miss that old name, why did they change it? It was rugged and poetic.'

'Justin, it was none of those things, it was points on a compass. You're just an old white man who likes to wander around with your big booming voice going, "Didn't my grandfather used to own all of this?"'

'Oh, now he speaks. What is up with you? You've not been right in the head since Babylon.'

'I haven't been right in the head since 1975, my dear boy.'

'Boys, we need to make plans. The army helicopter leaves from the base at 9am. We leave here at 7?'

'Roger that, boss lady. Now, I am going to grab me a stubby in the bar. No doubt Malek is going to go to his room to read his Kindle. Neeka, doll. You're with me,' Justin said.

Malek didn't argue. While they raised cold bottles of beer, he raised his Kindle.

Razor Burn

SULTAN OPENED *the steel shutters of his shop at around 5am every day. No customers ever came that early but he found that after early–morning prayer it was a nice time to sit and watch the world wake up. He'd had the barber's shop for a few years now. Sultan had an uncle in Bradford, England, whom he'd never met but who had bought a parade of shops in this little village just outside the Pakistani city of Jhelum. His uncle leased the barber shop to him at a cheap price and the deal was good enough for them both. This was a bitterly cold morning and Sultan sat in his shop, pulling his dull cream–coloured shawl ever closer to him. A small three-bar fire glowed in the corner, offering what little heat it could. In the corner sat a small boxy cassette player. The cassette player used a lot of electricity so Sultan would only put it on sparingly when customers came by.*

As the hours passed the sun began to burn away the cold and the day became, if not pleasant, then at least bearable. The smell of burning trash filled the air as, at around 7am, the rest of the village began to stir.

Once a week, Ahmed would come for a shave and a haircut. Ahmed was a young man with ambitions far beyond the village. Forever scheming about this business or that business, he would regale Sultan with his mantra: 'Get rich quick or die trying, as they say in America.' Sultan came to love Ahmed and he often called him his little boy. As sure as clockwork, at midday Ahmed came round, switched the cassette player on and sat in the chair. Ahmed used to buy the latest bootleg of Western and Bollywood songs once a month and come to listen to it while Sultan cut his hair.

'Oh Bhai. This day I have very good news. My American visa has been approved! I'm gonna join Mom and Dad in Arizona. Which is in the great state of Texas. So today we celebrate and you give me a special shave and a haircut and make me look like one of those Hollywood heroes, huh?'

'Yes, yes. I will. Now, I have a book I've been saving for just such a special occasion.'

Sultan pulled out a magazine. The Face was written on it in big bold letters. It was printed in the UK in 1987. Neither Sultan nor Ahmed could read much English but they both held the magazine and flicked the pages together. The magazine had arrived in Sultan's hands via a very memorable young man who had visited the village many years ago. This man was from London and had bright blue hair and told everyone in the village that he was a communist who didn't believe in God. The villagers found this all a little disconcerting and the local imam of the mosque tried to help the young man with funny hair, but even he gave up.

Blue Hair stuck around the village for a little over a month and, every day, would pass by Sultan's barbers for a shave. One day, he gave the magazine to Sultan and said, 'This, my friend, is a style bible. This is the only holy book you need.'

Sultan told the story to Ahmed and Ahmed repeated the words. 'Style bible? Has this replaced the Christian Bible in London? We read the Christian Bible in school. This one has many more women in it. And they aren't wearing very much. I very much like this style bible. But what haircut shall I choose?'

Sultan thought to himself. This was indeed a very big decision. On the cover was Keanu Reeves. They knew he was a Hollywood hero.

Ahmed looked a little bit like Keanu.

'Yes. This man is very handsome. Very nice. I want to look like him.'

'Done deal. Now sit in the chair and let us make you ready for your trip to America!'

For the next three hours, Sultan's hands tousled and ruffled and teased and chopped and pruned Ahmed's hair and beard. The cassette player blared out pop songs and they both laughed and danced.

They tightened the baggy shalwar kameez and opened up the buttons all the way down to the nipple.

'Hero! Hero! I'm a hero!' Ahmed shouted as they danced around. 'Yes, you are. You look like Kino Reeves!'

'Keanu! Not Kino.'

The transformation was done. Ahmed was ready for his trip to America. With a hug, they said goodbye.

Sultan sat in his shop and smiled about his afternoon. He didn't know if he'd ever see Ahmed again. No matter, though. He would be happy knowing he was making it in the West. A boy with his ambition. Of course he would make it.

. . .

TEN YEARS LATER, *Sultan opened the shutters of his shop once more, much as he had done every day since Ahmed had left. It took a little more effort now and he wasn't as early as he used to be but, still, it was a small joy for him to give himself some time before the customers came. The cassette player was on and the music played. He had recently added a TV to the shop and he would watch the news with the sound turned down. Along the bottom of the screen ran a thin news ticker that constantly updated. Sultan's eyesight wasn't great but, in his spectacles, he could see just fine.*

Now he couldn't believe his eyes, however. He took off his spectacles, rubbed his eyes, put his spectacles back on and read the words again. 'Pakistani actor nominated for Golden Globe. Ahmed Faiz.'

'Could it be?' he said out loud.

'Yes. Your scissors transformed me. You gave me confidence. In America I went to acting school. From there, a part in a TV show playing a terrorist and then a part in a movie playing a cab driver and now my own film. I owe it all to you.'

Sultan froze. In the mirror, he saw who was behind him. Ahmed was a little older but it was him. He was handsome and well dressed. It was him.

'Ahmed! Welcome back. I had no idea. You became Kino?! I'm so proud of you.'

'Don't be proud. Be happy. Here. I've bought you a gift.' He opened a parcel. Inside was a videotape.

The cover read, 'Razor Burn: Sultan's Barber and Magic Shop, directed by and starring Ahmed Faiz'.

They hugged and watched the film together. As the credits came up, tears were streaming down Sultan's face.

'I don't know whether I'm laughing or crying. The film is in English. I can't understand a word. But seeing you, my handsome boy. Wow. Ahmed the actor. Who would have believed that would ever happen?'

'You helped me believe in myself. Now it is my turn to help you. I have paid off your debt to your uncle in London. The shop is all yours.'

ACROSS TIME ZONES AND OCEANS, Fahad took a look out across New York from his office in Manhattan. The view was pretty spectacular, it had to be said.

His assistant entered. 'Good news, boss.'

'Oh yeah? What?'

'Remember that film company we invested in a few years back? AF Films?'

'Yes I do. Six million for their first production, as I recall. Last I heard, they were getting ready to release the film. My wife was keen on the film and on the young guy making it. She wouldn't shut up about him. I said yes just to keep her quiet. Six million dollars' worth of quiet.'

'Well, the lead actor just got nominated for a Golden Globe. Sets us up for Oscars season nicely and for a healthy profit on a low–budget flick.'

'Nice. What was the film again?'

'Comedy. Pakistani barber shop in Brooklyn.'

'Really? I funded that? I thought we funded some arthouse movie in French. That actually sounds funny. We should go see it. Are the figures for the last quarter in for BGW tyres? I really don't want to go and bang their heads together if they have lost money again. Have you been to Trenton, New Jersey? It is not a place you go to twice. Do you have the *numbers for layoffs in Singapore? I wanted thirty per cent. I am hearing the local management say twenty-five per cent. Fuck 'em. I want thirty per cent of that workforce gone. Thirty per cent raises the share price by fifty per cent. Once we announce, we sell the shares.'*

'They'll both be in later today. I'm on it.'

Fahad returned to looking out the window. Pakistani barber shop. Ha. It was two decades since he had gone to the village in Jhelum. He caught his own reflection in the mirror. He had come a long way from the blue–haired punk–rocker godless communist of his youth. He wondered what had happened to Sultan the barber.

Fahad, like so many people that Tuesday morning, didn't hear the plane hit his building.

MALEK PUT DOWN THE KINDLE. Fahad was an industrialist with a record of laying off thousands of people and destroying whole communities and the environment. He was as evil as they came. Rich man, camel, eye of the needle and all that. But he had changed the lives of Sultan and Ahmed, even if he had done it without realising it.

Still, though, he was evil.

Rubati took notes. She was starting to build up a picture of what made Malek tick.

'So, you're choosing hell because Fahad is greedy? But his greed helped Ahmed and, in turn, Ahmed gave Sultan enough money to retire on. That isn't worth anything?'

'He has wrecked more lives than he has helped. Besides, he had no idea what film he was investing in.'

'But he died in a terrorist attack on New York. His life was taken from him: doesn't that get him into heaven?'

'That's the argument. That innocents who die at the hands of 'rightly guided' pious men go to heaven. It's a stupid argument. Fahad didn't believe in God so he cared little about rightly guided pious bombers. If there is a hell, he goes. Which will be a surprise for him.'

13

Waziristan, Waristan

The next morning, they arrived at the army helicopter base just outside Islamabad at the appointed time.

After several security checks, they sat outside the tiny terminal building and waited for lift-off. Malek was quiet and spent his time staring at the helicopter in front of him. The Mi-17 wasn't a pretty-looking flying machine. In fact, it looked a bit like a malformed turtle with the uncovered frame of an umbrella sticking out of its shell. Something about it unnerved him.

Justin was making last-minute adjustments to his camera and Neeka was chatting away to the head of the Inter Services Public Relations department, Major General Kamar Ayoub. Take-off was around twenty minutes away and they were heading to North Waziristan in the country's tribal belt. Since 2011, the army had been involved in an operation to rid the region of Pakistani Taliban fighters and other assorted groups who'd established a base in North Waziristan.

This latest operation was code-named Zarb-e-Azb. Azb

122

was the name of the sword wielded by the Prophet Mohammed and Zarb meant 'strike of the sword'. The operation had begun in June 2014, when peace talks had failed and the Taliban had mounted a brazen attack against Jinnah International Airport in Karachi. After that attack there was a tremendous amount of anger in Pakistan, so the politicians and army had little choice but to go after the group. The operation even had its own theme song, which was at once patriotic, militaristic and religious, and had a video that Neeka described as '*Top Gun* meets Bollywood'. The major general was showing it to Neeka on his phone.

'You don't like the song, Neeka?'

'I love it. What worries me is the fact that you guys are using the same religious imagery as the Taliban and ISIL. Don't you think that by framing this as an almost holy war you're playing into the hands of the militants?'

'Quite the opposite in fact. We are reclaiming the narrative. For too long we – by "we", I mean we as a nation – allowed the Taliban to justify its campaign of violence through religion. They cannot justify it. We are a Muslim nation. Religion is our guide.'

'Hmm. I guess. Anyway, what is the plan when we land?'

They discussed a few more details and then got ready for the flight. The whole conversation had made Neeka uncomfortable. There comes a time in every journalist's life when they have to bite their tongue and not upset the people who are giving them access to something. Now wasn't the time to pick a fight over religion with the very men who were going to take you to one of the most dangerous places on earth to film a story. Any criticism could wait until they were editing the piece.

The helicopter fired up and its wheezy noise grew ever more high-pitched. They trooped into the machine.

It took around two hours to get to North Waziristan, and they landed at the headquarters of the army's 313 Brigade in Mir Ali.

In Pakistan, the army kept grand barracks for its soldiers and prided itself on the neat, perfectly groomed gardens and tidy buildings. This wasn't that. This was a forward operating base, in an area fiercely independent of Pakistan, despite being within its borders. The base was battle-scarred and muscular. Apache attack helicopters rested in the blazing sun. No army based here was received happily outside of these walls. The British had found this to their fatal cost. Now Pakistan's army had come here.

The residents of North Waziristan had known only war for the last decade. It was as if the chaos of constant disorder was what allowed this place to function.

Base commander Major General Saeed gave a briefing to Malek, Neeka and Justin.

'We are going into the town to show you the market, where much of the terrorism that has plagued Pakistan for the last ten years originated. Snipers are an issue but we've mounted several airstrikes over the last twenty-four hours, which should give us a clear run. Feel free to film whatever you want, but remember, speed is of the essence. The longer we are in one place the more likely that information will reach the terrorists and alert them to our presence and, while we welcome a fight, I'd quite like to bring you back to Islamabad alive. There will be some locals you can speak to. Any questions?'

Malek shifted a little uncomfortably in his chair. He wanted to ask about the returning residents. Millions had fled the region when the army had come in, and now they were coming back. They'd been asked to sign something called 'Social Agreement North Waziristan'. This was a pledge of allegiance to the government and the nation. The Taliban had also asked for pledges of allegiance.

Malek didn't ask the other question on his mind, which was who were the locals that the army would introduce them to? Probably not ones who were critical of the army. He didn't want to alert the major general to his thinking, lest he should find some excuse to stop them talking to non-sanctioned locals.

Embeds with the military, no matter who they were with – American, British, Iraqi or Pakistani – were a cat-and-mouse game of competing agendas. All sides were well-versed in the rules of the game which, in essence, were simple. The military wanted you to report what they showed you. In this case it would be a strong army, popular with locals, who had brought peace back to the area and chased the bad guys away. You, the journalist, would like to report what you saw, confirm it and speak to as many people as possible to build up a complete picture. Rarely did those two things match up.

'Let the games begin,' said Malek, mustering up some spirit to hide his doubt.

'That's the stuff. Let's go!' said the major general, with perhaps a little too much confidence.

They crammed into a SUV which had been modified to fit several M4 carbine machine guns in its carry rack. The flak jackets they wore were coloured dark blue, with the word 'Press' in the middle. While they were driving, Neeka pushed a finger into the word on Malek's flak. 'That joke never gets old for you, huh?'

'What? It says "Press". So I did.'

It would be the last time they would smile all day. As they drove through the streets of the town, the damage from war was everywhere. The brown mud-walled houses had stood little chance against the bullets and bombs. They stopped in the central market.

Justin began to film and almost on cue the major general began to speak.

'This was a terrorist bazaar. Suicide-bomber vests, car bombs and weapons were all available here. Everyone in this town relied in some way on this terrorist economy. Kidnap for ransom, the weapons trade: all helped fuel the war. After all, if everyone relied on this economy for food, why would anyone here want it to stop? But stop it we did. Street to street, house to house we fought hard and bravely. We routed the enemy and now people are slowly coming home.'

The major general continued his briefing as Neeka and Justin filmed him. Malek took the opportunity to slip into one of the nearby empty houses. A single room was littered with jihadist literature in every language spoken by the fighters. Some discarded small arms lay in the corner and the black flag of the Taliban hung on the wall. Malek looked through the books while, underfoot, spent bullet casings told a tale of the ferocity of the fighting. He picked one up. A spent bullet casing is an odd thing. The bullet has gone, but the casing remains, and looks quite innocent. There are some scratches on the side of this particular bullet. Malek recognised them. In very badly written Arabic script it said '*Allah O Akbar*' – 'God is great'. Clearly one of the fighters was hoping for some divine intervention, and wasn't a dab hand at calligraphy when writing with a sharp knife.

'Why are you in my house?'

Malek looked up from the bullet-strewn ground and saw a man holding a gun. It hadn't occurred to him that people might still live here.

'I'm so sorry.'

'You're here with the army?'

'Yes. Look, please forgive me. I'll leave.'

'Something troubles you. You're not at peace. My name is Javed Khudaullah. I'm a Pir. The Taliban took over my house and filled it full of hate. I can tell a disturbed soul when I see one. But you don't have hate in your eyes. You have pain.'

Malek had come across Pirs before. Self-styled holy crackpots by and large who took advantage of the poor to gain influence and money. He largely dismissed them but many in Pakistan didn't.

'Forgive me, I'll leave your house.'

'There is no need. Let's have some tea and we can talk about your pain. Perhaps it's a woman? No, that's not it. Perhaps it's war? We have all seen our fair share.'

There was one thing that was sure to annoy Malek, and that was self-styled holy men. Across the world he had met many of them, and they all seemed to have one goal: to get money. He looked at the Pir. He seemed harmless enough despite holding a gun. In this part of the world everyone had a gun whether they could use one or not. Malek noticed that the Pir's gun was without a magazine: not everyone can afford bullets. The Pir seemed harmless enough.

'Forgive me, but why should I tell you anything? In my experience, Pirs are nothing but frauds who take people's money in return for sketchy religious advice.'

Javed laughed out loud. 'This is true my friend. Frauds are everywhere. But I am a Sufi and we connect with God without the need for preachers and clerics. I can recognise a troubled mind. But if my credentials don't convince you, how about this: you argue with God, and you don't feel love for God.'

'Look outside. Take a look at what God has done. You tell me if God deserves anything from me.'

'Come sit. Let us talk.'

'Cross my palm with silver and your fortune I will tell? Is that what this is?'

'I don't understand. Why would I cross your palm with silver?' Clearly, fairground gypsies had yet to make it to Mir Ali.

'OK, so no silver, but what's your game?'

Malek recalled a tale of a Pir who had promised his local village that he could kill a man and bring him back to life. Somehow, he convinced a man to be his subject. He cut his throat and then prayed over him. The villagers watched as the blood emptied from his throat and he remained lifeless. The Pir closed his eyes and told the village that the man was speaking to him from heaven and that he was alive and dressed in golden clothing. The village hanged the Pir as a fraud.

'My game, as you put it, is to bring peace to the troubled and those who seek it. Clearly, you don't seek help, so forgive me, but this is my house and you are a stranger in it.'

As the Pir turned round he began to quietly sing. Malek recognised the song. It was an old Qawwali song called 'Allah Hoo'. Islamic devotional music, and a favourite of his father's. His singing was soft and low and a calm filled the air. The Pir noticed him listening to the song and began to sing a little louder. Malek relaxed a little as he remembered his father listening to the same devotional song. The Pir stopped singing. He looked at Malek

'You're not leaving my house I see. God knows best my friend. Perhaps we were meant to meet.'

'Your gun has no bullets. Why carry around an empty weapon?'

'Loaded gun or not, when God calls us we go. When it's my time to go a loaded gun will not stop that.'

The Pir was harmless, a devout man stuck in a war he didn't ask for. There was something gentle about him. He wasn't a crackpot hustling for a handout from people looking for spiritual advice.

'Please sit. What is your name?'

'Malek.'

'Well Malek, let us pray, and then we will talk.'

Both men held up their palms and closed their eyes. The Pir prayed in a soft voice. Malek was unsure what to do so he played it safe by keeping his hands up until Javed stopped praying. It was a trick he used to do when forced to pray to get on the right side of religious people he wanted to interview. Malek had long forgotten how to pray and hadn't been to a mosque without a camera crew in tow since 2001. When in doubt, mimic the others, and that's what he did. Mimic the Pir. The Pir stopped praying and asked Malek a question.

'Why did you not pray?'

Malek hesitated. 'Erm... Look, I'm sorry, but this might be a bad idea. I'm sorry.'

He felt like he had been busted raiding the cookie jar between meals.

'Please don't worry. We all have our ways to God. But why do you fight with God?'

Malek remained stuttering and hesitant at first, but then the floodgates opened. He told the man about it all. Throughout the story, the Pir nodded occasionally.

As he finished, the Pir raised his hand and said, 'Young man. You have been touched. We don't know by whom. This is unclear. You have been touched by the hand either of God or the Devil. This is the only truth we have right now. You must find more truth. But be warned. In truth, madness. The more truth you uncover, the more unreasonable it will be.'

Malek thought for a moment. 'The book says it can be used or misused. It depends whether I have malice or good in my heart. I can influence the outcome of someone's life. Or rather, where they go at the end of it. Can one man have that kind of power?'

'You all still misunderstand so much about faith. You have no power. God has a plan for all of us. The Devil wants you to deviate from that path. You, my friend, need to understand the power and purpose of this book. For now, keep reading. Keep reading and the book's purpose will become clear. Find out what it means, what the truth is. But, while you search for this truth, take this.'

He took a piece of green string from his pocket and tied it around Malek's wrist. 'Green is the prophet's favourite colour. It represented paradise and peace to him and has become the traditional colour of our faith. Go with peace in your heart while you find this truth and may this protect you from madness.'

Malek felt torn. Normally, this would be when he would open his wallet and give the crackpot holy man a few rupees and send him on his way. Insistent Pirs had a way of sticking to people until money was handed over. But something about Javed Khudaullah was different. He wasn't a crackpot holy man. To offer him money would be to insult him. Instead, he began to thank him. Suddenly the calm of the room was shattered by gunfire.

Malek rushed out of the house. Neeka and Justin were hiding behind the SUV, which was parked outside. The major general was calling for backup. A few minutes later, as the gun battle continued, muffled blasts of artillery started up.

'That's going to teach the bastards!' yelled the major general. 'Don't worry, it'll all be over soon.'

Malek flopped down next to Neeka. With each burst of gunfire their hearts pounded that much quicker. Malek put his hand on top of his helmeted head and prodded Neeka, who was weighing the odds of survival.

Neeka looked up at Malek. 'Oh, thank God. Where have you been? Have you been daydreaming again?'

'Sort of. I think I've figured out what the book means. We need to find more truth.'

'*Ay baba.* What do you think we are doing here? We are finding the truth!'

'Not the truth, more truth.'

'*Nemifahman?* Look, I can't even... Anyway, you know what you and Justin need to do right now? Are you ready?'

Malek looked at Justin. They'd been here before. A quick plan was formulated. Mics were switched on.

'Justin: keep shooting, no matter what. Stay behind the car. See that rock in the middle of the road? I'll start talking when I get there. Just shoot where I point.'

'Sensational. Don't be a hero mate. One take and you're back. OK?' 'OK. Here goes. *Bismillah!*'

Justin began to hum 'Bohemian Rhapsody' while he focused his camera on Malek.

Malek ran out into the street and began to record a report from the gun battle. It ran on the 2200GMT news hour.

Only the more eagle-eyed of viewers would have spotted the green string bracelet.

Malek felt better for having it on. More secure.

They spent a few more days in Islamabad until the call came through from Baher on the planning desk and, with it, details of the next assignment to Baghdad. Flights were booked and bags packed once again. And then it was on to Benazir Bhutto International. The worst airport in the world. It was essentially a military airfield with a terminal attached to it. It wasn't conducive to relaxing.

As the plane taxied onto the runway, Malek began to read his Kindle.

The Intentions of Men

MIKE GUILDSMAN TOOK the left turn into 675 North Randolph Street. He'd been working at DARPA, the Defense Advanced Research Projects Agency, for fifteen years now and was responsible for developing drone technology for military use. For the last five years, though, he'd changed tack and concentrated on artificial intelligence. It was slow moving. So far they had concentrated on replicating the cerebral neocortex, to try to mimic the bits of the brain that give us memory, awareness, attention and perception. They wanted to put into practice the ability to analyse huge amounts of data in real time to make decisions on the battlefield. The stereo in his car played some Crosby, Stills and Nash. He might be a responsible suit now but, somewhere, his Sixties youth still burned brightly.

His fifteen–year–old self would have been thrilled with his sixty–five–year–old self. It was truly the stuff of science *fiction that he had access to. Artificial intelligence. Wow. He walked across the car park into his building and into his office. They had a long way to go before they could build a self–aware robot, and it wouldn't be in his lifetime, but the research was fascinating and could lead anywhere. So far though, the only real breakthrough was developing a four-legged robot which, if you kicked it, would process thousands of pulses, correct itself and not fall over. While this was useful enough, it was mainly for amusement and as a test bed for new things that they wanted to try.*

But, on this day, Mike was to do something else. He'd just read the notes of a new programme he wanted to implement in Syria and Iraq. To be more accurate, he wanted the politicians and military to implement the weapon in those countries; he just happened to have built it.

'DARPA's Agnostic Compact Demilitarization of Chemical Agents program is exploring new technologies for neutralization of bulk stores of CWAs and organic precursors at or near the site of storage.' He was concerned about the overly scientific language that his colleague had used to write the report that he was to read out. He would have to brief the President's advisers on their progress, and there was no way they would go for overly technical language. He needed a simpler way of saying it.

Chemical weapons were a difficult thing to neutralise and often had to be shipped long distances to a safe site. Albania seemed to be one destination. Given that Syria and Iraq were at war, even gaining access to weapons was an issue. This would solve that problem. Destroy them on the site. This would quicken the process and save lives and money. At least, that was the hope. But there was something else. Something they'd found during research that had astonished even the jaded scientists. They had synthesised a formula that could be weaponised.

It was a sort of antidote. Basically, a chemical formula that could confirm, from a drone high up in the air, a chemicals weapons site, then, when dropped on that site, could neutralise the weapons by means of a vapour that degraded the chemical, causing a huge explosion. This meant that they could avoid the thorny issue of access to sites and simply vaporise the offending materials away. Imagine that. A weapon that would actually save lives in a real way rather than destroying them. The cost wasn't much: a few billion in development costs. All he needed to do was to sell the idea to the President's advisers and then let them go out to bat for him and get him the money.

Who could say no to this? It was perfect. And they could do it. They could have the weapon in less than a year. But Mike knew that he had a problem. He worked in defence, and politicians like snappy names for their weapons. He recalled Ronald Reagan's Strategic Defense Initiative. No one had remembered that moniker. The politicians took to calling it 'Star Wars'. It worked. People remembered it. 'Agnostic Compact Demilitarization of Chemical Agents' wasn't snappy. The acronym was dull. 'ACDCA.' Hang on, he thought, and scribbled down a note. That's it! AC/DC. I mean, who doesn't love Back in Black?

In the corner, a TV showed the news on Al Jazeera English. Reports had just come in about ISIL using chemical weapon gases on Kurdish Peshmerga forces. The reporter was live from Baghdad and wore a green string bracelet which Mike noticed because he wore a red one. Something to do with Kabbalah that his wife had introduced him to. He didn't quite get it but then he was more comfortable with science than animism. He knew from a variety of intelligence reports that he was privy to that ISIL were looking to steal chemical weapons, weapons that Bashar Al Assad had already used. ISIL would never allow weapons inspectors in and Assad would only allow them in after they had cleaned up the site and extracted concessions from the inter-national community. But this way, they could detect and destroy chemical weapons without the need for negotiation.

The briefing for the president's advisers was in thirty minutes. Mike left Arlington and arrived at the White House. It wasn't his first time, but he always got a little thrill walking into this iconic building. In the room sat representatives from Defense, the White House and the State Department. An uncomfortable triumvirate of competing agendas and political skulduggery. The women wore pant suits in various hues of neutral colour and the men looked even greyer. They listened to his proposal and he spared them the technical details that he so loved and they so hated.

As he wrapped up, he was confident that his work had been successful. 'So, gentlemen. I give you AC/DC. Let's put chemical weapons back in black.'

Somehow, had he managed to unite this triumvirate of competing agendas and political skulduggery?

Silence in the room. He wondered whether they knew who AC/DC were. The general looked the other way. It was the President's chief of staff who spoke first. 'You have got to be kidding me?'

'I'm sorry, is something unclear?'

'Yes. You're talking about building a weapon that can destroy chemical weapons for use in Syria?'

'And in Iraq, yes. Just today Al Jazeera showed...'

'Let me stop you there. You don't get it, do you? We don't

want a weapon that's easier to use. We need the chemical weapons to be a problem. That's how we negotiate, that's how we sell to the world that Assad is evil. That ISIL are evil. If we can neutralise chemical weapons with what you say is a perfectly harmless drone strike, then where is the fear? The world needs to feel fear in order to feel safe. This isn't the Sixties, there are no "happy hippy war weapons".'

Then the general spoke. 'I never want to hear the words Syria, ISIL or Al Jazeera out of your mouth again. You develop weapons. The President decides when to shoot the weapons. We shoot the weapons. It's fucking simple. We shut this programme down right now. Yes to on–site destruction, no to weaponising anything to do with this. I presume I speak on behalf of Defense and the State Department? Good. This meeting is over, Mr Guildsman.'

Mike swallowed his tongue and shuffled out of the building. He caught his breath on Pennsylvania Avenue. He was furious. This was the breakthrough he had been looking for all his career. A weapon that could help stop a modern war, one in which insurgents in civilian clothes, not uniformed standing armies, fought. Times had changed since Robert Oppenheimer, the father of the atom bomb, had given birth to his monster. 'I am become death, the destroyer of worlds,' as he himself had put it in a television interview years after inventing the atomic bomb. He was quoting Hindu scripture. Nuclear weapons had not made the world safer; they stayed in their silos, all brand new and shiny, while home–made chemical weapons and bombs killed thousands over the decades.

This time though, it wasn't just that quote that Mike remembered. There was another. Oppenheimer had also said, in 1955, that, 'There are no secrets about the world of nature. There are secrets about the thoughts and intentions of men.'

He had said that in an interview with the titan of American television news, Edward R. Murrow.

The thoughts and intentions of men in Washington had long gotten to Mike. But this, this was too much. It was now time for him to use television news. He called a friend at the US Embassy in Baghdad. They exchanged a few pleasantries before he got down to business.

'Mark. Do you know the Al Jazeera correspondent in Baghdad? I need a number.'

'Sure, I'll text it you right away. Let's speak soon.'

'Thanks. Speak soon.'

A few seconds later, the number came through. He tapped it in.

'Is that Malek Khalil? My name is Mike Guildsman. I want to go on the record as an employee of DARPA. You know what that is, right?'

'Yes.'

'Then you'll know we are serious people. Let me tell you about the weapon that could save lives in Syria and Iraq that no one in Washington wants...'

Suddenly the phone went dead. Malek tried calling the number back. There was no ringtone.

MALEK PUT DOWN THE KINDLE, his head swirling with thought. He remembered the man calling him some six months ago. No one could hear him over the sound of the jet engines, and he covered his mouth as he began to speak, just in case Neeka saw him talking to himself.

'Rubati. That phone call. I remember it. I tried calling him back, but nothing. I figured he had got cold feet.'

'He hasn't been seen since that meeting. No one knows

where he is. Well, I know where he is. His family don't. He is currently lying dead in a watery grave just outside of DC. Someone didn't want him to talk to you.'

'He developed weapons for a living. He played with fire. He got burned. What is it the Bible says about the wages of sin? "For the wages of sin is death, but the free gift of God is eternal life in Jesus Christ our Lord." He sinned. He used his gift to destroy lives. But then he did come up with a weapon of peace, if such a thing is possible. So maybe he gets into heaven on a technicality. That, and the fact he was murdered. They get you bonus heaven points, right?'

'Did you just turn heaven into a frequent-flyers programme?' Rubati sounded aghast.

'Yes. This book is stupid; you don't exist and so I can do anything I want. At the pearly gates, or whatever people think happens, you get a reading of your life. Gold members to heaven. Oh, you only reached bronze level. Sorry, my son. Take the lift downstairs please.'

'Malek.'

'What? That is what this whole thing is. Heaven reward points. Be good on earth, and get a place in heaven. It's like being at Starbucks and having a loyalty card except, in heaven, they probably get your name right.'

'It's not Starbucks. Why are you being like this?'

'I don't know. God is a dick?'

'You're the dick.' She sounded even more aghast. She also smiled. If he was calling God a dick, at least he had accepted that God existed. Why on earth did they choose this guy, she wondered.

14

Baghdad Blues

I t was just before midnight when Malek heard the noise. It was a dull thud. A deep, heavy, short burst of muffled sound, like hearing a snippet of a bass drum being hit in a different room while you had cotton buds in your ear. It was distinctive. He instantly knew what it was. He had heard this noise more times than he cared to remember.

In 2003 he was reporting in Afghanistan when his convoy came under attack on the outskirts of Jalalabad. They were filming a piece high in the mountains of Tora Bora about Osama bin Laden's escape into Pakistan, where bin Laden would remain in hiding for the next eleven years. It was a new team for Malek, and the producer Neeka and the cameraman Justin seemed switched-on and energetic. For this venture the Afghan security forces had provided them with a convoy of two pick-up trucks packed with soldiers armed with AK47s; the car carrying the film crew travelled in the middle. The road from Jalalabad to Tora Bora was quiet and the soldiers dispersed quickly on location. During a brief moment of tranquillity, Malek found himself looking out across the mountainous landscape around Tora Bora, marvelling at its fierce and austere beauty.

After filming, they got back into their vehicles and travelled back along the same quiet route. It was as they hit the road into Jalalabad that Malek heard the dull thud. The first pick-up truck narrowly escaped the bomb, which had been packed into the middle of the rough dirt road. Their own vehicle swerved off to the side as the soldiers began to shoot indiscriminately on all sides. Cowering in the car, they saw the crater the bomb had left in front of them. Justin grabbed his camera and Malek the car's door handle. They looked at each other. But it was Neeka who had her wits about her.

'Malek! Justin! Get out! Do a piece to camera and film some footage. Now!'

Malek's reply was less than gracious. 'Fuck, yes, we are going!' Justin burst out of the car, Malek following without another word.

As the bullets flew, Malek reported from the scene. And Justin shot as much footage as he could.

That night, back at the Hotel Spinghar, none of them talked about what had happened. Call it bravado or inexperience: that night was something they just wanted to forget. Over the years, though, that changed. Sometimes they'd shout expletives at each other after hearing a bomb. Other times, they would just be relieved that they'd only heard and not seen it.

Now in Baghdad in 2015, the bombs had, for a long time, taken on a constant miserable rhythm. It usually began soon after sunset. This time, it was coming up to midnight. The news broke, as these things often did, with a call from Osama, the Al Jazeera English producer in Baghdad. Osama had lived through the worst of Iraq's violence, yet still managed to smile and laugh. This time, however, he was serious and to the point.

'Malek, I'm hearing that seven car bombs have gone off in Baghdad. Give me five minutes and I'll get you more information.'

Malek's mood sank. He'd spent the afternoon with an Iraqi artist called Qasim Sabti at his gallery. Sabti was a gregarious man with an indiscreet manner, which he employed to tell tales of writers and poets under Saddam, and now under democracy. He had an infectious personality and his tales gave Malek a sense of optimism about the country. As they drank ice-cold colas he said, 'We love life in Iraq, and life loves us.'

Malek thought back to those words as the flurry of information came through. In the end, the death tolls and the scale of the attacks across the country shocked even him. Seventeen car bombs – twelve of them in Baghdad. Ninety-one killed, 245 injured.

We love life in Iraq, and life loves us, Malek said to himself.

After a night of on-air reporting, the morning gave Malek, Justin and Neeka the chance to visit one of the bombing sites.

They had decided on the Shia neighbourhood of Shaab to the north-east of the city, typical of the style of Baghdad: tiny apartments crowded above shops, with cafés and restaurants dotted around the streets where young men normally sat to play chess and sip tea. But in the aftermath of two car bombs, the chess pieces had been put down. Instead, brooms had been picked up and the sound of broken glass being swept made a screeching sound that grated Malek's nerves.

They were surrounded as soon as they began to film. Words, angry and full of hurt, began to tumble from people's mouths. For good reason.

The damage from the bombs was immense – the street was full of blackened metal, front doors hanging from hinges. Even though the cars had been removed, Malek could still see blast marks on the ground.

No one had been killed here, but plenty were injured.

They visited one of the damaged apartments and the blast-seared walls seemed to close in, the debris scattered across the floor. A young girl, six years old at most, sat crying on her mother's lap; the family had had very little to begin with, and now they had nothing. A lifetime's possessions had been consumed in seconds by the explosion. The Eid holiday was about to begin. A chance, as Qasim Sabti had put it, to enjoy life. Except there was no enjoyment here, no life to be loved. Only severe pain and fear for the future.

They said Baghdad was used to this violent life. Malek disagreed. No one could ever get used to car bombs ripping through their streets or gun battles raging outside their homes.

In his time in Iraq, Malek had seen neighbourhoods become no-go areas and, once again in Baghdad's history, the city was divided along sectarian lines. The attack on this Shia neighbourhood was claimed by ISIL. Its stated aim was simple: to transform the country into a Sunni Islamic state under its control. It had been able to take over huge swathes of Iraq, in part because the Iraqi army didn't have the US support it once had, although now that support was seeping back. Sunni tribal militias, formed to combat foreign fighters of the original Al-Qaeda, had been disbanded, and years of sectarian policies from Iraq's government had left Sunnis angry and isolated.

Malek asked the Baghdad producer Osama what he thought of ISIL.

His reply was bleak. 'This ends badly for Iraq. This ends Iraq, in fact. Unless we unify, we split along sectarian and ethnic lines. ISIL is the beginning.'

On the streets of Shaab, Malek shared a cigarette and a talk with Odai, a young guy who had been watching them since they got here. Odai was a member of the informal neighbourhood watch that had sprung up in different neighbourhoods all over the city. He'd call in the movements of strangers and anything odd to others, who would then be ready to act. They had weapons caches dotted around the neighbourhood. Malek had met these fiercely protective young men before. He asked Odai how he felt about what had happened.

'We will protect ourselves, God willing. No one else cares for us. Our politicians enjoy their money and sit and eat. We just die.'

'How can you protect yourself from these attacks?'

'Fear and suspicion. In this neighbourhood, we know everyone. There used to be a few Sunni families that lived here. But they left. The youth of this place told them to leave. Threatened them, in fact. Here we don't take chances. If we see a stranger we will ask what he is doing here. If a car is parked, and we don't recognise it, we take a closer look. Fear and suspicion are our defensive weapons now.'

'Do you ever leave here?'

'Where would I go? I have no need to risk my life to travel to another place in this city. I know everyone here.

They all know me. We look after each other. Go with God, my friend, and pray that your children never live like this.'

Malek smiled. 'I don't have any children. I have those two.' He pointed to Neeka and Justin.

Odai laughed and said, 'When we saw you arrive we knew you were reporters. But we never see reporters here. We just see misery. Who do you work for?'

Malek shuffled uncomfortably. This was a loaded question in Iraq. The government had banned Al Jazeera Arabic from broadcasting in Iraq and tensions remained between the governments of Baghdad and Qatar. Al Jazeera English was free to broadcast and to news-gather but, to most Iraqis, such reporting made little difference. Most of the tensions were stoked by groups with vested interests and Iraq's free media were never shy to take on the policies of Qatar or to criticise Al Jazeera.

But Malek's pride in his reporting and his network meant he wasn't about to lie. 'Al Jazeera English.'

Odai flinched visibly. 'They support ISIL! Why do you work for them?'

'We don't support anyone. We report. It was the Iraqi government that banned Al Jazeera Arabic from reporting. Bans never help anyone. I am here reporting on your situation. I can tell you, Arabic would do the same. I'm British Pakistani, I've seen first-hand what sectarian violence does to a country. The Taliban and the Americans have helped destroy what Pakistan used to be and you know this better than anyone.'

Odai drew on his cigarette and he narrowed his gaze towards Malek. 'Tell me. Are you Sunni or Shia?'

'Both. My father was Sunni. My mother Shia. I spent my

childhood in mosques and learning about Imam Hussein and Imam Ali. *Ya' Ali madat.*'

Odai laughed once more. Malek felt calmer now. Conversations with young men in Iraq can quickly get tense. 'What does this mean? *Ya' Ali madat?*'

Malek laughed in return. It was a line he'd used in Iraq many times before to diffuse a tense situation. 'It's an Urdu phrase some Pakistanis use. It means "May Ali help me", but it can also mean "May God help me". Ali, as you know, is one of the ninety-nine names of God. It means "the highest" or "the most exalted one".'

'Well, my half-Shia half-Sunni friend. Go with God and be safe.'

Malek returned the greeting but decided against telling the young man about the 'SuShi' nickname popular in Pakistan for describing people like himself. Trying to explain Japanese food and religious sectarian humour in one breath probably wasn't appropriate right now. The conversation though had left a sour taste in Malek's mouth. He was pissed off. In the car on the way back to the office, it was Neeka who broke the silence.

'Hey. What's up? What is it this time?'

'It's not what you think. I'm not an Arab. I don't have a dog in this fight. But, everywhere we go, people want us to pick a side. Shia, Sunni, Kurd, Jew, Christian, Israeli, Palestinian, Syrian regime or rebel, whatever. Everyone is so entrenched. It's so fucking depressing.'

'How long have we been on the road now?'

'The NATO summit was three months ago. On and off, it's been ten months since Babylon.'

'We need a break. How about I call the office? We are due to pull out next week. Justin has that gig in Kabul he wants to take. Let's go on holiday and meet back in Baghdad in a few weeks. Justin?'

'Cool with me. I can spend a week in Kabul filming the kids-on- drugs story then go and chill in Amsterdam.'

'*Aray*. Only you, Justin, could film a story about kids doing drugs in Kabul, then go get high in Amsterdam. Anyway, it's a deal. Let's all get out of here. Malek, I don't have anyone to go on holiday with.'

Malek realised that he didn't either. Neeka was the closest thing to a relationship he'd ever had. And she was a pain in the ass. Sometimes. 'Neither do I. I guess it's you and me against the world again. Where do you want to go?'

'Somewhere that isn't the Middle East. Vietnam.'

'*Yalla.*'

15

Vietnam

Neeka had organised an itinerary almost as soon as they landed. Excitedly she rattled off names and places as they sat in the cab. Malek gazed at her and took in the sights. Saigon. The scene of American defeat and now a hot tourist destination. For the next couple of weeks there would be no news desk, no cameras, no war and no misery. At least that's what Malek thought. Until they pulled up outside their first destination.

'Neeka. This is not what I had in mind when you said Vietnam. I was expecting great food, beaches and beer.'

'You'll get the beaches soon, I promise. But this is going to be fascinating.'

The War Remnants Museum in Saigon was a harrowing and thought-provoking place. The creators of the exhibition hadn't shied away from displaying the true horrors of war. Malek was more than a little perturbed.

One room was dedicated to the victims of an American chemical weapon called Agent Orange. The weapon, in one form carried as a grenade by US soldiers, was tossed into the tunnels the Viet Cong used to hide in. When that didn't work, the US Air Force just carpet-bombed the chemical indiscriminately across the south and centre of the country to clear the foliage that the Viet Cong used for cover. It also had the side effect of sticking to humans. Decades later, children and grandchildren still suffered horrific physical hereditary deformity. Neeka stopped at a corner of the museum and held back her tears.

The top-floor exhibition of pictures was by a variety of photographers, both foreign and Vietnamese, and were taken from a book called *Requiem for a War*. As dreadlocked hippies and well-fed Europeans walked around the room, the constant nagging flip-flop of their shoes on the stone floor provided an odd soundtrack to the war photographs and the nightmare scenarios that unfolded in them. A children's exhibition with a dove as its logo showed a lighter side, with its images of hope. Outside, old US army equipment – helicopters and fighter jets, big guns and boats – looked innocent, stripped as they were now of their noise, fury and fire.

'Neeka. What the fuck was that? I'm more traumatised than ever. Can we grab a drink now, please?'

'Yeah, we should probably do that.'

They found a small café and ordered a couple of beers. Neeka had arranged to meet an old friend who used to work for the BBC. He arrived and Neeka gave him a great big hug and exchanged warm greetings.

'Hey Phan, this is Malek. Phan is a journalist and tour guide who took me to the Viet Cong Cu Chi Tunnels Museum years ago.'

They chatted for a while until Malek asked a question about the history of the war and what Phan thought.

'I think what all Vietnamese think: we will forgive, but we won't forget.'

'That's in stark contrast to what Iraqis tell me. We will *never* forgive and *never* forget is more what I'm used to hearing.'

On the wall of the café was a cutting from the American *Life* magazine with the headline 'We wade deeper into jungle war'. If you changed the words 'wade' and 'jungle' to 'stagger' and 'desert' that headline could have been written today.

'Will this happen to Baghdad one day, do you think?'

'Will what?' said Phan.

'Look outside: motorbikes – and there are millions of them – and cars, and happy locals wandering the streets. The Socialist Republic of Vietnam is far from perfect, but it exists peacefully.'

Phan told Malek and Neeka at length about the problems of Vietnam: the costs of education, inflation and pollution. In short, the same problems that Malek had heard being talked about in Baghdad.

'But, Phan. At least you guys live in peace.'

'Yes, but we repelled and defeated the Americans. They left the embassy rooftop on helicopters. The Iraqis are still fighting. Once it was the Americans. Now it's each other. And we did the same. In the end, we just got tired of fighting.'

The war here had ended four decades ago. The olive-green drab of US soldiers had been replaced by the Day-Glo tie-dye of backpackers. Money was coming into Vietnam. As the three supped beer, they saw that things had vastly improved, including relations with the US. But neither Malek nor Neeka could imagine that one day the same back-

149

packers would wade through Mutanabbi Street in Baghdad buying old-looking books that Safa, had he stayed alive, would no doubt have thrown together in the back of his shop and sold as genuine Iraqi antiques. Neither of them could imagine US Army Humvees and Black Hawk helicopters being displayed in a museum in the Green Zone that you could walk into without seeing a checkpoint or an armed soldier. Could there be a desert tour to Anbar Province that would show tourists the effects of white phosphorus in Fallujah? Would taxi drivers snigger at blonde girls from Sweden and the way they wore their backpacks on their chests? Malek didn't know. But wouldn't it be great to think that war goes from life and hell to a picture on a museum wall?

'Neeka, Phan, I can see why Vietnam has survived and is at peace. The Socialist Republic remains and the red flag with a gold star in the centre sits next to Colonel Sanders' smiling KFC logo. Everyone loves fried chicken.'

'I don't,' said Neeka.

Malek continued. 'It's a maturing country, with realist ideals. Iraq is not there yet, but one day it will be. There are lessons to be learned, and new ideas to be gained from understanding history. I only hope that the powerful will understand those lessons and that we are alive to visit the Baghdad Museum of Coalition War one day.'

'Oof, Malek. You're so full of nonsense sometimes. Order more beer please.'

Malek called over the waiter. 'Can I have three beers and some fried chicken for the lady, please?'

'Ha ha. Very funny. Why don't you order up some freedom fries as well? How about a side of I'm going to kick you in the balls if you keep this up all holiday?'

This felt better to Malek. They were back to their old selves, exchanging barbs and smiles. He hadn't picked up his Kindle in a week. Tomorrow they would fly to the coast and to a resort. He looked at Neeka. She looked very pretty. The beer was clearly working.

16

Under a Socialist Sun

A couple of days later, Malek and Neeka arrived in Nha Trang on the south coast of Vietnam. They checked into a little upscale boutique hotel and spent some hours sitting on a tiny balcony overlooking the sea.

Dinner was steamed fish and rice. Neither of them said very much to each other; this time it wasn't because of stress or tiredness, just a comfortable silence. The kind that old married couples enjoy or young lovers in the midst of those heady early days. The only sound was the waves pushing up onto the shore. Even the waiters left them alone. There was no artificial noise. Everything around them was natural sonics. To a casual audience, they would have looked like honeymooners. Only they knew what they'd shared, what they'd seen and who they were.

Who were they really? News junkies. Travellers. Story-tellers. Hacks. Outside of that world, Malek and Neeka knew little about each other. They secretly adored each other and were certainly protective of each other. They knew each other's traits and personalities, but any knowledge of each other's lives pre-2001 was limited. There was never any need to talk about the past when so much was happening in the present. Like a twenty-four-hour news channel, the relationship was all about the events of that day. It was a constant cycle of birth and rebirth with them. Each day began anew and each night ended anew. *They'd* become a twenty-four-hour news cycle.

'Malek, I have an idea. No one is expecting us to call in for the next eight days. We can completely switch off. How about we do that? No Facebook. No Twitter. No WhatsApp. No Instagram. No nothing. How about it?'

'What? I have a social media following I need to maintain. People will judge me if I disappear. I'll lose followers. You realise it's a cold, competitive world out there.'

'Eight days isn't going to kill you. Besides, you check your phone more than a teenage girl.'

'At least I have a social media profile. You might as well be living in 1996.'

'Please Malek, let's get off the grid. Let's enjoy this. We are in paradise. Look at this place. There's hardly anyone here. You don't open the Kindle either. Not a single page for the rest of the time we are in Vietnam. The weather is perfect. It's beautiful. It'll still be beautiful if you don't Instagram it.'

Malek thought about her words. She was right of course. Again. 'No more Kindle.'

'Deal. No more being on the grid, Malek.'

'Amen to that.'

Around 10am the next morning they emerged from their separate rooms. About the toughest decision they had to make was whether to go down to the pool or the beach.

'I can do a beach. I prefer beaches. We could go snorkelling and read?'

'Read what, Malek? I thought we had a deal.'

'We do have a deal. I just meant something else. I have a copy of *Scoop* by Evelyn Waugh I want to read.'

'You're going to read a book about being a foreign correspondent? It's like you have a one-track mind.'

'Have you read it? It's amazing. The funniest book about journalism ever written. Besides, you took me to the war museum.'

'Really? Funnier than your reporting?'

'Fuck off, my dear.'

'Let me have a look.'

Neeka took the battered paperback from Malek. It was a very cute edition, a Penguin paperback with an orange-and-white cover. But, if Malek was to do this, if they were both to really switch off, then sacrifices would have to be made. No disrespect to the great writer but a man's sanity, not to mention hers, was at stake. She took aim. The sound the book made when it hit the surface of the pool was quite satisfying. It was the sound of switching off from the world of work.

'What the...?' Malek stopped mid-sentence and took a deep breath. 'You test the patience of saints. What am I going to read now?'

'I have a book for you. You'll like it. It's about a drunken, womanising screw-up like you are.'

'You hold such a high opinion of me. It's like you love me.'

'I'm not sure I even like you.'

'So no chance of a shag then?'

'*Nemishe*. Not bloody likely. If I haven't shagged you in

154

the – what is it now? Thirteen years? In the thirteen years I've known you, why break the sensible habit of a lifetime?'

Malek shook his head like the long-haired women do in shampoo commercials. He looked into her eyes and said, 'Because I'm worth it...'

The beach was completely empty save for the tiny crabs and assorted other natural companions that scuttled or flew around. The sun shone gently and the waves were warm and inviting. Neeka took off her beach dress and ran into the sea, looking astonishingly pretty in her red bikini. Well, it was astonishing for Malek, who'd never seen her that unclothed before.

Neeka bobbed around in the ocean and watched Malek take off his top. He wasn't bad for a forty-five-year-old. He could do with losing a few pounds but he wasn't fat and he certainly didn't look his age. In fact, neither of them did.

'Wow. This water is amazing. It's so nice in here, come in, please!' Malek waded into the water.

'I didn't see more than five metres in front of me until I was twenty. I've always lived in urban areas. Police sirens and Nigerian neighbours fighting about politics was my wildlife.'

'Wow. Twenty? That's sad. But you grew up in London, right?'

'I did. I went to a predominantly Jewish school in fact. When I was eighteen, all my friends were going on a gap year. I wanted either to go Interrailing or to go and live in a foreign country. Some of my friends sold me the idea of working on a farm, where they said I'd meet lots of cute girls. I said OK. I went home to tell my father. He looked at me a bit funny.'

'Why?'

'"*Ubu*, my friends are all going to go work on a farm in this country where the people are under attack from all sides by people who don't want them to live there. What the people are doing is building these walls and I want to go and help them because this is their ancestral land. It's going to be amazing and I'll help people." My father said, "What is this country called?" "Israel," I said. "And the farm is a collective farm called a kibbutz. Can I go?"'

'Oh my God,' interrupted Neeka.

'So my poor father was looking at me with this disappointment in his eyes that suggested he had failed as a Pakistani Muslim parent. For the next three hours I got a crash course in Israeli–Palestinian politics and history. That's what sparked the interest in becoming a journalist. Needless to say, I never went to the kibbutz.'

'Probably a good thing. If the settlers didn't shoot you, the Palestinians might have.'

'Yeah, it wasn't as bad as when I brought home a Jewish girlfriend who was also the daughter of a Conservative MP. That gave my life-long trade union member and Labour-supporting father a shock to the system!'

Neeka roared with laughter. It had been a while since she felt truly relaxed. In the distance, little boats bobbed up and down on the sea as their captains tallied up the day's catch.

'I spent my early years in DC. Mom and Pop were diplomats at the embassy there. They used to have these amazing parties. It was so glamorous. Hollywood and politics would come together. At the house, everyone would drink and laugh. I remember my mom dressing in beautiful gowns and looking like a princess. After the revolution, they remained in America, sought exile and got it. I became one of many exiles. It's only because I was born in Tehran that, when my parents went home for a year, I got an Iranian passport. I used to love the Shah and Queen Farah.'

'Used to?'

'It's complicated. So many people felt hope after the revolution that things might get fairer. Instead we replaced a paranoid king with a power-mad cleric. They are all corrupt.' Neeka sighed and continued. 'Malek. Why do we live in the Middle East? I mean, seriously. Look at this place. I could live here.'

'You'd be bored in a week. We live in the Middle East because it's a real-life chess game played on a multi-level board with devious players. Look what happened last week. Egypt asked Israel to help fight ISIL in Sinai. ISIL have threatened Hamas in Gaza, so Israel are de facto backing Hamas. Then you have Syria. The Americans will have to support Jabhat Al Nusra, who are basically Al-Qaeda, in Syria against Assad. So suddenly the Americans, fourteen years after 9/11, could support Al-Qaeda. But then next week it will be completely different and none of that will have happened. It's the politics that keep us there.'

'Oh my God. You're such a dick! Did you switch on your phone?'

'No. The pact still stands. I just picked up a few things at the airport while scanning the papers. Don't worry. I'm ignorant, blissfully and happily ignorant.'

She left the water, dried herself on the beach and lay in the sun. A while later, Malek walked back to the beach from the water. He was a little unsteady on his feet.

'How come when James Bond emerges from the water he looks super-hot, yet when you do you look like a slightly deranged ape? Try and impress a girl at least!'

157

'If you were Pussy Galore, I might just put the effort in, my dear.' They lay next to each other enjoying the afternoon.

Neeka began to giggle. 'Your poor father,' she said, as she remembered his story. 'You know people are constantly trying to revert me back to my faith.'

'Really? Your parents weren't religious?'

'They are more Persian than Iranian, more Cyrus than Ali. Islam is in the background. We call ourselves Shia Muslims but it's more ceremony than anything else. But we do take God seriously. Anyway, I was dating a Muslim guy from Delhi who took me home to his family. It was so much fun. I loved India. His mum took a real shine to me and brought out the traditional but beautiful embroidered Indian outfits from her wedding in the Fifties. We had a great time trying them on and then Jamil, the boyfriend, knocked on the door and said that the local imam had popped by. Like some blushing bride I sat in front of the imam while they had tea and stuff. Then the imam asked if I spoke any Arabic. I said no. He said he would teach me some. He did, and I dutifully repeated the words. The prayer is the same for Muslims all over the world and I saw no harm in repeating it. Jamil and his mother thought this was hilarious.

'So then the imam says, "Congratulations. You have spoken the Shahada. *Ash-hadu an la ilaha Illallah.*" Jamil and his mother burst out laughing. While I was wondering what was going on, the imam said, "You are reverted back to Islam. You are now a true Muslim, no longer the Shia heretic of your upbringing." I was angry. I take faith very seriously and while who doesn't appreciate an imam with a sense of humour, I wasn't happy. I didn't see Jamil after that.'

'I really liked you up until you said you loved India.'

For the next few hours they hung around the beach

swapping more stories of their childhoods and their lives before they met and the allure of the road had addicted both of them to the rush of delivering news.

Over the next six days, a pattern developed. Breakfast and lunch by the beach, nap, dinner by the beach, and then they'd gently walk to their separate rooms and smile and hug before the next day began.

Until the second to last night. They'd got back from dinner and looked at each other, lingering just a second too long but not in an uncomfortable way.

'You know how ridiculous this is, don't you?' said Malek.

'You correspondents never know when to shut up, do you?'

They kissed for the first time. Despite all the cities and hotels and dinners and drinks and breakfasts and wars and refugee camps and natural disasters, they'd never shared more than barbed banter and hard work. They stumbled into Neeka's room and shut the door to the world.

They didn't leave the room and spent the next two days and nights in each other's arms. 'We should have done this years ago,' said Malek, as he ran a finger down her back.

'You forget I had a husband.'

'Oh him. Shayan. The one you didn't see for years.'

'How was I going to see him? I spent eleven years on the road with you, before I got divorced.'

'You mean you spent eleven years running away from him.'

'I know. I just didn't get why he wanted to settle down so soon after getting married. I wanted adventure. I thought he did as well. Besides, Romeo, how many journos, diplomats and aid workers have you worked your way through these last thirteen years? It's not like you were available.'

'I'm not going to lie. I wasn't a monk. But I wasn't Hugh Hefner either. I think I was just looking for you.'

'*Jooni.*' The sarcasm was sharp and it hurt a bit. 'I should really learn to speak Farsi.'

'Malek, I am glad this happened.'

'I know! What's that Bollywood song again? The one about Jaanu meri Jaan?'

Malek then went into his best Amitabh Bachchan impersonation. 'Please stop. Now.' Malek didn't. She sat up and stretched her arms.

The flight to Doha and then Baghdad wasn't for another few hours. She rummaged around in her bag, naked on the bed, while Malek watched longingly.

'Here. It's time you switched this on. Let's hope it was all a bad dream.' She tossed Malek his Kindle.

'Count of three?'

'OK. One, two, three...'

Through the Looking Lens

JUSTIN HAD ORGANISED his equipment and left from Doha's Hamad International Airport to fly to Kabul. It was a trip he'd done a hundred times before, but this time it wasn't for work. Or rather, it wasn't for his day job. Over the last ten years, Justin had developed a passion project that he'd been filming on and off across various war zones in Iraq and Afghanistan. Every year, he would catch up with four orphan children he had been following since 2005. In Afghanistan, it was two brothers in Kabul: Hamid and Hamza. Both had lost their parents in the early days of the war and made a living picking through the rubbish dumps outside of Kabul and selling what they could find to merchants in the city. In Iraq, he followed two sisters, Inas and Najidha, who had lost their parents to Al–Qaeda when their home city of Fallujah came under attack.

For Justin this was a chance to really show, without filters or editorial influence from anyone, what it was like to grow up alone and in conflict.

His film had no reporter, no narration. The only sound was the children themselves talking. Every year at the same time he travelled to Kabul and Fallujah to film a little bit more of them growing up. In his spare time he would edit the film and put it together at home. He'd had interest from distributors but he wanted to wait until it was complete. He'd invested a lot of time and money in the project and, for him, complete control of everything was the aim of the game.

'Justin, welcome back. My dear friend, how are you?' Justin hugged Qais. The two men had known each other since 2001. He was Justin's guide.

'Better for seeing you Qais, better for seeing you.'

The two men had a tradition that went back a decade now. From the airport, they'd go straight to the Kabuli restaurant in Wazir Akbar Khan, Northern Kabul, feast on kebabs and rice and catch up. Qais said he was worried about Hamza and Hamid. The brothers had fallen in with a criminal gang and, although they were only ten years old, Qais had seen a change in them over the last year. They'd become hardened after living life on the streets.

'We can't get involved Qais, we just observe. Can we meet them in the morning?'

'It's all arranged. They have a house they stay at in the Sherpur district of the city. We will leave around 7am. For

now though, let's eat and you can tell me all about crazy Malek and Neeka!'

They drank tea and talked late into the night. In the morning, Justin got changed into traditional Afghan clothing and they took a cab whose driver Qais had known for years. This was a low–key assignment and was being done on a shoestring budget. There was no money for security or armoured cars. Justin put his trust in people he'd worked with for decades, but he was worried about what Qais had told him. He hoped that the boys hadn't gone too deep into the Kabul underworld.

He wasn't prepared for what he found in the house.

Hamza was chasing opium and selling it for the men who had put him in the house. All around, small squares of foil littered the floor. The boy barely stirred when Justin walked into the room. Last year, as a nine year old, he'd run up to Justin and given him a massive hug. Today, the dead look in his eyes barely registered the existence of anyone.

Justin fought back tears.

Qais spoke softly. 'Brother. I didn't want to tell you beforehand because I wanted you to see for yourself what is happening to our country. Hamid has disappeared. Hamza spends his days like this or running drug errands for the people who own this house. This isn't unusual in Kabul any more. The Taliban have flooded the local market with opium. There is a whole army of walking dead in our streets.'

Justin listened and knew he'd have to make a compromise. One that tore his soul apart. He couldn't cross the line and scoop Hamza up and get him help. If he did that, he'd disturb what was occurring naturally, the very thing that, ten years ago, he'd promised to observe without passion and with rationality. But ten years is a long time. Ten years of being an observer had taken its toll.

'Qais. Get the car ready. We are getting Hamza out of here.'

Qais made a phone call to the driver and Justin gathered Hamza up into his arms and onto his chest. They walked out of the building to the car, when Justin heard the sound of a rifle being cocked. A group of men shouted at them in Pashto. Justin held Hamza tighter.

'Justin. These men are going to take us away.'

A blackened SUV arrived. The three of them were forced into the back and the driver and the two gunmen made sure they made little noise.

Some thirty seconds later, Hamid arrived at the house.

He sat in the very room that Hamza had just been taken from. He opened up a small packet of brown powder. There was no sign that, just seconds earlier, Justin had been there, that Hamza had been there. Not for Hamid, who saw only the drugs and oblivion.

17

It Just Got Personal

Malek ran to the toilet and threw up. Neeka wept.

For eight days, neither had switched their phones on.

Had they done so they would have received the phone calls, ever more frequent and ever more frantic, from the news desk.

Justin hadn't been heard of for five days. The book had got personal. Very personal.

The trip from Nah Trang Airport to Ho Chi Minh City Airport was a blur. Neither Malek nor Neeka said much to each other.

When the flight arrived at Hamad International they finally had a decision to make. Malek thought back on everything that had happened since Babylon. The Pir had said, 'Find more truth.' His father had always taught him that, to understand, all you had to do was read. The bookseller in Babylon had warned him that this book had a power beyond a 'southern miner's understanding'. But he wasn't a southern

164

miner. His job was to find the truth and report it. He fiddled with the green string bracelet on his wrist. He knew what he had to do.

'Neeka. I have to go back to Iraq. If I'm going to find out what this book means and where Justin is, it's there that I'll find the answers. I'm going to take the flight to Baghdad. Why don't you stay in Doha and then go to Kabul? Figure out who is looking for Justin and keep kicking their asses until they find him and Qais.'

'OK. I'll cover you in Doha. I'll tell them you're speaking to some contacts.'

'Thank you, Neeka.'

'Malek. Be safe, please. You have to find out what this book means. For...'

'Justin's sake?'

'*Ay baba.* Yes, for Justin's sake find out what this book means.' They looked at each other and held each other close.

Malek looked into her eyes. 'I love you,' he said. 'I love you,' she replied.

Rubati said nothing, tucked safely inside the Kindle.

Part Three

Babylonian Tales of Death, Heaven and Hell

We who record the moments of others in our tales don't have the luxury of fiction. We cannot change what has happened. Now, Malek, you have found your friend's tale in our book. This was not malice on our part; it was always going to be thus. The Order of the Gatherers of Truths have no say in what appears in this book. Only God has that wisdom. But what happens when it becomes personal?

Dear Malek, we have all been here. We all know what it means to question the existence of God. The pertinent question is, can love for God bring your friend back? If you love, truly love, God, will God help you?

That is the challenge that you, my dear Malek, now face. You argue with God all the time, but now you understand that it requires faith in God to be able to argue with God. But you never loved God. Now, that lack of love will be tested, and it cannot be helped by religious counsel or visits to mosques, churches or temples. You will not find God in times of trouble if you didn't seek her in times of goodness. But you, Malek, did seek her in the good times. You may have had your quarrels

169

with God but you didn't ever stop believing in her. But you never loved her. In Kabul you screamed, 'Khuda is zaamen se Nikal Gaye hai' – 'God has left this land.' God has never left this land. People leave God. God remains. Let me tell you another tale.

In the mid–14th century there was a poet called Jahan Malek Khatun. She shares a name with you. But she shares more also. She lived in the land of ancient Persia, in the Fars district, in the glorious city of Shiraz. The city was hidden away just a few feet from the foothills of the grand Zagros mountains. To reach the city you had to take the mountain pass through the north. Often, travellers would catch a glimpse of the city from the mountain pass, and exclaim loudly, 'Allah O Akbar!' on their first glimpse of it. This reaction to the city and its lush orchards spread out in front of them was so commonplace that the locals began calling the pass 'Allah O Akbar'.

As a child, Jahan Malek Khatun was quite the individual. Her uncle was the ruler of Shiraz and a great patron of the poets of the time. Indeed, even Hafez was a regular visitor and many evenings would be spent with the members of the royal court listening in awe as the poets of the day enchanted them with their words.

Khatun was born to parents who bore no son. Perhaps because of this, she received an education unusual for a young girl. She was taught to read and write and became an accomplished woman. Her beauty was known throughout Shiraz and beyond and she took part in the political and cultural life of the city. Her father was king for a few years and was deposed in 1339. He tried to take back the throne in 1342 but met a sticky end. Her uncle, Abu Es Haq, took the throne in 1343 and looked after Khatun, understanding that she was a *special girl. The king was a famous lover of poets and encouraged her to write. It didn't take much of that encouragement. Her heart longed to write poetry and she recorded her words and thoughts. She learned from the visiting poets by simply listening, but it was her good fortune that she lived in the time of Hafez, who was without peer and the greatest living poet of her time. Whenever he visited Shiraz, she was sure to listen and learn. Her poetry largely dealt with her longing for the understanding of love. Much like you Malek, she wanted to know why love had such a hold. For you, it's a question of love for God but, in this context, both God and love are one.*

Her poetry though was not without controversy. Not for its content, but because of its existence. Khatun was a woman and such behaviour was frowned upon. But the king was clever and devised a way for her to write without gossip from the court.

One day she was sitting in her room in the palace when her uncles sent for her.

Abu Es Haq was a wily ruler who navigated the threats he faced well. Rival kings vied for his lands, religious clerics called him a heretic for his enjoyment of the finer things in life. His great rival, Mubariz Aldin Mohammed, was seeking control of the city of Yazd. Abu Es Haq needed a strong sense of command to keep control. He was not without brutality. Rebellions were dealt with by sword and fire.

Word had reached his royal ears that whispers were growing ever louder about Khatun and her well–educated and beautiful manner. She was quick to argue with those she felt were wrong, and would read verse to both men and women. This displeased some in the royal court and the king knew that traitors were everywhere. All it would take was some malcontent to take information about his kingdom across the moun-

171

tains to his rivals. He needed to do something. He spoke to Khatun about her poetry.

'*I would rather die than give it up.' The king understood that what he had watered and cared for all these years was now in bloom, and who was he to cut down such a flower?*

One night, his cup boy was pouring wine for the king and his best friend Amin Al din Jahromi. Jahromi was testy and sad. The king asked him to speak his mind. Jahromi did not. He was in love. The kind of love that he feared to speak.

'*Speak fool, speak!'*

'*It will not please you, this woman whom I long for.'*

'*I swear, if you do not speak my sword will do my speaking for me.'*

'*Jahan Malek Khatun.'*

The king roared with laughter. An opportunity and a marriage had presented themselves. His best friend would be with a suitable bride; the loose lips of the royal court would be forcibly sealed and, with the protection of a husband, Khatun could write without fear of gossip.

'*Her first love is poetry, Jahromi my friend. Will you let her continue because, if you don't, I fear your marital bed may be without merit.'*

'*It is her beauty first, her words second and her nature third, your highness.'*

Khatun was married to her uncle's best friend and her verse took on a questioning nature; some would say her verse became unhappy. Jahromi was a kind soul but his weakness for drink made him an inconsiderate lover and absent partner. Khatun had a poet's soul, which needed to be nourished. After a while though, even the drink couldn't stop a child from being born. But the child's life was short and she died in Khatun's arms, a few summers after she was born.

Perhaps the death of the child cast a dark shadow over Shiraz. In 1353 the king's arch rival Mobarez Al Din marched out of his base in Kerman and met the king on the battlefield. Khatun's uncle was defeated and Shiraz was now in the hands of the new, austere and ascetic king, who had no time for poetry or wine, things considered un-Islamic. Khatun was imprisoned and then marooned in exile. But such rulers never lasted in Shiraz and Mobarez Al Din was soon deposed by his son, Shah Shojah. Poetry and wine returned to the royal court and so did Khatun, where she lived out her days, still questioning love and still aching from a broken heart.

I tell you this tale because I feel you need to know that the quest for understanding is what you are also about to embark on. Understand the nature of love and God and you will understand the nature of this book. Maybe then you can know the fate of your friend. Even in exile, Khatun never stopped believing in love. Even after her child had died, her king had been deposed and her husband was lying drunk in a ditch she never questioned her love for love. This is what you need to find. Can you find love for God?

Khatun wrote a verse that I think will help:

At Dawn my Heart Said I Should Go

Into the garden where I'd pick fresh flowers, and hope to see his flower-like beauty there.

I took his hand in mine, and oh, how happily we strayed among the tulip beds, and through each pretty grassy glade;

How sweet the tightness of his curls seemed then, and it was bliss to grasp his fingers just as tight, and snatch a stealthy kiss.

For me to be alone beside that slender cypress tree cancels the thousand injuries that he has given me.

He's a narcissus, tall and straight! And so how sweet to bow my head like violets at his feet and kiss the earth there now.

But your drunk eyes don't deign to see me, although I really think it's easy to forgive someone the worse for love or drink.

And though it's good to weep beneath God's cloud of clement rain, it's also good to laugh like flowers when sunlight shines again.

My heart was hurt by his 'checkmate'; I think I must prepare to seek out wider pastures then, and wander off elsewhere.

Jahan, be careful not to say too much; it's pitiful to give a jewel to someone who cannot see it's valuable.

Now you, Malek, must find your own understanding of faith like Jahan Malek Khatun found her understanding of love.

We at The Order of the Gatherers of Truths know that you are about to undertake a journey. Without travel, knowledge is impossible. Go with God, my friend. Go with God.

18

Tebbel el Moustaheel: Damn the Impossible

As the plane taxied into Baghdad International, Malek put down his Kindle. He now fully believed in the power of this book. He didn't understand it, but he believed. He cleared immigration quickly and without fuss and his security detail, Saif and Riyaad, met him in the arrivals area. He was glad to see them. Two familiar faces. They caught up. A bombing in Khan Bani Saad in Diyala Province a day earlier had them all spooked. ISIL had been cleared from the area a number of months ago but the group had managed to drive a truck bomb into a busy marketplace. It was a massacre. In seconds, 115 people had died. A hundred more were injured. Saif and Riyaad had travelled down to the site with the crew that was covering Malek's leave from Baghdad.

'Man, I've never seen anything like it,' said Saif. 'We went up with Imran Khan, Osama and Ali Badri to do the report. There is a huge crater in the middle of the market and buildings all around have just disintegrated. There are coffins in the street. People were picking up body parts for hours afterwards, using tomato crates to put the limbs in. They couldn't bury people whole. Some coffins just had limbs inside. There is so much anger there. I'm worried that the militias will make a revenge attack. Sunnis will suffer.'

Once again, Iraq was facing an uncertain future. In this country, it only took one incident to plunge the country into hell. Sectarian violence was never far from the surface here. In 2006, Al-Qaeda hit the Askari shrine in Samarra, a key holy site for Shia Muslims. The blood-letting that took place afterwards lasted years and changed Iraq for good. Sunni Muslims were run out of their neighbourhoods. Death squads roamed the streets. The American occupiers were scarcely able to keep a lid on the violence and found themselves in the middle of a war they had helped create but didn't understand.

As they drove to the office, the streets of Baghdad looked shabbier than ever. The blast walls and security checkpoints made it difficult for trash collectors and other people to keep the streets clean. Plastic bags rolled around like tumbleweed and empty plastic bottles piled up. Malek found it difficult to imagine that under Saddam Hussein Baghdad was a beautiful city that was the envy of the Arab world. That's the thing about dictators, he thought. They might not be pleasant but the streets are clean and the trains all run on time. The state of Baghdad today, however, was pitiful. Once, a climate expert in the city had told him that the Americans had built so many concrete blast walls that they had raised the average temperature of the city by three degrees. He could believe it. In some of the more enclosed and secure streets you could feel the heat coming out of the walls.

Malek would be glad to get out of the city and go down south to Babylon. But that needed organising and, when things needed organising, there was only one person in town to speak to and that was Al Jazeera's Baghdad producer Osama. They greeted each other like brothers.

'Where's your on-the-road wife? We miss Neeka!'

'She misses you guys also, but I'm not here on business. Imran Khan will stay on in Baghdad. I have some business down south. Can we speak?'

Malek told Osama about Justin going missing in Kabul. He didn't tell him about the book or explain why he needed to go down to Babylon for a few days.

'I'll arrange everything for you in a beautiful and professional manner. For you Malek, anything. I'll get the permissions from the ministries and the Baghdad Operations Command. I'll find somewhere you can stay. But I'm going to warn you, it won't be luxury. You'll need cars and drivers?'

'No cars and drivers. I just need to be walking distance from the ancient site. Don't worry about anything else.'

'Malek. What the hell are you up to? No drivers, no camera. I can think of better places to go on holiday, *Habibi*.'

Malek hadn't bargained on anyone asking why he might want to go to Babylon, mainly because he'd been so preoccupied with getting there.

'I'm researching a book. Just for a few days, I need to get my bearings and taste for the site. You worry too much about me, *Habibi* Osama!'

'Of course I worry. You're likely to start daydreaming and get shot at. You seem to be good at that. You make us do things we would never do for other correspondents. During the sanctions, Saddam wanted to develop surveillance aircraft. His advisers said it was impossible. He said, "Tebbel el moustaheel! The Iraqi people will eat dates but we will beat the sanctions!" This is you, Malek. "Damn the impossible. I will go to Babylon."'

It felt good to be with Osama and the crew in Baghdad. Malek let Osama disappear into Iraqi bureaucracy and sort out his trip, while he talked with Ali Badri and Ahmed Khadim. These guys knew first-hand the violence that Iraq had witnessed. They were approaching the religious occasion of Ashoura, when the city's Shia Muslim community flocked the streets in their thousands to commemorate the death of the Prophet Mohammed's grandson, Imam Hussein. ISIL had promised to attack the processions. Ahmed left the office, planning to go home and gather his family so they could all go pay homage to Imam Hussein. As he left, Malek said goodbye and wanted to add, 'Be careful out there!' But he didn't, as Ahmed was grinning from ear to ear about something. He wasn't sure about what.

A few hours later, news broke of bombings in the Tunis neighbourhood. Osama got a call and relayed the information to Malek. Ahmed had been with his family when the bomb exploded. He had survived, but his two cousins had died on the spot, and his aunt had been seriously injured. The statistics had become personal and the hospitality tents had become casualty wards. The dead had passed, but the more heart-breaking stories were those of the injured, like Ahmed's aunt, who now faced years of physical pain even after many months of rehabilitation.

Few in Iraq have been spared this experience. Almost everyone has a family member or friend who has died or been injured in tragic circumstances. Malek thought of the book and of how many tales must have been written for Iraq alone. Between the years 2003 and 2015, some 160,000 Iraqi civilians had died violently. That was a huge number, but it hadn't surprised Malek. In the office, he looked back through some old articles on the Al Jazeera English website, and he found a post from 2013. He remembered it well: it was the first time he'd written about Iraq's war and the new one to come, a full year before it happened. It was called 'Iraq's Forgotten War'. He reread it:

IT'S NOT the way he hits the car horn. It's not even the frequency at which the high-pitched noise keeps coming. It's something else. It's the way he grits his teeth, pushes himself right back into his seat and presses hard with the flat palm of his hand. You can sense the anger and nervousness: this man wants to be anywhere else in the world right now.

I watch him from the window of my car as we inch through Baghdad's traffic. In other cars, other drivers pound away at the centre of the steering wheel, creating a grim symphony of car horns.

My driver keeps looking around as well. It is rush hour in Baghdad and no one wants to be stuck. Not because of the rush-hour commute, but because of the very real threat of car bombs.

October was the bloodiest month since 2008. A total of 979 civilians were killed – more than thirty a day.

Baghdad is a city that is afraid of itself. I have spent the last few days here embroiled in meetings and press conferences to try to understand how this has happened. How Iraq has become the world's forgotten war.

Ali is an old Baghdad character and a friend. He moved from the south to the city after the US invasion in 2003 to help protect his family. 'Once the Americans left, the old enmities re-emerged. Shia, Sunni, political, mafia. Then the revolution in Syria turned bloody. Sunni fighters leave to go and fight in the Jihad there and they bring their violence here because our government is close to Iran, who support al-Assad. But there are so many groups. Both Shias and Sunnis have blood on their hands.'

Ali and I have known each other for a few months through mutual friends. It seems that every time we speak he gets a little more afraid, a little more nervous. 'I can see a civil war coming. Just wait until fighters go into the Sunni areas and begin to kill there. The Sunni are in a minority. The blood will spill and the civil war will begin and no one cares. No one cares for us.'

Ali doesn't let his family travel around Baghdad. He stays in his neighbourhood. 'We have everything we need – shops, cafés – why risk our lives on the roads?'

The next day I have a news conference with Baghdad Operations Command. Their building is in the shadow of the crossed-swords landmark built by Saddam Hussein, which remains to this day. It is a reminder of a past which, while very brutal, was in many ways much more peaceful for civilians.

The BOC are in charge of securing Baghdad. At the conference, they are keen to show us that they are winning. We watch confessions of alleged Al-Qaeda operatives.

What they have to say is interesting, although I wonder how the confessions are obtained. One talks of how dangerous it is to drive around with heavy explosives such as C_4 and TNT because of the road blocks. So instead they build 'low-intensity' car bombs using household ingredients to avoid detection. Low-intensity they may be. Deadly they remain.

After the press conference, we are given an off-record

briefing by one of the most senior commanders in the country. I ask him what his biggest challenge is. His answer is
blunt. 'Al-Qaeda and its affiliated groups. They make the
people of Iraq the target. Everything is a target: the people,
mosques, shops, schools. Yet we have taken steps to beef up
our efforts on intelligence gathering to at least be able to take
pre-emptive strikes at terror groups before they can act.'

I ask him about the very recent trip to the US by Nouri
al-Maliki, the Iraqi prime minister, and whether it was a
success in getting the equipment needed for the security
services to do their job.

'The prime minister is also our commander in chief and,
as such, has a good insight into what we need, and what we
need are sophisticated technological devices to track down an
invisible enemy. As you can see, this is an open war and the
only way to beat the enemy is to be one step ahead of him.'

An open war. It's the first time I have heard such blunt
language directly from a senior official in the government or
military. But this 'open war' makes very few headlines across
the world anymore. Imagine if thirty people a day were dying
anywhere else? Imagine if car bombs ripped through a capital
city every couple of days?

This 'open war' is as deadly as any. I think back to Ali's
words: 'A civil war is coming and no one cares about us.'

Iraq braces itself for a future that no one can predict but
that most think will be even bloodier than it is right now.

Of course, thought Malek. Ali! Why hadn't he thought of
Ali before? Ali lived a few doors down from Malek's office. A
few minutes and a phone call later, Malek was in Ali's house.

'*Habibi, Shako Mako*? It's been a while!'

'Too long Ali, too long. *Mako shi Habibi.* How's your father?'

'Surrounding himself with long-dead people and ancient history. How's that Neeka of yours? You guys should really get together.'

'Possibly. Perhaps when hell freezes over.' Inside, he laughed a little.

It seemed that everyone but they themselves had thought they would make a great couple all these years. If only they'd known they would. 'Listen Ali. I have a favour to ask. Does your father still maintain that database of Babylonian myths?'

'Indeed he does. If it's not the most useless website in the world, then perhaps at least it's close to it. Still, it keeps him out of my hair.'

'Can we access it here?'

Tea arrived in tiny shot glasses called finjans and Ali switched on his computer. Ali's father was a historian of some note who had left Baghdad for London after ISIL destroyed Nimrud in the north. The destruction of that ancient site affected him more than any other. He'd gone to London to help those who were trying to put a stop to the very lucrative trade in antiquities and to lobby anyone in authority to put the defence of Iraq's ancient sites at the top of the list. A tough sell considering that ordinary Iraqis were dying every day.

'I'm in, Malek. What are we looking for?'

'I'm not sure exactly. Let's start with a group called The Order of The Gatherers of Truths.'

Ali scrolled through the text on the screen, scanning it with his eyes.

'There is an entry for them. First recorded in a clay tablet from Nebuchadnezzar the Second's Babylon in 526BC.

They seem to be a cult who reject the notion of many gods and preach monotheism, and the need to understand that the people we meet, we affect. We become unwitting members of a jury who can help decide if they go to heaven or not. Deceitful, opportunistic, crazy nut jobs if you ask me.'

It wasn't a whole lot to go on, but it did confirm that others had heard of the order. That was something at least.

'OK. Anything else?'

'Let me see. They go quiet for a while but pop up in Jerusalem under King David. There's a mention of them in the chronicles of the time. Then there's a mention of them in Bethlehem during Christ's time and in Medina during the Prophet Mohammed's life. Oh, this is interesting. They go quiet again until 2015. In January, a routine repair in Babylon reveals a fragment of another clay tablet that mentions them, but nothing beyond the name. Why are you so interested in this group?'

'I don't know. I just heard about them and it piqued my interest. That's all. Anything else you can tell me?'

'Dad keeps some private notes in a separate page on the site. Let me check those.'

A few keystrokes later, an entry came up.

The Order of the Gatherers of Truths

Likely to be an opportunistic occult group. Have changed ideology as faiths developed. Describe themselves as a pan-Abrahamic group that believes in no religion, but in one god. Have sent followers insane.

ALI SWUNG ROUND in his chair and faced Malek. 'That's all folks. Malek. What are you up to?'

Once again Malek thought silence and a change of subject were the better option.

'You know me, Ali. Predicting the imminent demise of Iraq. Next time we meet, Baghdad will be a neutral zone surrounded by the Republics of Shia'stan, Sunnistan and Kurdistan.'

'You always were a funny one. Enough tea. Let's have a real drink. *Chivas*?'

19

Spectacles and a Trowel

Thanks to the tenacity of Osama, Malek arrived in Babylon a day later. This ancient city was falling into ruin. The lack of visitors over the last decade meant that money for upkeep was scarce and the local economy was in tatters. The nearest city of Hillah used to be a place of artists and poets but was now a fading facsimile of a bygone era. Osama had found a disused mud farmhouse for him. It was basic, but he had roughed it before and he had brought with him tins of tuna and bottles of water. He would be fine. From the farmhouse it was a short walk to the city of Babylon itself.

Modern Babylon had a sad history, one of neglect and on occasion wilful destruction. One that all could see. Malek, though, could see it all through different eyes. Those eyes blinked twice as he slipped once more into an augmented-reality trance. He was now looking at Babylon not as a daydreamer, as he had earlier in the year, but as a traveller with a mission. As he approached the Ishtar Gate, he began to smell the city. He could hear the clip-clop of horses' hoofs and the entrance to the city came to life. Malek looked down at his robes. He was once again dressed as a southern miner.

Ancient Babylon, glorious in all its wonder, came alive around him. Few cities have captured the imaginations of men and women as Babylon has. It has stood as the gateway to knowledge and civilisation for over 2,000 years. Hittites, Assyrians, Persians and Greeks invaded, yet the city still survived. Evidence from various digs proved that, even in prehistoric times, this was a place that had life. But what hordes of earlier invaders had not achieved, archaeologists and more modern armies had. Babylon was relieved of whatever hadn't suffered the ravages of earlier invasions, and of time, by men in spectacles wielding trowels, and men in khaki uniforms wielding guns. The Ishtar Gate and the Processional Way were the perfect examples.

As Malek the southern miner walked through the gate, and onto the beginning of the half-mile Processional Way, he was able to summon a 21st-century perspective too, and reflect on how Babylon had been treated in more recent times.

In 1899, Robert Koldewey, a bearded German with a taste for the exotic orient, began major excavations at this site. Over the next eighteen years he explored the city, uncovering what had only been myth up until then. He excavated the walls around the city and the grand Ishtar Gate. Brick by brick, he took the gate down and shipped it to a German museum, where part of it was reconstructed. But the whole gate was far too big for the museum and so it remains in storage to this day. The distinctive blue glaze on the bricks imitated lapis lazuli, and gave the bricks a shimmer which made them famous throughout the ancient world. Adorning the gate were aurochs and dragons in golden-glazed brick friezes, but even they didn't survive these archaeological raiders. Dispersed across museums around the world, this once-grand gate had now disappeared from Iraq.

Koldewey would have taken more but the advent of the First World War and the British taking over Iraq put a stop to his pilfering ways. Pilfering? Perhaps Malek was being unkind. Perhaps the riches of Babylon were better off half a world away safely in storage and not under the jackhammer of ISIL. But Koldewey was no philanthropist out to save ancient relics. He was a competitive egomaniac by all accounts. Despite not holding any advanced degree in archaeology, he still managed to beat off the competition for the rights to dig at Babylon. He bullied and schemed his way into digs in Greece and Turkey, where he learned advanced techniques that he then put to good use in Iraq. From accounts of the time, Malek had learned that Koldewey was a dour man who remained a fervent anti-academic until he died. Malek had some sympathy for the anti-academic stance – nothing bugged him more than academics who had never spent any time in the region writing from DC and London on the Middle East. From 1917 the British had their fill of the site. The explorer Gertrude Bell took a particular liking to Babylon. To think I'm walking down the very streets that Bell could only imagine, said Malek to himself. Bell was a key figure in the modern Middle East. Alongside T. E. Lawrence, she helped the Hashemites rule over the deserts of Arabia. She loved Iraq and established a museum to try to keep antiquities in the country. In 1926 she died and was buried in Bab Al-Sharji in Baghdad. A wing of the national museum was named after her. The British finally let go of Iraq in 1954 after a variety of forms of soft power, and declared it a protectorate. The Baathists arrived in 1958 with their highly idealised version of pan-Arabism, which preached unity but never achieved it due to political rivalry. That eventually led to Saddam Hussein taking power in 1979, taking advantage of the disunity. Under pan-Arabism, Babylon was forgotten, becoming just another old city in the desert. But Saddam Hussein knew the power of iconography if nothing else, and he wasn't about to let the ancient ruins of Iraq disappear into the desert sand. In 1983, he began to build on the site. He ordered the reconstruction of the gate, albeit smaller and a little more Disney-like, and then built his infamous grand palace on a hilltop overlooking the city.

But nothing that Hussein could imagine held a candle to what ancient Babylon was really like. The fool, trying to compete with this city, thought Malek. He turned left into one of the streets near the centre. He was trying to keep a low profile. He looked around to see if any of the guards who policed the city had seemed to notice him. Despite Babylon's size, strangers still stood out. He saw where he was. After the invasion of Iraq, very different guards had watched over the city, for a while – guards he had seen in 2004.

In 2003, the Americans invaded and occupied Iraq. Perhaps it was General James T. Conway who did more damage than the bespectacled, bearded archaeologists or the brutal dictator. Conway oversaw the building of Camp Alpha. He dragged Babylon through the dust to build a US military-standard base. Contractors and the US military bull-dozed hilltops, turned ancient streets into gravel-laden car parks and drove heavy military equipment over roads designed for the horse and cart. The defensive measures for the base included barriers and embankments. Nebuchadnez-zar's pottery and bricks didn't stand a chance. Koldewey, Bell, Hussein, Conway. What a quartet, of vandal, colonialist, dictator and occupier. The Babylonians were always trying to predict the future. The high priests of Babylon didn't predict this.

Nebuchadnezzar's lust for building had always made Malek curious. He would often look at the scale models of Babylon and wonder at their size. If the Devil had all the best tunes, then God had all the best architects, he thought. The Tower of Babel was mentioned in the biblical Old Testament and was built 'so that its top may reach unto heaven'. The tower became a symbol of human pride and ambition. Back then, the known world only had one language. God, it is said, took his revenge on human pride by giving many languages to the people and dividing them for ever.

Modern-day Babylon represented modern Iraq, a once-glorious place that had been used and abused by various powers. Great cities rise and great cities fall, of that there is no doubt, but the fate of Babylon was particularly galling for Malek. He was reminded of a poem for another great city, Ur, a grand Sumerian city-state in old Mesopotamia. In its heyday, Ur was on the coast, but now the remains of the city lay stranded inland as the sands of time had literally, physically shifted. The book of Genesis says that the city of Ur Kasdim, which many believe to be Ur, was the birthplace of Abraham. A poet at the time of the fall of Ur in 2000BC wrote a lament. This poem was divided into eleven stanzas and told the sorry tale of the fall. Malek pulled his Moleskine notebook from his pocket and opened it to the page where he had written the poem down.

> *The country's blood pools like bronze or lead;*
> *Its dead melt of themselves like fat in the sun;*

Its men laid low by the axe, no helmet protects
them;
Like a gazelle taken in a trap they lie, mouth
in the dust...
The mothers and fathers who go not out of
their houses are covered in fire;
The children in their mother's lap, like fishes,
are borne away by the waters...
May this disaster be utterly undone!
Like the great barrier of the night, may the
door be shut upon it!

MAY this disaster be utterly undone, thought Malek. But how? He'd come here to find answers. To discover and undo the disaster that had befallen Justin.

He was here during Nebuchadnezzar the Second's reign, that much was obvious. He needed to find the bookseller and headed to the market. As he walked, he felt his wrist, and lifted up his sleeve. The green string bracelet was still there. This comforted him. He felt his purse jingling with small pieces of precious metals, so trade wouldn't be an immediate issue. Under his cloak was a dagger, hidden away, where he would normally keep his mobile phone. He had a canvas satchel slung over one shoulder. No Kindle. No nothing, in fact. It was empty.

He stopped by a water fountain and drank. The waters of the Tigris and the Euphrates flowed into his mouth and tasted of brilliant crystal.

A man was tethering his horse to a post. Malek spoke to him. 'Trust in the gods, but always tether your horse!'

The man looked at him and smiled. 'Praise be to the goddess Innana!'

'What year are we in, if you will indulge me?'

The man looked at Malek with a sideways, puzzled glance. 'I have no time for tricksters. If you're unsure of the year then perhaps your stock in trade isn't to work, but to relieve fools of their money. I'm no fool and I have no money, so perhaps your labours may be better served elsewhere.'

'I assure you I'm no trickster, just a simple, forgetful man in need of information.'

'I have no idea of the year, but the Ishtar Gate was completed a summer ago. Perhaps that is of use to you?'

Malek made some quick calculations in his head. He knew that the Ishtar Gate had been finished in 575BC. The Babylonian calendar was divided into two seasons, summer and winter, meaning that a year had passed since the Ishtar Gate was completed a summer ago. So that made this year 574BC. He also happened to know that Nebuchadnezzar's reign would come to an end in 562BC.

'Thank you, my friend. A good day to you and all praise to the goddess Innana.'

Nebuchadnezzar's reign over Babylon was perhaps its greatest. It was he who had constructed the buildings that passed into myth. But he was by no means a benevolent ruler. The Book of Daniel portrayed him as a powerful and ambitious king with grand designs on a wider world stretching as far as Egypt. He portrayed himself as a warrior king but spent seven years supposedly insane and lived like a wild animal. Perhaps it was here that he had had visions of a grand empire lasting a millennium.

He was the king responsible for the sacking of Jerusalem and the exile of the city's Jews to Babylon, where they then had to recreate their religion in a 'foreign land'. This was the moment when modern Judaism was formed, according to some scholars. The effects were still being felt in Malek's other world of 2015 and in modern-day Israel and Palestine. Neeka would laugh at him for drawing such a conclusion in this time and place.

Neeka. He missed her. Things had moved at such a pace that he hadn't quite figured out what was happening between them. He loved her. That much he knew, but he had to push all thoughts of her aside for the moment. As the sun began to set and the markets to close, Malek decided to allow himself the comparative luxury of a tavern for just one night before making his base in Osama's mud farmhouse. He bargained for a room, some beer and food. The plate arrived. It was bread containing ground barley and raisins and a leek broth. In his own time, he might have Instagrammed a picture of the dish, much to the chagrin of Neeka. Ah, Neeka. Once again his thoughts turned to her. If only he could get a message to her. He began to think of a grand plan to scribble a note onto a clay tablet that might wind up in a museum that perhaps Neeka could find in Kabul. He grimaced at the thought of his silly idea. Wow, he thought to himself. This beer is pretty strong.

20

A Bookseller's Woes

orning came and, with it, a sense of purpose for
Malek. The market would be open soon and he
needed to find the bookseller. In Babylon, the
market traders concentrated their stalls near the ruling palace
in a densely built rabbit warren of streets and squares. Local
fishermen would barter with the traders for the early-
morning catch. The rivers Tigris and Euphrates were home
to multiple types of river fish, but the most prized was the
meaty carp. Grain and bread from nearby villages arrived by
horse and cart, giving the market an aroma which made for a
pleasant walk, and, Malek thought, certainly a better smell
than the fishy one the carp brought with it. But the true value
of this market didn't lie in the daily supplies, the dry goods or
the dates and spices. The kings of the market were the barter
men: men who simply traded goods for credit. They sat
behind grand wooden tables scratching cuneiform symbols
onto clay tablets, keeping a running tally of who owed what
to whom. These men were the unwitting creators of a financial system that still runs in the modern world – which has

led to many conspiracy theories about the 2008 financial crash being foretold in the Bible. But, given that you can manipulate things to mean whatever you want them to, it wasn't something that Malek thought about much. As he walked past them, he noticed that they were looking at him oddly. One of them called him over.

'You, boy. You're a southern miner? Your clothes suggest so.' Malek cursed his outfit under his breath. A delay he didn't need. 'That is true, your eyes serve you well.'

'A southern miner so far from home. Perhaps you have something to trade? Our house welcomes you. I am Bellabarisruk, chief among the traders. For silver I can give you credit here in this market.'

'Your offer is very kind. But I have business elsewhere I must attend to.'

'Ah, we traders know the pressure of business. Perhaps credits in the tavern would be more suitable. The welcome warmth of a Babylonian beauty and a soft bed must be tempting for such a man whose travels bring him this far.'

'I have heard of the beauty of such women; I fear I don't have the deep purse you think I have to afford such luxury.'

'Nonsense. At the beginning of this winter a man such as yourself came to our humble market in search of knowledge. Knowledge of the darker kind. He swapped stones for this knowledge. Do you know of this man?'

Malek suddenly felt intense panic. The stone he had given the bookseller was worth far more than the clay tablet he'd received in return, if it had been any normal trade. The bookseller wasn't to know that the clay tablet had turned out to be beyond value for Malek. The guards of the trader stood with one hand behind their backs. Those hands must be clutching daggers. Malek put his hand to his stomach and felt his own dagger. He checked the odds. Two guards and only one way out. His purse must be tempting to the trader. He knew the trader wouldn't steal from him for, if he did, the reputation of the market would be sullied and trust, the coin of this realm, would be lost. But he also knew that a quarrel could be fabricated and that would offer ample opportunity for the trader to relieve him of his purse.

Malek sat down.

'I more than know him: I am the one who visited this last winter. The bookseller was kind enough to sell me a book but, I assure you, while the stones I paid may be rare in Babylon, where I am from they are merely children's toys. I am ashamed to admit that I may have profited from that trade a little unfairly.'

'We have all won and lost in this business. If the bookseller was so gullible, then the advantage was fairly yours. But tell me. The book. The knowledge it contains has been known to drive a man to distraction. I presume you are back because of some sort of distraction?'

Distraction was one word for it, Malek thought.

'What do you know of the distractions contained in this book?'

'I know what all traders know. That those who write this book live in darkness and peddle grand promises. The weaker-minded of us are susceptible to the tales that it contains. The more pragmatic of us dis- miss them as stories that are harmless. It is only the belief that the stories are true that causes damage.'

'Please tell me more.'

'This is Babylon, my friend. For every hundred people, we have ten gods. Gods to satisfy every kind of craving, every kind of greed; gods to forgive, gods to punish. Gods for events and gods for love. But, for some men, this isn't enough. So they invent more gods, or create one super-supreme being. The people of Judea say that their deity is the all-powerful one. I myself have little patience for gods and goddesses. This ledger is all I need. But the people who wrote your book are truly dark. They offer the ultimate power. The power to decide whether a man goes to heaven or the underworld. Nebuchadnezzar's men hunt this group of silent preachers whose words lie in clay and are not shouted from street corners like the rabble rousers who lay claim to divine understanding.'

'Why do Nebuchadnezzar's men hunt them? If they are harmless, why hunt them?'

'Because, southern miner, Nebuchadnezzar is a great but not a wise leader. The people of Judea already agitate against him. They believe their prophet Jeremiah will lead them to freedom after seventy years. And the king is paranoid. He believes that even his own holy men plot against him. Royal court legend has it that one day he had a dream. He ordered his holy men into his room. He asked them to interpret his dream, but he wouldn't tell them what his dream was. The holy men looked puzzled. The Jews in his court, who are among the king's holy men, prayed for guidance all night so that they could understand the dream that only the king knew. One of the Jews, Belthashazzar, described the king's dream in vivid detail. Nebuchadnezzar was impressed. The Jews praised their god and said that he had given them guidance. So Nebuchadnezzar paid homage to the Jewish god. He built a gold statue and commanded all to worship it. But he still thought *himself* above the Jewish god and made no secret of it. Now, not everyone worshipped the gold statue. Three Jews, Shadrach, Meshach and Abednego, refused to bow down. This angered Nebuchadnezzar. He ordered the three Jews to be cast into the fire, and into the fire they went. But then a fourth appeared in the fire and, without so much as a singed hair, they all walked out of the flames. The fourth was an angel, who had saved them. Nebuchadnezzar once again paid homage to the Jewish god, but this time he declared the Jewish god above all gods, and also above the king.'

'An interesting tale. Do carry on.'

'This is the tale the Jews tell each other about the great Nebuchadnezzar's belief in the one God above all. But the Jews still agitate for freedom. Take a look around you, miner friend of mine, take a look around you. One god or many, power is power. Trade is trade. Nebuchadnezzar knows this better than all. With gods, comes power. He who talks to God or the gods can rule above all. That is why he hunts those who may by such means subvert his power.'

Malek listened intently. He wasn't bargaining on seeking an outlawed group. But he wasn't fazed. He had met with the Taliban in Pakistan and Afghanistan, he had spoken to members of ISIL. Hunting the hunted wasn't unfamiliar to him. He decided to make friends with the trader. And the best way of making friends with a trader was to trade.

'You are a wise man, and a southern miner such as myself would be honoured to do business with you. These beauties you speak of, would they make the goddess Innana blush?'

'For Sumerian silver, I would say even the Jewish god may go crimson.'

Malek took a weight of silver from his purse and placed it on the table. Better to trade than be robbed, he thought. The trader pulled out weighing scales.

'If you wouldn't mind, I'd like to take a closer look at your scales.' Malek inspected the bottom. Such scales were still in use in rural Pakistan and his uncles had taught him as a child always to inspect before use. A dead weight on the bottom would always tip in the trader's favour.

'You are an experienced trader, and one whose insult I shall forgive as you're a guest here and one I am fond of. Everything is to your satisfaction, I trust?'

'It is. I presume this will buy me the comforts you promised?'

The trader smiled, scratched a few cuneiform words onto his tablet and summoned a young boy.

'Go to Annunaki's tavern and tell him to expect a guest. His name is...'

'Malek.'

'A strange name befitting of a stranger. Go with the gods. But be careful. It's dangerous to travel without friends. I trust you regard us as friends now?'

The guards relaxed and brought their hands back into view.

'Of course. But I have one last question. Didn't Nebuchadnezzar wander the deserts for seven years like an animal?'

'He did. But even then, many believe he did so as a political act to prove his own worth as a leader. The Jews say he went into the wilderness because their god commanded him to do so. Depending on who you speak to in the royal court, Nebuchadnezzar either believes in one god or all of them. He may not be wise. But he is wily and he hunts those who threaten him.'

'I thank you for your counsel and I bid you good day. Perhaps later we could meet at the tavern?'

'The tavern is not for me, my friend. But every day I am

here, and my stall will welcome you whenever you wish. Be
well, southern miner.'

Malek was relieved to exit the trader's stall. He recognised where he was. The bookstall owner was reassuringly in
his place.

'The southern miner returns!' Zamama the bookstall
owner boomed. 'Come, let us sit. You brought me great
fortune when you last came. My children laugh and my wife
has never been so welcoming.'

'I have had less fortune, my friend. It seems that my
arrival last time didn't go unnoticed by the traders.'

'What can I say? The fools around here only gossip for
lack of any other ideas. I trust there was not a problem?'

Malek knew that there was. He needed to move quickly.
His presence in Babylon had been noticed.

'The tablets you sold me last time. I need to find their
authors.'

'This is a dangerous game you play. I told you the book
had power beyond a southern miner's understanding. Now
you wish to trouble those you don't understand. I worry for
your safety. Tell me, are you well versed in the defensive
arts? You may find need of them should you continue this
fool's errand.'

'I look not for trouble. Only understanding.'

'With understanding comes trouble.'

'The truth never brings trouble.'

'The truth only ever brings madness, in my experience.
You brought me good fortune the last time you were here and
for that perhaps I owe you a debt that can be paid with information. Your business is now in the Hanging Gardens.
Climb until you cannot climb any more. Then look for a man
in silk with fire in his hair. He is the one you seek. But, before

you go, tell me. Does your purse contain one more gift for a bookseller in woe?'

'Woe? You just spoke of a welcoming wife and happy children. You seem to have vanquished woe I think.'

'It is true. Those things I have. But it is another I seek and she will be most welcoming for one of your trinkets.'

'Then, for your wife, my purse remains sealed! I thank you for your answers.'

'Be very careful, my friend. Those you seek are not welcomed by all in this city and a stranger could find himself without freedom very quickly.'

21

A Happy Garden

The Hanging Gardens of Babylon. To most, a myth. A green, lush mountain built on the banks of the Euphrates. To others, a mistranslation of a cuneiform tablet, and the gardens did exist, but 300 miles to the north.

Whatever the Hanging Gardens truly were, Malek was now looking at a multi-level pyramid with greenery on every level. How fortunate he was to be gazing on this: it had captured the hearts of men and women, one of the original seven wonders of the ancient world. Somewhere in heaven, Koldewey must be looking at Malek and smiling to himself. At a guess, he figured that the pyramids must be at least 500 feet tall, with intervals at every hundred feet that contained gardens. Right at the top though, the grandest was saved for last. There was a forest. A sky forest. What an imagination these Babylonians had, and the industry to make it work.

Magnificent date palm trees stood at the sides of the structure on each platform. Emerald-green grass lay well kept and people sat enjoying its freshness here, in the middle of a desert. Flowers grew from bushes with colours that, even across from the riverbank where Malek sat, could be seen to dazzle and sparkle.

A lattice of wood cascaded down the whole structure, which allowed for climbing plants to snake upwards. Legend has it that Nebuchadnezzar built the gardens for his home-sick wife, Amytis, who found the deserts of Mesopotamia a stifling encroachment after the green and mountainous land she was born in. Her home was the Medes in ancient Persia, and she had been married to Nebuchadnezzar to cement a political alliance between the city state and the Median empire. Her beauty was renowned throughout the world, though it seemed to Malek that any noblewoman mentioned in any texts throughout history was described so; he wondered if anyone ever described any noblewoman as ugly or plain, with a manner only a father could love. Amytis was never truly happy in Mesopotamia and longed for Persia. It was said that she would sometimes disappear from the royal court for months at a time, dressed as a commoner, and travel a thousand miles just to catch a glimpse of Media.

The small boat across the river took just a few minutes and Malek now stood at the bottom of the pyramid. The smell of the flowers and grass surrounded him and he began to climb. The bookseller had told him to climb until he could climb no more and look for a man with fire in his hair. Had Malek been wearing a watch he would have realised that it had taken him nearly an hour at a steady pace to reach the top. The rooftop terrace was expansive. Persian squirrels, a favourite of the queen, jumped from tree to tree. Osprey flew overhead, and one of them would occasionally dive head-first into the river below and re-emerge with a fish in its beak and fly to the top of the garden. Other birds with luminous colourings and splendid plumages stood lazily in the forest. Not being much of a birdwatcher, Malek did not know the names of the avifauna of Mesopotamia but he did spend a few happy minutes taking in the garden. He wished Neeka was with him. For a few minutes, he forgot all about the book, about Justin. He forgot about war and violence and destruction. He stood at the top of the garden and saw the world as it could be. A happy garden, which would be complete if Neeka was with him. No wonder the king had built such a testament to his love for his queen. It clearly cast a spell on anyone who visited.

The entire pyramid was watered by a manual chain pump with a series of clay pots attached to the chain, powered by oxen at the bottom. The oxen walked around a wheel which, in turn, rotated another sideways wheel that dipped into the Euphrates. A chain was attached to a third wheel at the top of the pyramid and the clay pots to this chain. Every few seconds, the water-filled pots passed over the wheel at the top and the water tipped into a series of narrow irrigation canals and trickled down the pyramid, allowing this garden to bloom. Malek grinned. A smaller, cruder version of this technology still existed, and watered his grandfather's farm in the village of Gujarpur in Pakistan's Punjab Province to this day.

A ladybird flew onto his hand and rested for a moment. Malek watched it walk around on his wrist until it flew away. He followed it with his eyes for as long as he could when, at the edge of his vision, he saw a man resting in a shaded clearing. His hair was as carrot-coloured as anything a rabbit might eat. The man with fire in his hair.

Justin. The book. Kabul. It all came rushing back to

Malek as he wondered how to approach the man. He didn't even know what to say to him.

Hi. I'm the guy that bought a book that... Oh yeah – I'm also from the future.

Any opening gambit he rehearsed in his mind sounded ridiculous. Even 'Hi. I'm Malek', his standard opening line, sounded weird. He needed an excuse. The few people around him seemed to be relaxed and comfortable. Picnic baskets were opened up and the whole place felt wonderfully sleepy and lazy.

The fire-haired man was resting. He lay on the ground with his legs crossed and his hands upon his chest like some fattened Egyptian mummy. He looked absurd. His expansive girth was dressed in yellow silk and he had a kink in his hair which meant it grew upwards. What an odd-looking man.

Malek rummaged around in his canvas satchel and found a piece of raisin bread and a small sheepskin bag of wine. It was nearing lunchtime. Malek was sure that the offer of bread and some wine would be welcomed. Malek had a more pressing problem, however. How do you disturb a sleeping man?

'By hovering like a dragonfly. That's how you disturb a sleeping man.'

The man's voice startled Malek. He offered a stuttering apology. 'No need to apologise. Come, sit next to me, Malek.'

'How... how do you know my name?'

'Your tongue is loose and your clothes odd. My name is Shamesh, but I suspect you already knew that. You should know better than to talk to gossiping booksellers. It was he who told me you'd be coming. He sent a boy this morning.'

'Then you know why I am here?'

'Like the others, you want to meet the man who wrote

the story "Seven Severance", I expect. It's always my early work. I cannot make a sliver of silver from the work I do now. It's only the early work they want. Well, you've met him now and you can tell the tale in the taverns of Babylon. Please. Leave me. I don't have time to talk to my admirers all day.'

'It's not your early work I admire. Although I'm sure that, if I was aware of it, I would admire it. What do you know about The Order of the Gatherers of Truths?'

For a fat man he sure sat up quickly.

'Shush! Of such things, I know nothing. Be gone with you, fool!'

'I think that you do. You see, I bought a series of tablets from the bookseller. He – '

'I told that imbecile not to sell that book! I curse my gambling debts.'

'If you're a gambling man, I'll make you a wager. I have bread and wine. I'll bet by the time we finish lunch you will want to help me. If not, I'll leave this place and never cast my shadow upon the Ishtar Gate again.'

Shamesh paused, but not for long. 'Well, I'll accept the wager. Give me the wineskin. I'll put it in the irrigation canal so that the waters can cool it. The bread we shall break together. Tell me what the book did to you.'

The two men sat in the shaded clearing. Malek said nothing. He didn't know where to begin.

'Come come, boy. Say something.'

'These stories you write. How do you come by them?'

The man grabbed Malek's hand. He pushed up the sleeve. The green string bracelet was visible.

'You're a follower of the future Prophet Mohammed. Peace be upon him. Many centuries from now I will sit next to him in Medina and I shall hear him preach the word of

God. As a follower of one true God you must know it is not I that write the stories. I am a mere vessel of God's words.'

'Are you a prophet?'

'Heavens no. There are plenty of prophets walking the streets of Babylon. Nutcase charlatans all of them. No. I am an angel. The Order of the Gatherers of Truths, such as it is, is a division of heaven's religious affairs department.'

'Religious affairs department? What would heaven want with a religious affairs department? Sounds Orwellian.'

'Ah, George Orwell. He is destined to be a fine fellow. He will hate the church, be an atheist – who can't stop talking about religion. One day, we will seek him out also. We find people like you, Malek, who struggle with God and faith, and we help them to see. I can tell from your eyes that we have failed in that task with you. Tell me. What did the book do to you?'

'It told me about people I have met. It told me about their stories. About how they may or may not go to heaven. But one story shook my faith. The story is about my friend Justin. He is missing in a land and time far from here. If the book is correct then he is about to die. I want to save him. That is why I sought you out. I have to save him.'

'We are all slowly dying from when we take our first breath. Why is his soul more important than any other?'

'Because it is. Because I know him. Because I love him. Because I know it's not his time to die.'

'Then perhaps you've already saved him. There is a Hadith, a saying of your future beloved prophet, who heard the words from God: "I was a hidden treasure and I loved that I be known, so I created the creation in order to be known." Malek, you need to know the hidden treasure that is God. You have quarrelled with God for long enough, Malek.

Love and believe in God and perhaps your friend will return to you.'

'But I do believe in God.'

'You don't. You believe in a god you're desperately trying to rationalise. You cannot believe in a god that you wish to command, whether it is to save Justin or, like Nebuchadnezzar, to use to glorify your own achievements. As impressive as this garden is, it is not as impressive as the love God will give you if you just let go of the idea that she is fallible and to be manipulated.'

'Why does Nebuchadnezzar hunt you?'

'He fears the truth. He fears that we bring the love of God and that when the people realise that love is more important than hanging gardens and gold statues then Nebuchadnezzar shall be exposed for the false king that he is. But please don't misunderstand our order. We are not revolutionaries or agitators, we are merely gatherers of truths, truths that we wish you to understand. When we say that you influence the lives of people you meet, what we are really saying is "Love the people you meet". If everyone did that then what a happy world this would be.'

'Hippy...'

'Oh, heavens no. Jesus was a hippy. I'm afraid I like the finer things in life too much to be a hippy. I'm more silk than hessian. The book that you read is to help you understand. That you can have an impact on the lives of others.'

'All I need to do is read.'

'It was your father who used to, or will one day, say that to you. He was – will be – a wise man. You've read the book we gave you. I have told you who I am. I have offered you a solution. Love God, don't just believe. Love. In Arabic they say, or rather will say, *Wahdat Ul Wujud...* God's uniqueness of being. Nothing exists independently or endures like God.'

'You're a strange man.'

'Malek, I am many things to many people. Come, the day is growing older and with the night comes the wisdom of things you've learned that day, and then temporary death. Be reborn in the morning and let us meet again. I have friends I wish to introduce you to. Perhaps through them you will learn to love God, and will not blame her for humanity's failures.'

'You keep saying "her". The book says "her". What is the truth of it?'

'The truth is what you believe and, let's face it Malek, you have always loved women. By making God a woman it might be easier for you to love her. By the way, congratulations.'

'On what?'

'You won your bet. I shall help you. Let us meet at daybreak by the Tower of Babel.'

22

She is More Than a Voice

The tavern felt stifling and hot. Malek was drinking beer through a straw. This made him giggle to himself. By some accounts, beer was invented in Mesopotamia by the Sumerians, but this wasn't the beer that you might be familiar with back at home. This was a stodgy concoction that had bits of bread and grain inside it. The straw, another Sumerian invention, was necessary to get to the liquid inside. Beer was an important part of this world. The gods would drink and strike bargains with each other. Mere mortals would do the same. It was part of the daily diet.

It was also disgusting to drink.

Barley bread that had been fermented. It smelled yeasty. Malek, though, wanted to fit in so he nursed his beer and gave the events of the day some thought. Love God. The advice was as useless as it was simple. How can you love something you don't understand? Shamesh was an angel. OK, got it. He was an angel. If I believe that, Malek thought to himself, and I believe that God exists, then I have to find

my love for God and that will save Justin. This wasn't
working out as well as Malek had hoped.

Malek occupied a quiet table in the corner of the tavern.
He had chosen it deliberately so that he could keep an eye
out. The trader had given him ample credit for his silver.
He'd renegotiated his deal with the tavern owner. The Babylonian beauty promised to him was changed to food. His love
of Neeka meant that the favour of the tavern whore wasn't
appealing, even though he had seen one in particular whose
charms seemed manifold. She looked a little like Neeka.

She noticed him looking at her, and walked over. 'You
stare, yet you don't take?' she said.

Malek nearly fell off his chair. 'Rubati!'

'The one and the very same. I told you I was hot.'

'You're also a whore in a bar. I'm so confused.'

'I need to keep an eye on you; still, for the right price you
could have me...'

'My heart belongs to another, Rubati. You know this yet
you still try and tempt me?'

'Let her have your heart. It's your purse I want for now.
In return, I shall be a comfort to your body and leave your
heart to her. By the way, you're from London – why are you
talking like you're in a Shakespearean tragedy?'

'Because I'm in disguise, obviously. Jesus, Rubati. You
really are kind of a dick. Or rather, you're a wicked woman.
Perhaps I should pay for your words and not your body?'

A sudden crash made her swing round. Some men had
entered the tavern and didn't look the sort who wanted to
party.

'It's the Incendiaries. I dare say they've come for you.
Quick. There is a back way out of the tavern. Leave through
that door and I shall meet you in the alley.'

Before Malek had the chance to move, an arrow entered his cloak, pinning the material around his left shoulder to the chair. Another inch to the right and he would have been meeting God.

The tavern fell silent. All eyes were on the archer and the men who surrounded him.

'In a hurry? I see you still have beer in your cup. It seems a waste. My name is Aruner. I'm the commander of the Incendiaries. You know who we are? We find those who peddle false gods and deal with them by fire. Our loyalty is to King Nebuchadnezzar the Second. We are his special guard. Tell me, who are you?'

'A southern miner looking to trade. I am to leave Babylon in the morning.'

'Your plans have changed, it would seem. The king would like to see you, southern miner. You are to be spared the fire, for now at least. Guards. Take this man.'

'Before you do, let me take what I am owed,' said Rubati to the Incendiaries. She picked up Malek's purse and whispered in his ear. 'I will send word to Shamesh. Don't worry, my dear Malek. We at the Order will save you.'

Malek didn't react to her words, fearful that any reaction would give her away.

The archer ripped out the arrow and roughly handled him through the tavern doors and into the back of a horse-drawn cage. The streets of Babylon were dark. Malek sat in the back of the cage in silent worry. The king had summoned him and this could only go one way. Badly.

The cage must have been bouncing around the streets for about thirty minutes when they arrived at the gates of the palace.

He walked through the palace with two guards, who had

placed him in chains. The archer strode in front of them. As they entered the blue-tiled throne room, Malek saw that the royal court had gathered in full, with holy men, priests and priestesses, advisers and traders thronging round the king. They made for quite a sight in their silks of bright colours. The king sat on his throne as the guards made Malek kneel.

'He doesn't look like much.'

'He isn't much. Shall I prepare the fires, my lord?' said the archer. 'The Incendiaries have always served me well. But, this time, let us find out what words will give us, as we already know what fire gives us. Unchain him. What is your name?'

'Malek, sir.'

'And to which gods do you pray?'

Technically Malek hadn't prayed to God in twenty years. He was a Muslim, but that would mean little to a Babylonian king.

'I believe in one God your highness. One God and no others.'

'Are you from Judea? The Judean god saved the lives of three men I had thrown into the fire. At least, this is what the Jews tell each other. My memory isn't what it used to be. Perhaps I forget things that have occurred in this court.'

'I believe in one God, your highness.'

'Do you praise him above your king?'

Malek remained silent.

'Your tongue betrays you, even when it does not wag. Perhaps the fire will help loosen it and let you admit what your silence so obviously shouts?'

The royal court looked at Malek. They looked at Nebuchadnezzar. The grand fireplace remained unlit, but the torches that lit the throne room seemed to burn brighter, perhaps in the hope of igniting Malek. 'You're a heretic. I charge you with heresy, blasphemy and conspiracy. Where is my judge? Oh, there you are. What say you, judge, to these charges?'

'Your Highness is a just and fair king. He has allowed the stranger his right to speak and to defend himself. As judge, I serve at the pleasure of the king. Command me to deliver justice and I shall.'

'What say you, Malek of Judea? Shall I allow justice to run its course? Or do you have anything to say?'

A voice broke from the back of the throne room. 'His Highness King Nebuchadnezzar the Second is indeed a just king. He is a rightward king. I ask him humbly to allow me to defend this man. After all, the great Babylonian laws allow for the accused to have counsel.'

Malek looked at the man speaking and recognised Shamesh, and by his side stood Rubati.

'Our great laws do allow for counsel. We have the defence. We have a judge. Do we have an accuser? Who will act on my behalf?'

'It would be my honour to act on your behalf, my king. I humbly offer my services as the accuser.' It was the bookseller, Zamama, who spoke.

Malek panicked. The bookseller could prove heresy, blasphemy and conspiracy.

'Zamama, you shall be my representative. I set the trial date for the morning. Take the prisoner to the cells and allow him time with his counsel. Zamama, come sit with me and let us discuss strategy. It has been a while since we have seen a courtly trial. This is going to be diverting.'

The royal court records from the time noted that Nebuchadnezzar the Second was greatly pleased with his decision. The thoughts of the prisoner were not noted.

23

Does a Cockroach Have a Soul?

'My my, Malek. What a pickle you seem to have found yourself in.'

Rubati, Shamesh and Malek sat on the cold, stony floor of the prison cell somewhere under the palace. For all Malek had ever read about Babylon's beauty he had never read a word about its prison, but then why would anyone write a single word about such a hellish and unforgiving place?

'But before we discuss justice, I feel you have questions you would like answered, no?'

'Who are you?'

'We are your friends. We are Neeka and Justin. We are Rubati and Shamesh. We are your guardian angels; we are here to help you.'

Malek looked at them. Who were they? If they were Neeka and Justin, then perhaps he could trust them. But Rubati was a mischievous minx and Shamesh was, well, unknown to him. A virtual stranger with fire in his hair. He spoke slowly.

'To help me to love God? God doesn't speak to me. I'm in despair.' In the faint light of the candle, Malek saw a cockroach on its back, blackened and fat. It was dying. As life ebbed away from the insect, its legs twitched. Perhaps its soul was leaving its body.

Rubati saw him stare at the dying insect. 'From him we come and to him we shall return. You're a Muslim. Offer submission, Malek. When was the last time you prayed to the East? Can you even remember how to pray?'

It had indeed been a very long time since Malek had prayed. He wished he had his rucksack with its beaten-up copy of the Koran inside. He could use some words of comfort right now. Instead, he had Rubati and Shamesh, or were they Neeka and Justin? He couldn't be sure.

She continued. 'Take a look at the cockroach, Malek. The last prophet taught us that the soul gives life to a body. In its absence, the body dies. But the soul is eternal and on the day of resurrection will be reunited with the body. Praise God and let your soul be filled with love.'

'*Allah O Akbar*,' Malek said, somewhat mockingly.

Shamesh spoke. 'Even in the face of death you still argue with God. Make your peace, Malek. Make your peace.'

Rubati spoke softly. 'Let's pray, Malek.'

'It's not prayer time.'

'Salah times are fixed, of that you are right. But Dua' you can make any time. Like now for example.'

Malek's mother had taught him a little prayer as a child. It was simple enough. 'God is great. Mohammed is his prophet. Send thy peace Lord so that we can rest and praise your name.' Malek said the words over and over again.

The cockroach stirred, flipped back over onto its legs and scurried away.

'See the healing power of prayer? You've just saved the life of a cockroach,' said Shamesh.

'I think our dear cockroach just needed to flip over.'

He didn't feel any better for the prayer. But he didn't feel any worse either and the very act of prayer had given him some clarity to think about the immense problem facing him right now.

'So, how do we save my life?' he said.

'That is somewhat more troubling. Blasphemy, heresy and conspiracy are easily proved and the sentence is death by fire. Zamama the bookseller knows that. He has us on conspiracy. Blasphemy because you professed to believe in one God. Heresy because you didn't praise Nebuchadnezzar.'

'Are you my defence or my accuser? Besides, you're an angel. Can't you just use your powers to get me out of here?'

'Our powers are limited here on earth. The Order is here to help you find your path to love. Find love and you'll find freedom.'

'*Allah O Akbar*,' said Malek, this time a little more convincingly.

They left him in his cell and walked through the palace, which was alive with the organising of tomorrow's trial. Rubati spoke to Shamesh in an alcove just outside the throne room. 'Shamesh. This is a dangerous game. Zamama could expose the whole Order.'

'He could. But we need Malek to learn to love God and, for that, we need to seek some advice. I'm going to have a chat with the big guy. I'll see you in the morning, Rubati.'

24

Beautiful Sedition

Once again the throne room was packed. The king, this time with the queen in attendance, sat on his throne while the judge, the accuser and the defence took their places in the middle of the room. The gallery was packed and every available space was filled with the curious, there to learn the fate of the southern miner.

Nebuchadnezzar stood. Everyone in the room kneeled.

'In the presence of the gods we stand, to witness judgement and justice being carried out. We offer our sacrifice to the gods of twelve head of cattle to be shared among the poor of Babylon so that the gods may bless our proceedings. I charge the judge to open the proceedings. Bring in the prisoner.'

Malek was brought in. He looked different, confident even. Shamesh and Zamama stood. They looked at each other with mutual respect.

The judge, in a red silk ceremonial robe, and holding a staff of gold, opened the proceedings. 'I command the prisoner to sit.'

Malek remained upright. 'I said sit.'

Nebuchadnezzar spoke. 'For the sake of the gods let him stand if he so wishes. But I warn you, southern miner. The choice you have made to stand is a choice you have made for the length of this trial. If you sit, you shall be found guilty. Now, get on with this trial before even the gods become impatient.'

The judge shuffled a little and began to speak.

'The charges are grave: heresy, blasphemy and conspiracy. They carry with them the sentence of death by fire. You have the charges, prisoner. How do you plead?'

Malek looked around the room, scanning the faces. They feared him because he was an unknown. He looked directly at King Nebuchadnezzar and Queen Amytis. She wasn't the great beauty that myth had led him to believe. He should probably change the Wikipedia page on this particular point, if he survived. Rubati, who looked exactly like Neeka, was a welcome sight. If hers was the last face he would see, then perhaps he could face death. Or did he see Neeka because he wanted to see Neeka?

There was something about Malek that captivated the room. They all stared back at him. No one spoke. Not a word was uttered. Shamesh wondered what Malek was up to. Everyone wondered what Malek was up to. Everyone apart from Rubati. She knew. The cockroach, she thought. The cockroach.

Malek began to speak. 'Last night, in the depths of this palace in a cold and stony cell, came my darkest hour. I was left alone without my counsel, to spend the final few hours in solitude before being brought in front of you. I was left with nothing. I had no faith. I wept. I wept out of pity for myself. I wept out of contempt. I wept out of desperation. I wept because it was something I could feel. Then, when I could squeeze no more tears from my eyes, I howled. I howled like a wolf. I screamed into the night and, like an animal, I became basic and primeval. I stripped myself of reason and screamed. Then, when my voice was hoarse and I had no more tears, I began to pinch my skin hard just to feel something else. I strangled myself with my coat and I took my hand to my own throat and squeezed as hard as I could. I felt like my soul had left me and my body was empty. As I was contemplating my own mortality and my soul and trying to find the most efficient form of death, I noticed my green string bracelet. Many months ago, a man tied this around my wrist as a reminder of who I am. A believer in one true God.

'My flesh was weary from the self-abuse. I had no more tears and my voice was hoarse. The man who tied this around my wrist also told me to find more truth. So I prayed and prayed to God. At first, my prayers took the form of a quarrel with God. But God took no part in my quarrel. My thoughts turned to insults but God did not respond to my insolence. When I had nothing left, I prayed that I might see my dear Neeka one more time before I entered the fires in Babylon. It was then, when nothing else had worked, that God filled my heart with hope. I thought of her and felt at ease. My heart was full of love. But it was also full of love for God, who offered me hope. I may never see Neeka again but I know she exists and I was lucky to meet her. So you ask me if I am guilty. I am guilty as charged. I am a heretic who believes in one God. I am a blasphemer who places God above Nebuchadnezzar. I conspired with others to understand the nature of God. I am guilty. You will not have to force me to enter the fires of Babylon. My faith is strong. I will enter the kingdom of heaven and take my place with God.

'In truth, madness. That sweet madness, the brilliant, sweet madness that comes from God. A God you cannot see or hear and yet is everywhere around you. You will call me insane. You will say I am mad and therefore must be sentenced to death. Well, I take your sentence as glad tidings. I have made my peace with you all. We are all equal in the eyes of God. I hold my arms out towards you. They're bound in chains, but these chains are not bondage to me, these chains are freedom. Nebuchadnezzar, I challenge you. What can you do to me now? What can you, King of kings, Lord of lords, do to me? How powerful are you really? You praise the gods yet you don't believe in anything but your own power. Accept the one true God and repent your sins.'

There was a collective intake of breath throughout the royal court. No one had ever insulted Nebuchadnezzar in such a public manner.

The king rose from his chair. The subjects of the royal court kneeled. The judge kneeled. Zamama kneeled. Shamesh kneeled. Rubati kneeled. Malek did not. He stood firm.

'You dare insult me in such a manner? The Jews of my kingdom tell a story that I have accepted the god of Judea above all. Shamesh? Where are you? There you are. Shamesh. Did the god of the Jews build the hanging garden?'

'No, your Majesty.'

'Who built the hanging garden?'

'You, your majesty.'

'I shall make an example of you, boy; no one shall ever question my authority ever again. The gods, all of them, speak through me alone. Remember that, boy. I see we are adding sedition to the list of charges facing you. I have no need of a judge to pass the sentence. Incendiaries, prepare the fires. This day shall bring justice.'

Malek stared with righteous intent.

The king stared back. 'Those eyes will be the first to burn.'

Queen Amytis stood up and walked down into the royal court. She faced Malek. 'You're a fool if you believe a word of what you just said, and we would be even bigger fools if we believed you. No woman has the power to make you love God, just as no man has the power to make you believe he is bigger than the gods or God. My king is the gods' only equal.'

Malek remained silent.

'Speak, fool. Your queen commands it.'

'It was worth a try. Worth it actually just to see the look on your husband's face.'

Shamesh spluttered. 'Forgive me your majesty, he is not of sound mind.'

'Of that I am sure, counsel. Tell me Malek. Why the deliberate insolence?'

'Cockroaches.'

'I'm sorry?'

'Cockroaches. They die on their backs. They survive on their feet. Better to stand on your feet than to die on your back. I made my play.'

'Incendiaries, take him down. Let the fire have its way with him. Why I was hoping for more from a southern miner I shall never know.'

Part Four

Babylonian Tales of Death, Heaven and Hell

Oh dear. We seem to have broken you, my dear Malek. Cockroaches, my dear boy? What on earth were you thinking? Your plan was to insult Nebuchadnezzar with a display of religiosity so dazzling you thought he would kneel before God and submit and, in the process, set you free? We should come clean about the very nature of our Order. You see, we are not what we led you to believe that we are. We work for the other side. We are a Satanic order. We were sent to take your mind and send you into madness. A task we did rather better than any of us dared hope. Cockroaches? Just wait until I tell the rest of the Order that story. Yes, yes, I know we told you to love God and to get right with the Lord our master. Well, that was your first failing, Malek. You see, God is all right with you not loving him. That's kind of the point, that God loves you regardless. That's God's thing. We just tell that story about loving God to people like you so we can control you.

Heaven and hell are in an eternal struggle for the soul. Both sides need the numbers. We like taking down bad souls and so capitalism, and the late 20th and early 21st centuries, have been pretty good for us. But then all centuries have been pretty good to the Devil. Most of humanity misses the central point that God teaches us. I mean God gets it right, generally speaking, with parents and with lovers and with friends and the people that you meet – like the book says, people whom you influence. We struggle with those personal relationships. We are better at the big–picture stuff. We have our successes in the social arena for sure. Gun–control laws in the US help immensely in that regard. But, generally speaking, we are better when power *is involved, be you a car park attendant or a dictator.*

Give a human any kind of power and he or she forgets to act kindly, and that's where we come in. What we do is simple, what we are is intricate. We are the front–line force in the other battle that goes on between God and the Devil.

You see, souls are souls are souls and we shall always collect souls. But what we really want are the minds. You see, minds we manipulate. We can break minds. With minds, we can keep the world in chaos. Keep the world in chaos and what do you get? More souls for hell. You understand, Malek? Good.

We even have a whole department of evil angels, The Qareen, whom we assign to you all individually, to do our bidding for us. The Qareen can appear to you in many different forms. The simpler, some would say lazy, Qareen just get you to eat one more slice of chocolate cake. The more devious take your darkest thoughts and make them into a real-ity. Those Qareen scare even me. I am your Qareen, Malek. You know me as Rubati, but throughout your life I have taken many different forms. At school, I was a friend who wanted you to bully other children. Sadly, I failed on that one as you weren't much of a bully. Ever the lover, not the fighter. But

Malek, you have a huge heart, and that's the one thing we can't fight. You love. What can we do? This is God's gift to you. You, all of you, have the capacity to love but for some of you it just comes easily. For you Malek, it comes easily. This is why we had to find a way of breaking you. There was no reason to break you, it's just that sometimes we get bored and when we have a challenge it's fun. Does that sound cruel? I work for the Devil. You don't get that job because you're a nice girl. There you have it. We tricked you, Malek. You were a challenge, but we did it.

Devil, one. Malek, nil.

It was a close–run thing. You might ask why we turned you into a gibbering wreck for amusement, and why we sent you to a farmhouse outside the ancient ruins of Babylon? Good questions, all.

To answer that we need to go back a little, to the dawn of mankind itself. Iblis, the Devil, refused to bow down to Adam, who, God claimed, was his greatest creation. Iblis was made of fire, Adam of mud. Iblis thought that fire trumped mud. He refused to bow down to Adam. God cast Iblis out of heaven, and created heaven and Eve for Adam, and Adam was pretty happy.

But Iblis wasn't. In comes a snake into the garden and the rest is history, if you choose to believe.

Iblis tempted Adam and Eve to take the one thing God told them they couldn't have. God cast them out of heaven to go live on earth. But Adam and Eve felt very guilty about what they had done so God forgave them, because God loves. On earth they stayed.

Iblis has been playing the same trick ever since. And for millennia, humankind has fallen for it. That disproves Darwin's theory of evolution right there. If humankind could evolve you'd have figured out Iblis's trick by now. Any time anyone has been given any sort of power over others we have stepped in and manipulated the situation. My personal favourite was the international banking crash of 2007 and 2008. While maybe not the worst thing ever to happen to humanity, its deviousness was breathtaking. What mankind has never understood is that it was a plague sent by the Devil. We did it.

It was a plague better than any the Israelites say God sent to Egypt. Those plagues were just local. OK, there were ten of them and they were pretty grim, especially the locusts and the slaying of the firstborn, but they were still local, because local was what God wanted at the time. God has always thought small. The Devil thinks big, real big. We went global with the pox on anyone who uses a bank.

That was inspired. We plunged the world into massive amounts of debt by offering easy money for any kind of thing you might want. Houses, flat–screen TVs, holidays? Hey, you want it? Here, have it, no, don't worry about paying, we will figure it out later. We got the banks to lend you all so much money that you didn't have a hope in hell of paying it back. Then we got the banks to be even more greedy. We got them to invent financial products even they didn't understand. We got them to give loans to people who could never pay them off. We basically got the whole world high on the dream that easy money was the solution to everything. Then, like all good drug dealers, we got the banks to charge you extortionate interest rates once you were high on easy money. The next hit was expensive. People defaulted in their thousands. The banks then sold so much of this bad debt that the bank that guaranteed a lot of the debt didn't have the money to pay when the debt was called in. Then we persuaded the governments of the

US and the UK to use your money to pay the bank's debt off. Brilliant. You lost all your homes and money and cars and whatever else and the banks kept all their money and the bankers paid themselves huge amounts of it. The US and the UK and Europe didn't realise it was a plague. That was our most genius move. The European Central Bank didn't bother trying to keep money in the system. You people don't learn. It's coming again. Iblis is whispering in your ear again and you, humanity, are falling for it again. We just completely screwed Greece. China is feeling the pinch. The US is leveraged up to the hilt. Then we have you, Malek.

Poor, deluded Malek who is now broken of mind and body. You, Malek, made some very poor investments and now have no money. Not your fault. You just thought that buying up stocks and shares and getting a huge mortgage was what you did. A sound investment. Then things came smashing down: your house was worth forty per cent less than your mortgage, your stocks nothing.

You stayed on the road and in a job that was hurting you because you needed the money. You should clearly have sought some professional or spiritual help. We screwed the banking system and, suddenly, millions of people like you, Malek, got screwed in turn, making decisions that they wouldn't ordinarily make. We found a weakness in you, just like we will always find a weakness in anyone and exploit it. My dear boy, you belong to us now, and the broken mind we have inflicted upon you is our prize.

We win. God loses.

In the farmhouse in which Malek had made his home, outside the ancient ruins of Babylon, there was no electricity. Malek cursed the fact he had no electricity, he cursed the fact that he was sweating in the midday sun. In modern-day Babylon he had been here for a few hours. In ancient Babylon it had been days. His augmented reality had sped up time in the ancient world.

He grabbed his Kindle. The battery had run out. There were no answers there and he hadn't brought a portable charger with him. He began to sob uncontrollably; he hadn't found any answers in Babylon. He had failed Justin. He had failed Neeka. He was now a wreck in a stinky Iraqi farmhouse, alone and without hope.

25

To Be a King

Neeka moved behind Justin as he smashed through the rickety door and they burst into the farmhouse. The intense shaft of daylight blinded Malek. He was huddled in the corner like a wounded animal and covered his eyes. Neeka pushed past Justin and threw her arms around him. Malek howled with tears.

'*Jaani Jigar*, baby. Shhh, I'm here. Malek, look, it's Justin. Look, it's Justin.'

'No, no, I couldn't save him. No, I couldn't save him.'

'Malek, he is here. His captors released him a few days ago, unharmed.'

Justin sat down next to him. They made quite a sight, Neeka holding a broken Malek in her arms, Justin crouching next to them.

'It's you?' Malek finally managed to get the words out between sobs.

'It's me, mate. It was kidnap for ransom, mate. They were just a handful of goons and chancers looking for a few quid. They didn't get any. Qais pulled some strings with the

Afghan police using a phone he bribed one of the guards to give us. They came and got us. Apparently, the leader of the group was the nephew of the police chief, and a pain in his arse, so the chief had no qualms about shutting his operation down and getting me out. So I was out, unscathed. But, like you, I stank. Mate, tuna and sweat are fucking foul. Let's get you out of here. Look. Here's the hat you hate, put it on. It's blinding outside.'

Justin pulled the fisherman's hat off his head and gave it to Malek. He had always hated this hat. It was one of those ten-dollar affairs with a tiny zippered pocket on the side that you get from camping shops. Malek never knew why anyone would need a tiny pocket in their hat and what it contained was a mystery. He unzipped the pocket and out fell a folded picture of the three of them.

Justin nodded. 'It's not what you think it is. I'm not that sentimental. Have a look at the back.'

Written in a very neat hand were next-of-kin details and blood types for each of them. Malek remembered where the picture had been taken. It was in Jordan, on the border-crossing with Israel. The year was 2005. They looked younger.

'You were better looking back then,' said Neeka.

'And I was thinner,' said Justin.

Malek sat clutching the picture. The tears came slower now. 'The book, Neeka. The path to heaven and hell...'

'*Jaani*. I know. It's OK.'

'The book, the book of The Order of the Gatherers of Truths. The tales of death, the tales of who might get to heaven and who to hell. The book.'

Neeka gazed into Malek's eyes. 'Malek, why are you here? You said you were coming to Baghdad to find your

Pakistani contacts in ISIL to see if they knew where Justin might be. Why are you in Babylon? Osama said you came to research a book. What book?'

Malek stared at her. The tears had stopped.

'I don't know what's happened to you. Look at this place, it's disgusting. Come, let's get some air. *Moosh Bekhoratet,* Malek.'

They walked out of the farmhouse. In the distance they could see the new Ishtar Gate. Malek closed his eyes, and imagined the markets, and the Processional Way leading to the Hanging Gardens. Nothing came to him. He blinked in the late afternoon blaze of the sun. Nothing worked. None of the neural waves inside his head connected to anything. His eyes darted from side to side as the sunlight filled them. Nothing made any sense. His hands shook, from fear and lack of water. Neeka pulled a water bottle out of her bag. Malek put some in his hands and washed out his eyes. Still nothing. He stared at Babylon a little bit harder. It looked sad and pathetic. Neeka threw her arms around him and pulled him closer to her. Justin looked a little uncomfortable.

'I hate to interrupt love's young dream, but we are in a Muslim country and things are pretty conservative around here.'

Neeka let Malek go and put a scarf around her head. In Iraq and Iran she had reluctantly chosen to wear one, despite her general protestations that she never would. 'Baby, can we go back to Baghdad now? We can talk in the car. There's air conditioning and a cooler full of water.'

Once again, the three of them made their way to the red SUV like they had a thousand times before. The air conditioning gave them welcome relief as they hit the highway to Baghdad. None of them said very much for the first thirty minutes of the drive. Usually they would be asleep, but this time they all stared out of the window watching Iraq go by. Who knows what their driver made of all of this? But whatever he was thinking he was keeping it to himself.

The towns along the road had witnessed fierce fighting between ISIL fighters and Iraq security forces. ISIL had come in from the west and from the strongholds in Anbar Province. The buildings of Jarf Al Sakher remained empty, bombed-out shells, blackened and burned. Spent ammunition covered the side of the road, as if someone had thrown grain onto the soil hoping it would grow. The only thing that would grow here was more hate, thought Malek to himself.

More hate and more war. His rucksack lay at his feet. He reached inside and pulled out his Kindle. Sand had not been kind to it and he wiped off a thick layer using his hand. He plugged it into the nine-volt cigarette lighter and began to charge it. After a minute or so, it came to life. He pressed the little home icon and his books came up. He scrolled and scrolled but couldn't find the book. He typed in 'The Order of the Gatherers of Truths'. Nothing. He raised his hands to his face, wiped them downwards and broke the silence.

'There is no book, Neeka.'

'What do you mean?'

'No, I mean there is a book. It took me to Babylon. I was there. But it's not here on the Kindle.'

Malek felt his anger rising. Why wasn't the book there?

'Malek,' said a female voice that wasn't Neeka's. He looked around the car. No one else seemed to hear the voice.

'What do you see in that girl?'

'Rubati! You evil little b – '

'Now, now, let's not be mean. We had you fooled, right?'

'What is happening to me? Am I losing my mind?'

'Pretty much. I did tell you I was fucking with your head.'

'But why? Can I have a reason now, please?'

'Because you will be mine, and together we will rule Babylon.'

'Yours?'

'Oh, Malek. Yes. Your destiny lies with me. I am here to bring you your true destiny. To rule Babylon as my king. Why fight it? Come to me, Malek.'

'I can't marry a book.'

'I saw the way you looked at me in Babylon.'

'But the book, the trial, everything has gone.'

'It'll come back. When you have no enemies within, no enemies outside can hurt you. Just accept the truth. You have seen Babylon and survived it. Nothing can touch you once you take my side, dear Malek.'

She blew him a kiss and, with that, the Kindle switched itself off.

Neeka turned to Malek. 'You're muttering to yourself. While that is not unusual for you, I said we should talk. Perhaps we should now.'

Justin shifted to face them from his shotgun passenger seat. 'Yeah, I think Neeka is right. We should talk. What is this book?'

Once Malek began to talk, it all came out. Everything. The tales. Babylon. Shamesh and Rubati. Nebuchadnezzar. Everything. He must have talked for an hour. As they reached Baghdad, he finished.

The Al Jazeera villa was occupied by other journalists and so they had moved into the Hotel Babylon.

Neeka took Malek's hand and they walked into the lobby. From modern Babylon to Hotel Babylon via ancient

Babylon.

'Malek. You need a break and some help. Tomorrow we fly to London. We are going to stay in my flat. We need a couple of days' rest and then we go see a specialist. But first things first. You stink. You need new clothes.'

'Neeka, I'm tired. I just want to shower and eat.'

'Look, there's a menswear boutique in the lobby of the hotel. Sit down a minute and let me pick some things up for you. Give me your wallet.'

'What for?'

'You don't think I'm paying for your clothes, do you? You haven't even bought me flowers yet.'

Neeka took 300 dollars and some change from his wallet. She walked over to the tiny boutique selling high-end designer wear – t-shirts with Italian names emblazoned across them; jeans so tight no one's blushes would be spared. This was going to be a challenge. Malek wasn't fashion guy; his style was more casual and hadn't changed over the years as clothes trends came and went. As she picked out a shirt and some normal-looking jeans she felt strange and mildly thrilled doing something as intimate as clothes shopping for him. She steeled herself. This was a practical errand. Now there was the thorny issue of underwear. Glancing around she grabbed the first pair of boxer shorts she saw. She put them on the counter, hidden underneath the jeans, t-shirt and jacket she had managed to find on the sale rail – 300 dollars didn't go a long way in this shop – and didn't meet the eyes of the sales assistant as she handed over the money and waited while everything was carefully wrapped.

She came out at last and gave the enormous shiny carrier bag to Malek. 'You can shower now. Seriously, you are truly disgusting. And throw those other clothes away. I'm not going to sleep with you otherwise.' With those words, Neeka smiled and her eyes sparkled in a way that made Malek feel safe.

Justin and Neeka needed to discuss last-minute travel plans. So Malek went on up to the bedroom. He took off his clothes. They were stiff with dried sweat and dust. He stuffed them into a laundry bag and threw them into the trash chute. He stepped into the shower and switched it on. The water flowed from his body into the bathtub, turning everything brown. The sand kept coming off his body. He caught a whiff of himself. They'd need to disinfect the car. After an hour he stepped out of the shower and looked at himself in the mirror. He'd gotten older.

Downstairs, Neeka and Justin were sitting in the lobby of what was once a proud metropolitan hotel but now looked wilted and provincial. They toyed with their cups of tea and made small talk. Very small talk, until Neeka broached the subject.

'You think he is mad, don't you?'

'I don't know what to think. Mad? I mean he sounds convinced. He clearly believes it and he thinks you believe him. Let's face it, he has always been a bit odd, but we all have our funny little ways. You got me. I don't know. What do you think?' Justin swilled his tea around in the tiny finjan.

'I'm scared. Petrified, in fact. He and I are in love except I don't know which Malek I love. The pre-Vietnam one or this one. Has he even changed? London will be good. We need to stand still. Get off the rollercoaster for a bit. Justin, you have to promise me something, though. We can't tell the management what has happened these past five days. I told them he was ill. If they find out he's making bad decisions, they might fire him. There is always someone younger, cheaper and prettier in this line of work.'

'I'm leaving this whole thing to you. As far as the management know, I'm in Ireland recovering from my kidnap ordeal.'

'Justin, I'm sorry. With all this crap going on I just felt we needed to come here... I – I was relieved you got out.'

'I know. But it was a storm in a teacup, darling, and I live to fight another day.'

Neeka walked into the bedroom an hour later. Malek was in the foetal position on the bed, fast asleep. He was wearing nothing but his brand new boxer shorts. Neeka blushed. The tiger print she had accepted in her rush to get out of the shop. But the words printed on the front – 'Beware. Beast of Baghdad Inside' – how had she not noticed those? She blushed even more, and hastily covered Malek with a towel. The other new clothes were in a dishevelled heap beside him, still half-wrapped in tissue paper. He had crashed while unpacking them. Neeka smiled. She put them on a chair and went to the bathroom to brush her teeth. She came back and looked at Malek again. She put a couple of drops of perfume on the pillow and undressed. She spooned into him and took his right hand, tucking her thumb under the green string bracelet and wrapping her fingers around his wrist. She kissed the back of his neck and said, 'I love you. Please don't be crazy.'

26

London – Two Weeks Later

Neeka lived in a small Victorian conversion flat on the first floor of an old, grand house in Brixton, SW2. She had bought it years ago when she had moved from DC to London, back when no one wanted to live in Brixton. Malek stared out of the window at the mass of trees at the end of the gravel driveway. London looked orderly, pedestrian even. He hadn't been in this city for a while. It was stifling and oppressive, albeit in very different ways from the Middle East. Still, he was happy here. Neeka had taken a job on the London news desk at the Al Jazeera English office in the Shard.

Malek was officially on extended holiday. Unofficially, he was in therapy.

But before therapy came research. He switched on his journalist's brain and spoke to a variety of doctors and researchers in academic institutions. He told them he was working on a mental health article and wanted some background. He concocted an imaginary case study of a man of similar age to him who had a history of an overactive imagination and now firmly believed that he'd been given a book that foretold the future. The doctors and researchers went along with the hypothesis and Malek was able to ask several questions that allowed him to form an opinion as to what he might or might not be going through.

Neeka thought this was an insane idea. Malek thought it was inspired.

'You're like one of those people who diagnose themselves on the internet and find that the symptoms of a common cold are the same as those caused by some exotic airborne pathogen that can kill you. You can't do that. They are called mental health professionals for a reason. Just go and get some help!'

'I am getting help. Some of the country's finest mental health professionals are talking to me. I'm getting a pretty good handle on what the current thinking is on someone with an issue such as this.'

'Firstly, it's not someone with an issue such as this. It's you. And you need specific help. Secondly, this is not a job!'

'You asked me to seek help. I'm getting it.'

'*Pedasag.* You actually might be insane. This week has been awful. You've been glued to that computer like some digital hypochondriac. You barely say anything and, when you do, its psychobabble gobbledygook. Get some real help! Now!'

Neeka had once again become uber-Iranian and was waving her hands around in despair.

'*Ay baba*, I think I would find this easier if you were watching porn. Will you go and get some help?' she said once again, but this time with a little more force.

'But look, my case study seems to be suffering from this.' He pointed to the screen and read a sentence that went something like this: 'The criteria for schizophrenia have never been met. Note: hallucinations, if present, are not prominent and are related to the delusional theme e.g., the sensation of being infested with insects is associated with the delusions of infestation.'

'Well, that's OK then. You don't have insects crawling over your body. I'm glad we cleared that up. Malek. I told you in Baghdad that this was only going to work if you sought help. Not reading websites called... What is this one called?'

She peered at the screen. 'Amateur Psychologist and Fisherman's Weekly dot com.'

'It's not called that. It's the American Psychiatric Association.'

'*Pedasag*. It might as well be American Psycho for all the good it's going to do you. Looking at that is like trying to treat malaria with an aspirin. Just a week ago you were a gibbering wreck in Babylon and now you're an expert in mental health. I am this close to throwing you out. I mean it, Malek. It's not just you. This affects me as well. You think I want to live with a man who might break down at any second?'

It had been a tough week. But, ultimately, Malek applied some rationality to his problem. The symptoms had lasted over a year. Most people he had spoken to suggested that this was a good baseline to try and diagnose what was occurring. Most of those people also suggested that the case study was an example of something called 'delusional disorder', which was 'grandiose' in nature, multi-episodic and in partial remission. Grandiose. If you are going to be bat-shit crazy you might as well suffer from a disease with a cool sub-name, thought Malek.

Neeka was right, of course. He held her fast in his arms

241

and said nothing. The act of holding her was agreement enough.

It was time for Malek to find a therapist.

He decided that the best course of action was to check out some therapists and then look at the number of second-hand bookshops within a bus ride of each therapist's clinic. The one with the most bookshops would win. It seemed as good a criterion as any other. One name jumped out at him. Dr Semera Khan. She must have been in the book for a reason. Then he thought about Rubati. Was this a trap?

God works in mysterious ways, the Devil in devious ways. Was this the work of the Devil? There was only one way to find out. He picked up the phone and dialled Dr Khan's office number to book an appointment towards the end of the week. Neeka was happy that he had finally done it. He didn't tell her it was with the psychotherapist from the book. No use in alarming her unnecessarily.

The doctor was pleasant enough, a formal woman a few years younger than Malek. Her office was suitably clinical but without the feel of a medical surgery. Perhaps it was better described as clinical chic, or as having an atmosphere to alleviate the aura of absurdism. He wasn't really thinking about the therapy at this stage.

'So, thank you, Malek, for coming in today. It would be useful for me to hear what has brought you, so shall we start there?'

He thought about the question. 'I'm experiencing something odd. Yes, odd. That might be the best way of putting it.'

'Can you describe it?'

His mind raced through the last few months. Images of Babylon and Iraq, with fragments of conversations from his travels in the ancient city. Justin and Neeka and Shamesh and Rubati filled the gaps between.

'Not really.'

Dr Khan smiled. 'I understand that this might be difficult for you, especially if you've bottled things up for a long time. Perhaps we should start instead with a little bit about yourself and your work.'

Professional Malek was a subject Malek could talk about for a very long time. He ran through his CV for a bit, including his recent work in Iraq, Pakistan and Turkey.

The therapist's next question was obvious, but it still took Malek by surprise. 'Are you worried that you are suffering from post-traumatic stress?'

'Possibly. I actually think I might be suffering from a delusional disorder that is grandiose in nature. It's multi-episodic but currently in partial remission. That is to say, I haven't felt any of the effects for several days.'

'Has anybody told you they think you are delusional?'

'I spoke to a few professionals in the course of my research.'

'Interesting. Please tell me more.'

Malek went through the research. He described the case study. Saying it out loud to a professional, he could see why Neeka thought it was a dumb idea. He was having his own doubts right now.

'So, no one has told you that you are delusional, but your research has led you to believe that you might be?'

'Yes. And I have been looking into treatments.'

'And how would you treat this disorder?'

'Medication seems a good idea.'

'You would self-medicate?'

'Does wine count as self-medication?'

'How often do you drink?'

'Not as often as I'd like.'

She made a note. 'I'm actually quite interested in what you think a course of treatment might be.'

'Well, there has been some success with antipsychotics like olanzapine and risperidone. Those, mixed with some antidepressants, seems like a pretty good fix.'

'Psychiatric medication is a dangerous road to go down. Without proper medical supervision, combining medications in that way could be lethal.'

'Still, it would be a fun way to go out.'

'I am glad you've not lost your sense of humour, but this is a serious matter. A matter you felt serious enough to seek help for.'

She was not a warm or funny woman. Malek felt like he was in the headteacher's office.

'Let's get back to self-diagnosis. You wouldn't trust a journalist not practised in his or her craft. It's the same for us.'

'Not a fan of citizen journalism, then?'

'I'm sorry, I don't get that reference.'

'Anyone with a smartphone thinks they can do what I do.'

'I wonder if we can get back to the day-to-day. Let's build up a picture of what's happening with you. Maybe we can make sense of it together and think about what might help?'

OVER THE NEXT MONTH, the sessions bore fruit. Malek opened up and told her everything, as he had done with Neeka, Justin and the Pir, and spared her no detail. After the session, he'd visit the secondhand bookshops that he'd identified in his search for a therapist, picking up volumes of poetry. He was particularly excited at his latest purchase. He had found the *Gulistan* by the Shirazi poet Sa'adi, who was born in 1210BC.

The translation from Persian was made in the late 1800s so the old-fashioned English matched the Persian warmly. It was an enchanting book full of old idioms that were familiar to Persian speakers, just as Shakespearean idioms are to modern English speakers. It was a beautiful edition. Its full-leather binding gave it a substantial feel resembling tree bark and the gold tooling on the edges of the paper still shone if you looked closely. Inside, a swirling Paisley pattern gave it some colour. Whoever had printed the book had spent time thinking about its design. It was heavenly, and the kind of book Safa would have appreciated.

Malek sat in Battersea Park, just by the Peace Pagoda, on a bench near the river. He read his book and ate a cheese and pickle sandwich. He had missed cheese and pickle sandwiches. With all the amazing food the world has to offer, the simple can seem just ordinary. Not to him. A cheese and pickle sandwich was a taste of home. It was September and the weather had turned autumnal. After the heat of the Middle East Malek welcomed it and, with his scarf, he looked just like anyone else enjoying the last mild days before the onset of a chilly English winter. He put the book down and thought about the sessions so far with the psychotherapist.

Dr Khan had told him that, although delusional disorders were rare, they did exist. Malek's ego took this news quite well. Malek had insight into his delusion. He was living alongside it and understood it on one level. He was able to be his normal self, not trapped inside the delusion 24/7. She'd also told him that he wasn't alone, despite the relative rareness of the condition, and that with understanding came respite. She was taking a holistic approach and encouraged Malek to exercise and eat properly. Neither of these things he did. Together, they explored why he was imagining, in such minute and clarion detail, things like the book and Babylon. Dr Khan had jokingly – well, as jokingly as she could – coined a term for this. She called it cognitive journalism therapy. She pointed to Malek's natural inquisitiveness, the thing that had led him to become a journalist, and told him to apply that to understanding what had happened to him. This was all helpful. It helped Malek feel in control of what was happening. At home, Neeka and Malek were close, and spent many happy evenings binge-watching TV series and films. The Middle East was in turmoil but, for a few more weeks, it was to be someone else's problem.

Under a golden Buddha, Malek looked at his watch. He needed to pick up some wine and go home to be sous-chef for Neeka. He had a few minutes. Enough to read another Sa'adi poem:

> An ill-humoured fellow insulted a man who patiently bore
> it saying: 'O hopeful youth, I am worse than you speak of
> me, for I am more conscious of my faults than you.'

Perhaps that was the takeaway message from the therapy: *I am more conscious of my faults than you.*

27

A Crushing Inevitability

Dinner looked great set out on the table, like Lahore had come to south-west London. Neeka and Malek had made chicken pulao, dahl and keema aloo. There was plenty of warm naan bread, salads and wine. Dima and her husband Rami had come over. Dima was a Lebanese human-rights lawyer who was currently handling the case of a man accused of providing material support to Al Shabab. Hamad was a British Palestinian and a researcher for Chatham House specialising in European–Arab relations.

A lapsed Maronite, a lapsed Sunni Muslim, a Persian and a confused Muslim eating Pakistani food in London and discussing global politics.

Neeka looked at the spread on the table and rubbed her hands. '*Bah, bah, bah,*' she said out loud, and with that the feast began, and with that the conversation.

'What do you expect when the Saudis' biggest exports are hard-line religion, oil and used luxury goods?'

'You know, Nawaz Sharif used to be as bald as a coot, I tell you.'

'Jesus couldn't get into Jerusalem now. He'd be turned away for not having the right papers.'

'Assad has run out of money, time and options. Perhaps ISIL could lend him a few quid to tide him over.'

'FEMA should run Middle East outreach. They'd do a better job than Tony Blair.'

'The Palestinians should move Ethiopian Jews into the West Bank. Israel would stop building settlements then.'

And so it went on and on and, the later it got, the less politically correct and more hilarious the discussion became. For both Malek and Neeka it was a relief to be doing something normal. A dinner party was a welcome change from grabbing junk food on the road between assignments. The allure of the road would always be there but, right now, they were happy.

It was Dima who asked the obvious question.

'So, when did this all happen? God knows you two should have got together years ago.'

'That'll be my cue to go and wash up,' laughed Neeka.

'Don't be silly. If I leave it to Malek, he will tell me of long-lost love and some Persian poet I've never heard of predicting the future. Come come, I want the truth from you, missy,' said Dima.

'I think it was a case of crushing inevitability mixed with a lack of more suitable options.'

'Neeka, it was your romantic sensibility I fell for. Clearly,' Malek said.

Rami chuckled. 'I think what my wife is asking has much more to do with the practical elements of your coupling rather than the esoteric.'

Malek shook his head. 'With that, Neeka, the floor is yours. Regale our guests with the greatest love story of our time. I'm off to the loo.' In the bathroom, he splashed some water on his face. The food and wine had made him fuzzy, and the cold water felt good. He looked up and into the mirror. He wasn't entirely surprised by what he saw behind him. 'Rubati. Hello.'

'My, Malek. Is this your life now? You turned down my charms for this... How shall I describe it? Domestic oddity? The confinement of love?'

'Oh, I think it's more freedom than confinement, don't you think?' Rubati looked odd in a London bathroom. Her clothes suited an upscale Babylonian whorehouse. Her flowing black dress revealed everything and nothing at the same time, and the gold jewellery braided through her hair made her look like someone's fantasy, perhaps even his own. He'd clearly fallen for the idea of the exotic orient. Edward Said would be most disappointed in him. Still, this was his delusion, so he had no need to pretend to be anything other than he was.

'Oh, Malek. This is no delusional disorder, or whatever that apothecary has you believing, you know this is real. Perhaps I could persuade you. You never found out how skilled I am in the more lustful of the arts. I know you want me: your eyes have never mastered the ability of your tongue to deceive. Your eyes, dear boy. They have the truth in them.'

'My eyes might have the curse of truth in them, but banging on the bathroom floor isn't my idea of a good time. Not since the mid-Nineties anyway. My heart and soul, the things I truly desire, are next door, Rubati. What do you want?'

'Well, I guess if fucking is out of the question than perhaps a little chat? You can spare a moment for one of your oldest friends, now can't you?'

'Perhaps a moment for an elderly friend.'

'Malek, this foolishness must cease. You found your answers in Babylon. You defeated the great Nebuchadnezzar in verbal combat. Your words echo around the city to this day. Everyone in the court still speaks of the southern miner. You are a hero to the people. You have the love of the people. They know the queen threw you into the fire but, like the Jews, they expect you to come back. Children even play with cockroaches in your honour. They say you fooled Nebuchadnezzar by pretending it was a ruse. The people speak about you with hushed reverence. Come back home to Babylon and topple the king. Rule with me. I shall be your queen. Shamesh has it all arranged. Leave those fools in the next room to their selfish stupidity.'

'A conspiracy to topple the king? My my, I was guilty after all. Your words tempt me, Rubati, they really do. But my life is here, with Neeka. I'm home.'

'Then I have failed, for now. I leave you a gift. The morning shall reveal it.'

Rubati moved in closer to Malek and kissed him on the lips.

'I pray for you to come over to the side of the truth. I know my prayers will be answered.'

'I know who you pray to, and I want no part of it.'

With a flirtatious wave, Rubati walked backwards into the wall and faded away. Malek returned to the living room.

'Everything OK, baby?' asked Neeka.

'You know me, just talking with myself, telling myself how lucky I am for having met you. I trust our guests are thoroughly bored with our love story?'

He picked up another bottle of wine and made an announcement to the table.

'I have a game to play. It's called "Persian Incursion". It was invented by the Pentagon to role-play a possible Israeli airstrike on Iranian nuclear facilities. Who is in? I bagsy Iran.'

'Brilliant! I'll take the Israelis. It'll be ironic,' said Rami. 'I'll be the Americans.' Dima rubbed her hands with glee.

'Oof, I guess I'll be the UN then. I'll just sit in the corner and issue the occasional pissant statement,' said Neeka.

'Oh, it's better than that, Neeka. There are a bunch of UN statements that you can read out. No, you get to play "rogue actors and sideline nation states". Hamas, Hezbollah, Iraq, Turkey, Saudi and Russia.'

'Great. My Iranian parents are so happy with me right now.'

Food was cleared away. The board game was put onto the table. The Middle East was about to be put to fire. Again.

Rami began. 'Gentlemen, Israel shall prevail. Our orders are clear. We have refuelling rights over Saudi Arabia, who have joined us in our mission to take down Iran's nuclear facilities. We are to begin a seven-day bombing campaign. Godspeed and *Heshbon bevakasha.*'

Dima looked at him in a funny way. 'You know that means "Cheque please!" Right?'

'Yeah, it was the only Hebrew phrase I could remember from my fact-finding mission to Jerusalem last month.'

'The only fact you found on that trip was that Israeli beer tastes like shit,' said Neeka.

'I'm Palestinian. What did you expect me to think?'

The scene was set. The friends began to play. If any of them had been paying attention they would have noticed Malek's Kindle come to life and begin to download.

28

The Perfect Gift

For a moment, the dark outside threw Malek. He rubbed his eyes and sat up in bed. Neeka had left for work and the house was still. Last night had been fun. He brewed a coffee and looked over at the Persian Incursion war game on the table. If he read it right, Israel had attacked Iran via Saudi Arabia. In turn, Hezbollah and Hamas had launched attacks on Israel. The Israeli army had then occupied southern Lebanon and the Gaza Strip but couldn't hold on to the territory. Iran had launched S200 anti-aircraft weapons at Israeli jets on the third day of bombing and shot down and captured two Israeli Air Force pilots. IRIN State TV had put them on display for the whole world to see. That had forced Israel to stop bombing Iran, and the US fifth fleet was now almost entirely stationed in the Strait of Hormuz. The UN Security Council was paralysed, with Russia and China vetoing almost every move the others made. Hundreds had died. No one had won. No one had lost. Iran and the Iranian civilian nuclear facilities were still standing. Israel was still standing. Palestine hung on for dear life. The Middle East was a mess again. As was the lounge. Scrabble might have been a better choice.

He cleared up the wine bottles and switched on the dishwasher. Being a house husband suited him right now and brought with it a sense of order and satisfaction. He flopped on the couch and flicked on the TV. Iraqi authorities were reporting a series of suicide bombs in the capital. Lebanon was in the throes of street protests. It was business as usual in the Middle East. He grabbed his Kindle and switched it on. On the screen was a message.

A gift. From your Rubati.

Malek noted his lack of surprise. He thought back to last night and how casually he'd taken her appearance in the bathroom. None of this had freaked him out. None of this had seemed unusual to him. He sat on the couch and wondered why he was so blasé about the whole thing. Three weeks ago he'd nearly lost his mind in Babylon. Today it was as normal as could be. He looked at his Kindle. The book was back. He could delete it. He could read it. Or he could ignore it. He deleted it. A second later it was downloading itself again. He switched off the WiFi connection and deleted it again. The WiFi switched itself back on automatically and the book appeared again. He decided to read.

Tonight a Comedian Died in New York

HE STUMBLES TOWARDS THE MIC, *fiddling in his jacket pocket. He begins to speak: 'Phew, they make detonators a lot smaller these days. I thought I had lost it. Salaam aliekum. My name is Mohammed Anwar. Here is my passport to the Islamic State. You can call me Anwar.*

'*Is this an open–carry state? Phew. I can drink this whisky then. Oh, wait. That's not what you mean by that.*

'*Any Muslims in the house?*' (*He speaks into his collar like the secret service.*) '*Third row. Fifth along. Make sure you grab him.*

'*I grew up a Muslim, so our prophets were the same as those of Christianity and Judaism. Moses, peace be upon him, was hanging out with Jesus and Mohammed, peace be upon them, one day, when Moses threw his hands up in the air. I gave them the tablets. What did they do? They trolled me hard. Jesus said, "Well, at least they didn't turn you into a blond–haired, blue-eyed white guy. I am Palestinian for Christ's sake." Mohammed said... Oh wait, Mohammed actually wasn't there. Delta wouldn't let him fly.*

'*Seriously. What is up with that? People being thrown off planes for doing math? I know Muslims invented algebra but that's a bit much. One woman was reading a book about Syrian art and got thrown off a flight. She was gorgeous as well. Fuck J-date. If she was a terrorist, then sign me up to T-date.*

'*I love this country, America. I think I want to be a WASP, they seem like such nice, nice people.*

'*So well dressed. Who doesn't want to look like they just stepped off a tennis court in 1929? I tried joining a country club in Tennessee. It didn't go well. I spoke to my friend Jack. "I want to join your country club," I says to Jack. Jack says, "Anwar, forget about it. They don't want Muslims at the club."*

'*I insist. "OK, fine," says Jack. "Just don't tell them you are a Muslim. Just ask the concierge at the club if you can*

*become a member." So I get down there. The concierge asks
for my name. I say Ian Kohen. He says, "Sorry, we don't take
Jews." So I gave up becoming a WASP. They hate everybody. I
used to live in Qatar in the Gulf. Persia, not Mexico. But think
brown people.*

'*You're only allowed to be in the country if you have a job.
So that can get awkward if they don't understand your job.
My friend got asked by the cops, "What is your job?"*

"*I sell condos," he says.*

"*To single ladies?"*

"*Sometimes," he says.*

"*You're under arrest for encouraging sex outside of
marriage!" That one took a little bit of explaining I can tell
you. Anyway. I'm glad to be back here in the States. Qatar was
a weird place. Think Vegas but all the women are covered and
there is no gambling. My friends here are all really funny
though. They keep taking me to Middle Eastern restaurants,
because they think that's what I like. No, motherfucker. I
want a pastrami on rye. Take me to a bar, goddamn it. I love
American bars. People are friendly in bars. Until you find out
I am Muslim. Then you get confused.*

'*But then I get confused as well. I went to Brooklyn the
other night. So many guys with beards, I thought I was at a
Hamas rally. If New York was an open–carry state I could
have been in Gaza, if Gazans dressed in vintage clothes and
carried guns. Actually, Gazans do dress in vintage clothes.
Israel restricts imports to the Strip. They have no choice.
Except there, they call it oppressed–as–fuck clothing.*

'*Anyone been to Israel? You should. They all talk in thick
New York accents. It's basically like if a synagogue in the
Bronx moved to the Middle East. I love America. We kicked
the Brits out just like the Indians and Pakistanis did. But then*

we discovered we needed a lot more oil than we had here, and we went to the Middle East. This time with drones. We learned from the Brits. They don't have beer and the women are all covered? Fuck it. We will send in robot planes instead. Ah, you guys have been a great audience. I won't blow you up. Mind you, it wouldn't make a difference. Can you imagine? What God would be like? You blew up a late–night comedy club? Those guys are all atheists. What was the point of that? Go to hell asshole. And tell Bin Laden he still owes me money...'

Anwar felt good as he walked offstage and into the cold New York night. He stopped and lit a cigarette.

'Trump is coming! He's got my back you, Sharia mother-fucker. You can't force your Muslim shit on me. Fuck you, asshole.'

The punch came from nowhere as Anwar swung around to see who was shouting at him. It hit him square in the side of the head. He fell to the floor and remained there until the ambulance arrived. The time of death was 0103.

ANOTHER MESSAGE FLASHED up on the screen.

> Our rule shall be the greatest Babylon will ever know. Our names shall ring out, in our time and in the future and forever. I said I had a gift for you. I sent Anwar to hell. That is my gift to you. Beware of what I can do. Rubati.

Malek needed to get out and go for a walk. He threw the Kindle into his rucksack, put the bag over his shoulder and left the house, walking to his usual spot in Battersea Park, by the Buddhas, near the river. He nibbled on his cheese and pickle sandwich and wondered what to do. The book and the vision of Rubati didn't worry him. They couldn't be real. He had that feeling again. One where the neural waves in his brain weren't connecting to anything, where he wasn't making any sense to himself. How could he be so accepting of what was happening to his mind? He pulled out his phone and was about to dial Dr Khan's number to book an appointment at short notice, but changed his mind. Instead, he pulled out the Kindle. Nothing. No book. No messages from anyone. It was as if the whole thing had been a bad dream. He wished it was a bad dream. A message came through on his phone.

> Tickets tonight at the South Bank. Artist a surprise. You'll like it. We haven't been out in ages. Meet at RFH at 7.30pm. Neeka xx

God, he loved that woman. An evening out couldn't hurt. No sense in wasting the day. Time to confront his demons, as it were.

He rang Dr Khan's office. Her receptionist squeezed him in for a session in fifteen minutes' time.

In Dr Khan's office, Malek took a deep breath, began with the dinner party and Rubati and ended by handing her his Kindle. 'You can see that the book isn't there, but I read a story on it this morning.'

'I think, Malek, we should continue with our treatment. We know what you are experiencing isn't real. We need you to keep functioning in normal society. Now, you're not socially isolated or purposefully withdrawn. You have a social system around you that is healthy and normal. You aren't in your delusion all the time. You need to use that to regulate your own thought. Think of these delusional thoughts as your brain working overtime. You can let the delusions continue to work themselves out or you can find an alternative that can combat them. It's about living with this disorder and eventually finding a way for it to go away. It's good that you're not freaked out by the appearance of Rubati or the book, but it is a delusion. I'm going to start to look into alternative therapies. Maybe together, Malek, we can find a way.'

Malek frowned. 'So, I'm mad, but socially functional, so that's all right then? Isn't that a bit like saying OK, so he drinks a lot, but he is a successful person holding down a great job, his kids love him and his wife thinks he is great, so let's not worry about the damage the booze is doing? His booze is Châteauneuf-du-Pape Grande Reserve at home and not Special Brew in the park swearing at the kids. So, you know, it's all good.'

'Not at all Malek, but we have to concentrate on the positives. You are socially integrated. You are successful. That's a step beyond the norms of your disorder.'

'I'm not convinced, but OK.'

'We will figure this out together, Malek, I promise. Perhaps you should think about dumping the Kindle for a while and only reading physical books. Also, eat better and exercise. I keep telling you, it'll help. And lay off the cigarettes and booze, or at least go easy on them. Now, I have a question for you. Are you a religious man?'

The question was a fair one, but still unexpected.

'I believe in God. Everything else is up for negotiation. Do I think the Koran was revealed to the Prophet Mohammed and is the unchanged word of God in Arabic? I can buy it on one level. I'm not sure the Hadith, which are the basis for Islamic law, are reliable or can be taken at face value. Take the Taliban, for example, who put the Koran and Sunnah, the way of the prophet as recorded in the Hadith, on an equal footing...'

'Malek, Malek, let me stop you there. That's an academic answer and one you have clearly rehearsed and said a lot. I want an emotional response. Does God exist? You have just spent months trying to love God. I mean, that's the story you have told me. That has got to have left a mark.'

Malek thought back to his childhood and to the toy soldier. He thought back to his arguments with God. He thought back to the damage he'd seen done in God's name all over the world. He thought back to all the murders that had been committed. He thought of Neeka, a woman so loving and kind that she had to be proof of the existence of God. He thought about the love he felt for his close ones. 'I do believe in God, absolutely. *Mashallah.* All praise to him. And I mean that sincerely. But do I love God? I'm not sure. Do I have to? Where is it written that we must love God?'

'In all faiths I think loving God is pretty standard.'

'Fair point. I don't know. There has to be one pure thing in this world and that, to me, is God. We are flawed in our understanding of God. How about you?'

'My thoughts on the subject are not important. But, as you've asked, I'm an atheist.'

'Wow. I wasn't expecting that. Really? An atheist? With the dowdy dress sense and the name and the whole serious outlook I was expecting a little more from you.'

'Well, there you have it. You, a clean-shaven, heavy-drinking British Pakistani, believe in Allah almighty. I, a dowdy, teetotal British Pakistani, am an atheist. Looks can be deceiving. And thanks for the "dowdy" comment. I was going for "professional". Tell me, do you often talk to women like this?'

'I admit my jokes can fall a little flat. OK, so I crash all the time but, no, I don't "always" talk to women like this. I'm sorry.'

'I'll take that. Anyway, I ask because I read about a 2008 study. They compared the treatment of delusional disorders in Saudi Arabia and the UK. Small samples: thirty-three in each country. In Saudi, sixty-two per cent used religion as a source of treatment. In the UK, less than three per cent. Worth a thought?'

'Saudi also beheaded more people than ISIL last year. Perhaps that's the most effective way of dealing with mental problems. Certainly effective. No head, no problems in the head.'

'That's one way of looking at it. Let's talk about you though. Think about religion, maybe?'

'I'd really rather not.'

'Well, our time is at an end. I think we have made great progress. You seem calm and in control. That is a positive step. We have to concentrate on the positives.'

'Before I go, we need to talk about something else. Have you ever treated a woman called Roya Farishte?'

'I don't discuss other clients.'

'That's not a no.'

'Why do you ask?'

'Roya was in my book.'

Dr Khan shuffled her papers nervously.

'Malek. These stories in the book. You say they are people you know or have briefly met? Correct?'

'Yes.'

'What if I said that your brain was conflating stories you

have worked on or read with those in this book? That the book is actually fragments of the news but told to you in a fantastic way? The book is your way of processing information, and the concept of heaven and hell is you trying to bring about some real justice for the dead.'

'OK.'

'Roya died a few years back after she threw herself out of my office window convinced she could fly. Her death made the national papers. You read about her and created a story in your book to give her a happier ending in death. You chose me because you recognised my name. You recognised it not from the book, but from newspaper reports at the time.'

'Logically that makes sense. But what about the daydreaming? The augmented-reality thing?'

'That feels like you're justifying your intense daydreams with something tangible, something logical, rather than confronting what they are.'

'And what are they?'

'We will find out. It's certainly a delusional disorder, but one we can get you to deal with. Let's keep our appointment for tomorrow.'

Malek walked out onto Lavender Hill and back down towards the park. He felt good. Conflating news reports and the book seemed a reasonable explanation. For the book at least. He wasn't sure Dr Khan could offer him any more help, but he would keep coming. He seemed to be coping with his delusion.

The wind was picking up and autumn was definitely dying. He pulled his scarf a little tighter and pushed up the collar of his winter coat. Not working was making him feel guilty. He flicked through AlJazeera.com on his phone, saw that his colleagues were in all sorts of far-flung places and felt like he was missing out on the action.

He would talk it over with Neeka tonight. Maybe it was time to get back on the road.

Just off Lavender Hill was a tiny jewellery shop. On a whim, he popped in. He read on a card that the owner made some of the jewellery and the rest was from small independent designers she had tracked down. One of the necklaces caught his eye. It was a Hamsa, a symbol common throughout the Middle East, and used within both Islam and Judaism. In Islam it represented the hand of the prophet's daughter Fatima and was said to ward off evil spirits and bring good luck. In Judaism it was a symbol adopted by Jews from North Africa living in Muslim communities and reminded the wearer to praise God with all five senses. More importantly than that for Malek was that the symbol annoyed fundamentalists on all sides, who claimed that the use of talismans was forbidden. For that reason alone, the Hamsa had always appealed. He and Neeka had officially been dating for a month. What better present? The necklace was gorgeous. A silver chain with the Hamsa made from lapis lazuli, which shone bright blue, like the bricks of the Ishtar Gate in Babylon. The hand was subtle, no bigger than a twenty-pence piece. It was perfect.

The jeweller chatted to Malek about her recent trip to Turkey where she had picked up the necklaces from a designer called Ayse. 'The collection is wonderful. It's named after Ayse's friend, who passed away. With each necklace, she is remembered.'

Malek smiled. The story of Damla came back to him but instead of freaking him out, it gave him comfort. 'The universe works in funny ways. Let's hope Damla watches over my girlfriend and protects her.' He watched the jeweller gift-wrap it and put it into a silk drawstring purse. A southern miner's purse, thought Malek. He handed over his credit card, paid for the necklace, put it into his pocket and went on his way.

'Oh, Malek. A gift, and not for me? You tease me. Show me what it is?' Rubati walked alongside him.

'Such things are not for you, my dear.'

'You honestly don't believe what that quack told you in there, do you?'

'Why not? It makes perfect sense.'

'But I am here, and you can touch me.' She took his arm and put it around her waist as they continued to walk.

'Rubati, it's freezing. You might want to put something warmer on.'

'See, you do care for me Malek. Give up this foolhardiness. This isn't the life for us. Put that chain around my neck and let it forever bond us. Show me you love me...'

'Be gone with you, Rubati. My heart is not yours. And your heart belongs to the Devil.'

Rubati stopped, stamped her feet and Malek continued to walk. He didn't look around, held the silk purse in his hand a little tighter and pushed his hands further into his pockets.

'That bitch, Neeka Shirazi,' Rubati muttered under her breath. 'I shall show her the ways of a queen.'

29

Rubati's Song

It was around 2am and Malek was wide awake. He picked up the Kindle but couldn't muster the mental strength to switch it on. He thought about saying Rubati's name out loud, but he knew trying to summon her would probably lead to more questions than answers, if she heeded his call. Rubati was up to something. Something different from the book. Did she really want him to rule ancient Babylon with her? He shook his head quickly, like a dog drying its coat, hoping the movement might clear his head. Neeka remained asleep. The only light in the room was the flicker from a fading candle. The flame danced as he stared at it. He blinked twice. He saw a room. It wasn't the room he was in.

She carefully placed Malek's picture by the candle. She flipped open the cover on her iPod.

The song was going to be important. It needed to be perfect. To sum up Malek, yet also sum up her feelings for him. She had a mission.

To bring him back to ancient Babylon from 21st-century

London. This was her chance to get out of the Order and take power for herself. With Malek by her side, she could topple Nebuchadnezzar and live as queen in one of the greatest cities, in one of the greatest times in history.

She flicked her thumb up the screen and the songs scrolled by, artists and titles blurred into one.

The word 'love' appeared a lot, but what Rubati needed wasn't love. It was power. A spell. She recognised the title instantly.

'Drink to Me Only with Thine Eyes'.

It was a song she had first sung in a village in Suffolk, England in 1627.

In a candlelit house she had gently whispered its lyrics to another they had sent her to get. It had worked. She began to sing it once more:

> *Drink to me only with thine eyes,*
> *And I will pledge with mine;*
> *Or leave a kiss but in the cup,*
> *And I'll not look for wine.*
> *The thirst that from the soul doth rise*
> *Doth ask a drink divine;*
> *But might I of Jove's nectar sup,*
> *I would not change for thine.*
>
> *I sent thee late a rosy wreath,*
> *Not so much honouring thee*
> *As giving it a hope, that there*
> *It could not withered be.*
> *But thou thereon didst only breathe,*
> *And sent'st it back to me;*
> *Since when it grows, and smells, I swear,*

Not of itself, but thee.

THE SONG HAD MORPHED from a poem by Ben Jonson, who had written it in 1616. Various singers had sung it since and, in 21st-century London, it still made sense to Rubati. She had crossed lines trying to get Malek. She had sent Anwar the comedian to hell out of spite and without consultation with Malek. She had done it just to get his attention, but that wasn't the end. She was about to do it again. Rubati continued to sing as she picked up her Kindle. She stopped singing for a moment.

'My sweet Kindle, on it these words I write, and these words you read. You poor foolish boy. I am the author of this book that has so captivated you, and will make you mine.' She began to sing again.

As she waved her arms in the manner of an orchestra conductor, more words appeared on her Kindle. In the darkness of the Brixton flat, Malek's Kindle buzzed and he picked it up. The ellipsis once again appeared.

If You Play With Fire

'THOUGH IT MIGHT BE FADING, *I can still taste you on my lips. I still catch your scent if the wind blows my way. But even if it fades the memories of that kiss still remain and the anticipation of perhaps another thrills me. I sleep dreaming of what is to come. I hope you awake with a smile on your face and a song in your heart.'*

She read the words not once, not twice, but many times.

She was locked away in her bathroom. She was far away from London, far from where he was. Far from her torrid affair. Back in her home town, she had surprised her boyfriend with a romantic reunion. She had booked one of the best hotels in town. She had overcompensated for the guilt she had felt for all the messages and hours she had spent with him, the other man. The affair in London. Him. The one who should never ever have been anything other than a passing acquaintance. Perhaps a shared cigarette, maybe even a smile. Not this. Not this guilt. She was locked in her grand bathroom in her grand hotel with her grand idea of a grand night with her boyfriend, and all she wanted was to speak to the guy who was 1,500 miles away and not the one 150 centimetres away in the shower.

Having an affair didn't suit her. Both men right now gave her a headache. She concentrated on the headache.

The headache was not like the usual dull pain. This was something else. She looked in her mirror. Her northern European alabaster skin felt darker back in Sweden than when she was in the Middle East. She held her nails up. For the other him she had painted them fire–engine red. Not for her boyfriend. She opened up her palms and spread them. Her fingers tingled. Her headache sharpened. She closed her eyes. Without thinking, she blew on her nails. A tiny grey puff of smoke rose. She dropped her hands suddenly to her thighs. What had just happened? Slowly, she raised her hands to her face again. She blew. Again. The nails spluttered and belched out smoke. Once again she slammed them on her thighs. What was going on? From each red nail, fire rose. She had complete control. Like a switch she could turn them on and off. She rinsed her face. Walked out of the bathroom. She asked her boyfriend what he thought of her nails. He said nothing. Her *phone beeped. It was him. She caught a glimpse of the message before the notification disappeared. It said, 'If it is red, then let it be fire.'*

MALEK RECOGNISED THE WOMAN. They'd had an affair a few years ago at a counterterrorism conference in London.

Another message appeared on the Kindle.

'Hey? Remember that Swedish researcher you had an affair with a few years back in London? Sent that bitch to hell. You will be mine and we shall rule. Rubati.'

Malek closed his eyes and breathed deeply. Rubati wasn't real, this was all a delusion.

Neeka sleepily snuggled into him. 'Can't sleep?'

'I'm OK. Just thinking about the Kindle.'

'You give that Kindle too much power. Maybe we should destroy it?'

'Then I'd have to talk to you all the time.'

Neeka smiled and fell gently back to sleep. Malek spooned into her and closed his eyes.

30
Thirteen Years, One Month

There is something so very ugly about London's South Bank that gives it a charm unique to the city. It's grey and industrial-looking but full of life, even on a weekday autumn evening.

The Royal Festival Hall was the height of sophistication when it opened in 1951. It hadn't changed much. Hosting cutting-edge bands, world-class orchestras, singers from every corner of the globe, cabarets, festivals. It was a space that occupied a special place in Malek's heart.

When Malek was six years old, his parents had brought him here to see a concert. It was all very special and exciting. They walked through the foyer. Malek got an ice cream. His mother warned him not to spill any of it on his new clothes, which had been bought specially for the night. His father took his hand and they found their seats in the auditorium.

He sat between his parents and watched as a number of very large Pakistani men entered from the side and sat down on the stage. Their instruments were all strange-looking. Small drums sat atop cloth bases. A tiny keyboard was pumped by hand. One man sat cross-legged like the rest of them but slightly to the side. A microphone was in front of him. The strange keyboard made a haunting sound in the darkened hall. Then the drums began to come in, played by hand. The sound rose like nothing he'd ever heard. Suddenly, the men behind began to clap. There were only four of them but, as they joined in, it sounded like hundreds. The man with the mic began to sing. The music and voices rose once more. The man sang and his hands swayed to the words and to the beat. When he hit the high notes, one arm was raised high above his head, his eyes half closed, as if he was reaching out to touch God. Which might well be true. The singer, Nusrat Fateh Ali Khan, sang a form of South Asian music called Qawwali, which meant 'those who utter the words of the prophet' or 'those who testify'.

The memories of that night returned to Malek as he stood waiting for Neeka outside the Royal Festival Hall. She broke his daydream by throwing her arms around his waist from behind.

'Happy one-month anniversary, baby,' he said as he turned around.

'You're ridiculous. Who celebrates one month?'

'Two people who should have started dating thirteen years ago?'

She smiled, pulled out a card and gave it to him. The handwritten message read

Happy 31 days. Dooset Dharam xxxx

Inside were two tickets to tonight's performance. The group was Rahat Fateh Ali Khan and party. He was Nusrat's nephew and heir to the throne although, in recent years, some would claim he had squandered his talent on cheap Bollywood songs. Tonight, though, he was playing a tribute concert to his uncle, whom he'd learned from and sung with since he was three years old. His voice was said to match his father's. High praise indeed.

Malek kissed her and pulled out the small silk purse and placed it in her hand. She read the note first that said,

Thirteen years and one month xxxx

and then opened the purse.

'Oh my God, I love it! I shall wear it with pride. Particularly in front of imams and rabbis.' She tossed her head back and laughed.

They walked into the foyer and towards the auditorium. The place was packed with a crowd that spanned hippies in dreads and families who had made the trip up from the suburbs, much like Malek's family had done years earlier. The fathers wore blazers and slacks. The women were resplendent in elegant shalwar kameez and the children were wearing whatever the latest fashion was. It looked to Malek like the latest fashion involved having half a haircut. Scattered amongst them were members of London's arts and music community. One of the blazered men approached Malek.

'Excuse me. I just want to say that I am a huge fan of your reporting. My wife and I watch Al Jazeera all the time. It's the only news channel that brings us the world! Stay safe and keep up the good work!'

Neeka waited until the man had left. She almost didn't, but she did.

'Can I have your autograph, Malek?'

Malek blushed. Despite all his years of appearing on television, he was rarely recognised. Out of context, meaning away from a tragedy somewhere in the world, he was ignored.

'Please, Malek. I want to show my mother that I know you!'

'You have one more gag, then we never mention it again.'

Neeka thought for a second. 'Did you ever meet Osama bin Laden?'

'Yes. He was at your mother's house for Nowruz.'

They took their seats and waited for the show to start. Three rows behind them sat Shamesh and Rubati.

31

Allah Hoo

The auditorium darkened as the players entered and began to play. Instantly, Malek was transported back to his childhood. The smell of samosas filled his nostrils, the cassette tapes his parents would play in the car were alive on the stage. He sat transfixed. Neither he nor Neeka said a word to each other. They sat listening, each transported by the incredible voice.

Qawwali began by taking it right back to the basics of devotional music. 'Allah Hoo'. The same song the Pir had sung in Mir Ali. It was a song Malek must have heard a million times growing up, but this time the neural waves in his brain connected. He could feel them fizzing into fusion. For the first time in months he felt connected and normal. The song, with its near-constant refrain of *'Allah Hoo, Allah Hoo'*, made sense. There is only God. In Urdu they sang: 'Hindus see you in their idols. Muslims see you in the Ka'aba, this is limited. I believe in one thing. There is only you. There is only you. In the mosques, in the temple and in the *gurdwaras* there is only you, there is only you.' For the next two hours, Malek's heart and mind were as one, as were his and Neeka's hands.

The concert finished and they walked out onto the South Bank, heading towards Waterloo.

They strolled hand in hand, until a boy ran past them and pushed into Neeka.

'You little...' She stopped mid-sentence.

Malek was frozen to the spot. The boy was holding Malek's Kindle in his hand. Like the Artful Dodger, his touch was light and Malek hadn't even realised the Kindle had been stolen from him.

Facing them were Shamesh and Rubati. The boy handed Rubati the Kindle and ran off.

'Erm... Neeka. You are seeing what I'm seeing, right?'

'Yes, I think so. If you're seeing two oddly dressed people looking right at us.'

'We mean you no harm. Please allow us to introduce ourselves. I am Rubati. My rather grandly dressed companion is Shamesh. Our quarrel is not with you, my fair Neeka. It is with Malek, who simply refuses to accept his destiny.'

'You don't exist. You are a delusion,' Malek murmured.

'Malek,' Neeka said. 'Who are these two?'

'Rubati is the woman from the Kindle. Shamesh is my lawyer from ancient Babylon. Both of them work for the Devil.'

'Well, that explains that then.'

They stood side by side facing each other as the crowds flowed as normal.

'We have come to take you away, Malek. Come with us and let us not fight.'

This needs to be over, thought Malek. If it's a fight they are trying to avoid, it's a fight they'll get.

32

The Last Tale

Neeka clutched the talisman around her neck, the Hamsa. Malek opened his mouth. He sang with a voice he never knew he possessed. The words in his song mirrored the words he had heard at the beginning of the concert.

'*Allah Hoo, Allah Hoo*, Hindus see you in their idols. Muslims see you in the Ka'aba, this is limited. I believe in one thing. There is only you. There is only you. In the mosques, in the temple and in the *gurdwaras* there is only you, there is only you.'

Shamesh began to fade as Malek's words got louder and louder, his voice matching the clapping of his hands. Love for God was being sung. He walked towards Shamesh and, with every clap, Shamesh dwindled a little more.

Rubati was proving to be a bit more resilient.

Neeka unbuttoned her coat and exposed her necklace. Locked in each other's arms, Malek and Neeka walked towards Shamesh. One singing songs of devotion and the other holding out the talisman. Shamesh cowered and withered.

'Everything begins with your name, everything ends with your name. For you are the God of Mohammed, *Allah Hoo, Allah Hoo.*'

Shamesh spat and uttered curses in an ancient tongue long dead to this world to try to combat the living Urdu chorus.

It didn't work. Living chorus beat dead language. Shamesh was sent back to the fiery pit where he belonged.

Rubati screamed and promised revenge. She pulled out Malek's Kindle from underneath her flowing robes. 'Just one more short story, Malek. Just one more soul that you decide goes to heaven or hell. Let's just have one more tale, shall we?'

She began to read. On the South Bank, reading from the Kindle, she looked like any one of a number of buskers and street performers.

Malek and Neeka looked at each other. Earlier the four of them had been ignored, almost unseen by the hundreds of people on the South Bank. Now a small crowd gathered. What was real and what was not?

A Heart Casts the Darkest Shadow

FIVE TIMES A DAY *I turn my heart East. I do this every day. I have done this since I was a child in Pakistan. I did this when I moved to London when I was nineteen. I continued when times were good and when times were bad. I'm an old woman now. I have three grown children, and growing grandchildren from my youngest son. Malek, my eldest, was always too busy working to have children. I use my prayers to pray for them. I pray for my husband, whose side I haven't left since I married forty-five years ago. I pray for those I loved and who have passed away. As I get older, those prayers come a little more frequently. I pray for guidance. I pray for love. Last year, my husband and I went to Mecca and fulfilled our duty and performed hajj, the pilgrimage. I pray that the prophet has been granted the highest level of paradise and sits in the presence of God. I pray for all these things with my heart turned East. I have always avoided those things that God has forbidden us and I have spent my life praising his name. But I have a dark secret that I wish to unburden. I have a shadow in my heart. There is a darkness in my heart that I cannot lighten.*

I am a teacher in a school. I love my job and I thank and praise God for it. I studied hard to get this job. I juggled my children and my home life. When money was tight we found, with the blessing of God, ways of making things work.

I teach at reception class. Many of my children come from ordinary houses in the working–class enclaves of north London. They live in tight–knit communities that have been established for decades Some of the children don't speak English. Some do a little, others a bit more. My job is to bring their English up to scratch so that they can go through school and make the most of an education. I do this with the grace of God. We read together and we write and we sing. I've been doing this so long that I've seen the young girls and boys in my school grow into adults and I have seen them get married and succeed in their lives. I've seen them bury their own parents and I have been to their houses when their children were born. I bless God for this. I have seen their children come into my reception class and I watch them go through the school. They are good boys and girls. I pray for them also.

I tell my grandchildren about my other family and they laugh about it. When they are not here, my husband and I sit and talk about things for the house and children and grandchildren, but we talk in hushed tones. There is no need to shout as the house is quiet. When they come and visit, our quiet house comes alive. Every room has laughter and noise and joy. I make them breakfast and then lunch and then dinner and they tease me. Grandma is in the kitchen again! Grandma is in the kitchen again! I bless every meal in God's name. Granddad spends his time chasing the grandchildren around the house and our children sit and watch this spectacle. But I have a shadow in my heart.

When the Twin Towers fell in New York my heart fell also. At school, we lit candles for those who passed and prayed no more harm would come. We prayed in many faiths and many languages. I stopped watching the news. It was too much. At school one day a little girl came in upset and crying. Her daddy had been taken away by men in black uniforms in the middle of the night. She was frightened. With God's grace we helped her cope until her father was released without charge a few days later.

Over the years, I noticed a change amongst the mothers. Jeans and long shirts and scarves wrapped around the neck turned into headscarves and flowing black robes. At pick–up time, I would speak to these young mothers. They had fear and anger in their voices. Their fathers and husbands and brothers were harassed on the pavement. Their worlds had shrunk to a few local streets, they were afraid to travel further. They were suspicious of vans parked on the corners of their roads, they feared that men were inside monitoring their movements. One day, one of the mothers asked me why I didn't wear the hijab. I was shocked. I'm Pakistani by birth, but sixty years of British life has taught me to be happy in this green and pleasant land. The hijab was an Arab thing. Not my thing. My traditional shalwar kameez was conservative enough. I wear my head-scarf around my neck. I put it on my head when I enter a mosque or another house of worship. This mother told me that she didn't want me teaching her child any more. That the school and I were too secular. She had heard of an Islamic school nearby and that is where her child would go. She was fed up with people looking at her with hate because she had chosen her faith. She was angry that the school wasn't putting faith first, like she did at home. If they want us to be the enemy, she said, then she would gladly become the enemy and, in her faith, she would find strength to endure their hate.

I was saddened. My whole life, my heart has been turned East and now I'm not Muslim enough? I walked away realising that Britain, my home, had changed. When my grand-daughter was born that year I bought her an England football shirt. My son was surprised. He didn't have much time for football being the cricket fanatic he is and I certainly didn't have a clue about the game. But it was important. We should show this country that we are British also. That our faith is important, but so is our passport. I do not want my grandchildren to live in fear of what is outside their front door. My son laughed and neatly folded the shirt away. I saw some of the former pupils from my school become older and more aloof. I switched the television news back on. It seemed every sentence began with the word 'Muslims'.

My heart has a shadow. My heart carries with it a dark secret. I do not pray with my heart turned East in joy like I once did. I pray with sadness in my heart that this is our coun-

try, that we are divided and frightened. I cannot believe what is happening in the streets that surround my school. People are frightened, and sometimes young white men drive by and scream 'ISIL bitches' at the mothers playing with their kids. In turn, this community becomes more inward. People become more conservative and religious, hoping faith will isolate them from hate. But faith is supposed to bring love, not hate.

My heart remains forever East, but the joy has gone. I hope my grandchildren have their hearts turned East but their minds turned West and that they live in joy.

33

A Mother's Death

Malek froze as Rubati finished speaking. The small crowd clapped and moved away. Rubati took a bow, delighted with the attention. She looked at Malek. The story was familiar to him, but not in a vague way like the others. This was intimate, personal. This was about his own mother. Except his mother was in Pakistan on holiday. If she had passed away, he would have heard.

His phone rang. The voice on the other line spoke in Urdu. His father told him that his mother had passed away a few hours ago. She was seventy-nine years old. Her death had been quiet and dignified, much like her life.

Before Malek could digest the news, Rubati spoke, and she revelled in the hold she had over Malek and Neeka. 'Oh, what shall we do with this mother of yours? Shall I make the decision like I did with your Swedish bitch and stupid comedian? Shall I make the decision? Or shall we chat? I miss our little talks dear Malek, I really do. You were such a dear, with your wide-eyed disbelief at what was happening. And the

282

fight against your destiny! Lord! I have never seen another man fight so hard and choose that whore and this filthy city over Babylon and my chamber. Oh, what shall we do? It seems the choice is obvious: come with me Malek, and guarantee your mother eternal bliss in the kingdom of heaven, or stay here and condemn your own mother to hell.'

'*Haramzadeh*,' Neeka muttered. She launched herself at Rubati, grabbing her arm and twisting it behind her back. She pushed it up and Rubati screamed in agony as Neeka wrapped her other arm round Rubati's neck. 'I am so sick of this. *Khaarkosteh!* Who are you?'

'I am a member of The Order of the Gatherers of Truths, I am an angel, I am a lady of the gods, and, as far as you are concerned, I am the Devil's representative on earth. Who are you? An ageing singleton with bad shoes.'

Neeka squeezed her neck tighter. 'You are a myth, a figment of Malek's overactive imagination. I always told him he needed to stop daydreaming. You are nothing. You are a satanic whore sent to bring out the beast in Malek, and a pain in my ass.' She snatched the Kindle and threw it on the ground.

The two women faced each other on the south bank of the river Thames.

Rubati spoke first. 'You will regret that.'

'I highly doubt it, because I know how to get rid of you.'

The screen of the Kindle glowed dimly and you could just make out the title of the book, which was placed squarely in the middle.

BABYLONIAN TALES OF DEATH, HEAVEN AND HELL

Neeka took aim, raised her leg, looked at Rubati. Rubati

screamed, 'Nooooooooooo!' as Neeka's spiked heel smashed into the middle of the Kindle.

Neeka hit it with such power that the heel went right through it. As it did, Rubati whirled around, spinning faster and faster as she disappeared inside the smashed e-reader.

Neeka looked down at the Kindle. She looked up at Malek. '*Kisofat*, these are vintage Gucci. Bad shoes, my ass.'

34
Vulliamy's Dolphin

Malek and Neeka stood by the Thames, framed in the light of the lamp post above them, holding each other close. The dolphins wrapped around the post had been the only witnesses to the last few moments.

Everyone else had gone about their business, completely unaware of what had just happened. It was as if Rubati was able to make them visible to the crowds, and then invisible, on a whim.

Malek let Neeka go for a second and picked up the smashed Kindle from the ground. It was intact save for a very neat hole all the way through the middle of the screen.

'Neeka. Don't ever get angry with me.'

'I won't, but you might want to keep your Kindle in a tougher case.'

'How did you know how to do that? To break the Kindle and so break the spell?'

'Do you know what a Djinn is?'

'As in the drink? I could do with a G and T.'

'No. God, you're an idiot. As I have said before. Thank God you're pretty because you ain't smart. No, not the drink. A Djinn is a creature made from fire who inhabits a parallel world to ours. Some are good and some are bad. The Djinn come from an old Islamic folk tale that says they inhabited the earth before humans, but then they became infidels so God sent angels to kill them. But not all of them died, and they live amongst us, some in human form. You can only kill them through true faith in Islam. Rubati started off by trying to help you understand and love God. But really, she wanted to destroy your spirit and have you all to herself, and she ran amok. I guess that is what deceitful devils do. She had to die. But how? Remember the other night when I said we should destroy the Kindle? Well, I thought about it in the morning and I nearly took it off you to smash it, but then I didn't. I didn't understand then what I do now. Tonight I realised what gave her life was the book on the Kindle and your belief in the book on the Kindle. Destroying the Kindle would destroy her. Break your belief in the book, and she dies, and you stop being delusional. You needed to see the Kindle break. The vintage Gucci through the screen was just a flair of my own.'

'Qareen.'

'I beg your pardon?'

'Qareen. The Qareen are a type of Djinn. They accompany every human being. Basically, they're like your evil twin, pushing you to do bad shit. Rubati was my Qareen, stopping me from seeing the love that was right in front of me. The love that was you. By the time we hooked up, she got desperate and tried her hardest to make my delusion permanent, and make me believe that I could rule in ancient Babylon with her and not live in peace with you.'

'How do you know that?'

'It was in the book.'

Neeka thought for a moment. 'London is better than ancient Babylon anyway. Can we go home now?'

'There is something I have to do.'

He aimed high and far. As it left his hand it spun through the air, arcing upwards, with its busted screen fading into the night. They never heard the sound of it hitting the river above the noise of London.

'Malek, what the hell? We call that pollution, don't you know? How many environmental stories have we done together? Do you ever, ever learn?'

'Shit, sorry.'

'Typical TV correspondent, always going for the big finish. Anyway, I am cold. Can we go home please?'

'Not before we stop by a bookstore. I seem to be without anything to read on the tube home.'

His phone blinked. It was a message from his mother. 'Hello, darling son. Love you. Speak soon. Back next week.'

'It's from Mum. She's not dead.'

'Of course she isn't. So far as I can figure out, the people whose stories you read have passed away. When she read to you, she figured she had your mind and that you would believe anything she said. Using your mother is such a low thing to do. It's almost Iranian. I kind of admire it in a way. What she didn't reckon on were my vintage Guccis. I do have a question though. Why Babylon? We only ever went for a few day trips there in all our time in Iraq.'

'It's the birthplace of civilisation. We humans are

supposed to be better than we are. Ancient Babylon is an example of how ingenious we can be, and how evil. I think Babylon just sums up how mad this world is.'

'Even now, even after everything, you remain full of shit.'

35

Folie à Deux

A common grandiose delusional disorder is an impossibility. For two people to share the exact same delusion and react to it in the same way just cannot happen, but cases of shared, rather than common, delusion have been recorded. The condition has rather a quaint name, actually. Folie à deux. The madness of two. The disorder, however, is far from quaint. There is normally one dominant psychotic individual who shares the delusion with another who buys into it. When visions occur, there has never been a recorded case where both sufferers have seen the same vision. Hallucinations are common in shared psychotic disorders but it is always the dominant psychotic who hallucinates and it is never shared. Women with high IQs tend to be the dominant psychotic and lead the charge when sharing the problem. Normally, separation of the two leads to successful treatment of the disorder.

Malek was self-diagnosing again. This time, Neeka was helping him.

'You have a high IQ, Neeka. See, you are mad.'

'Fuck off.'

'I'm serious. What they describe, we don't have. This is all about sharing a scenario, like perceived persecution. They don't see devils together.'

The treatment for shared delusional disorder is separation. This wasn't going to work for Neeka and Malek. They vowed never to be separated again.

They had also made a few more decisions.

No more therapy. Dr Khan would be disappointed, but her treatment was to help Malek manage his delusion. Now they would both manage it together. Whatever this madness was, it couldn't be explained or treated. It was madness as a gift. For some reason, they had been chosen to receive this gift. It had bonded them closer than love could. It came with a sense of belief in each other. They were to act as mirrors to one another. If the madness ever got too much they would reflect sanity back at each other. This much they promised. Outside the flat, London began to stir into its morning routine.

'Do you believe in ghosts?' Malek was staring out of the window as he spoke.

'I am Iranian. I told you about the Djinn, didn't I? After last night there isn't a single thing I don't believe in, from the Loch Ness monster to the Devil from below. It's all true, if you ask me. Also, I'm cancelling our *Guardian* subscription. From now on we are getting *Occult* monthly magazine. They report the truth. Look.'

Neeka turned the laptop towards Malek. The headline read: 'The lost gospels. What is the truth of Jesus?'

'We said we'd support each other. Not encourage each

other to go after every loony theory out there and drive ourselves bat-shit. Although maybe I could persuade Al Jazeera English to give me the paranormal correspondent's job. "This is Malek Khalil live from hell, where the Devil faces a funding crisis. Devil?" "Yes, Malek. We can't cope with the huge numbers of people we got down here. We need more money. Our supplies of torture equipment are running dangerously low. The international community must step up.'"

'Why does the Devil have an American accent?'

'Why wouldn't he? America is *shaytaan-e-borzog*, the great Satan. Ayatollah Khomeini said so, remember.'

'I've changed my mind. You really do need help.'

'I just need you.' With that he kissed her.

'Malek! Stop it, you'll break my laptop!'

Later, they both lay exhausted in each other's arms, in a huddle of discarded clothes.

Malek reached over and picked up a book. 'We should probably both seek some help.'

'What kind of help? No one is going to believe us, ever. And if they did, what kind of treatment would they offer. Dr Khan was stumped, remember. Some people bond over their children, others over matching leisure wear. We have your evil twin Rubati.'

'The Gulistan of Sa'adi.'

'I'm sorry?'

'A book of poetry from the 1200s. I picked up a beautiful copy from a place in Chelsea. I've been reading it. It's going to help us.'

'How are long-dead Persian poets going to help us?'

'Let me read you something from it. Listen: "Tie thy

heart to the heart charmer thou possessest and shut thy eye to all the rest of the world.'"

'Malek. Are you asking me what I think you're asking me?'

'Yes. I don't have a ring, but I do have the words of Sa'adi. Will you marry me?'

36

'Dheeme, Dheeme'

Preparations for the wedding were under way in the garden of a friend's house in Istanbul that overlooked the Bosphorus. It was going to be a smallish occasion with see-through plastic chairs arranged in a circle around a silk-covered gazebo. A November wedding in Istanbul. It was cold, but not freezing. Just crisp enough, just bright enough. The ceremony was a suitably mixed affair, with an imam and a priest in attendance. The priest was Justin's father, who was a guest, and not officiating in any way.

The imam was an old family friend of Malek's from Damascus who had settled in London. The food was Pakistani. The setting for the wedding was to be Persian, with a Sofreh Aghd, a wedding-spread reflective of the couple's background. The Sofreh Aghd for the soon-to-be Shirazi-Khalils contained traditional items such as bread and walnuts, but also the Gulistan of Saa'di book, the battered translation of the Koran given to Malek by his father, and, in a moment of whimsy, Malek and Neeka had included a small

Velcro patch with the word 'Press' on it, which they had ripped from Neeka's flak jacket.

The ceremony was to follow British civil law, with a few changes. The first part would be read by the imam, which covered the legal part of the marriage. He would then join the couple for the giving and receiving of rings and perform the rest of the ceremony as the registrar would normally do. There would then be some poetry readings from their families, and a prayer in Farsi from an imam who was a friend of the Shirazis from Tehran. Once the religion was out of the way, the imams would sit down and the bar would open.

They had ordered wine from Lebanon and Turkey, as a homage to their travels. Malek couldn't think who had first told him about Turkish wine. If he had thought hard about it he might have remembered that she had been a project manager of sorts in London who had worked in Istanbul, and who had died nearby, and whose memory was honoured in the necklace he had given Neeka.

But by now, try to recall them as he might, the stories in the book had faded from his memory.

The desserts were all Iranian. It was the first Muslim–British–American–Pakistani–Iranian wedding either of them had attended. In typical producer style, Neeka had spent weeks going back and forth between the parents. She had probably spent more time on shuttle diplomacy than both the Israeli and Palestinian negotiators had spent in talks in recent years. Neither her parents nor Malek's really cared about the religious part of the ceremony. So long as God was invoked then that was settled. The food, however, was the real issue. Both the Shirazis and the Khalils wanted a traditional feast from their home nation and neither wanted to back down.

Iranians and Pakistanis can get a bit fundamentalist about cuisine.

Neeka, however, was nothing if not a skilled operator. She talked both sets of parents into accepting a ceremony that would bring the best of each culture together. Her husband-to-be was flabbergasted and very proud of his soon-to-be-wife and her wily and charming ways.

That just left the wedding outfits. That was something Neeka refused to negotiate on. A traditional dress from Tehran for Neeka and, for Malek, a long, traditional Pakistani frock coat, both with matching embroidery. They'd travelled to Lahore and Tehran for the outfits specially. The guests were flying in from all four corners of the world, which was one of the reasons for choosing the bridge between Asia and Europe as the venue of the wedding, but there was also one other reason.

They were planning to buy a small place on the beach in Bodrum where their idea was to retire, after a fashion. They'd still hit the road on occasions as a team but not as often and certainly not to the kind of places they'd visited in the past. Neeka and Malek both wanted to stand still for a while and maybe do some writing or whatever it was that journalists did for kicks. To be fair, that was probably just more journalism. Old dog, new tricks and all that.

Malek's mother had been wary about visiting Istanbul, as had Neeka's mother. Turkey had seen protests in recent weeks and Syria's war had spilled over into the border areas. But Istanbul endured as Istanbul does and the mothers had bonded over their fear and become firm friends. They'd even spent a day in the grand bazaar haggling over the prices of cushions. The fathers had spent their days exploring the museums of the city debating the finer points of religion and politics. All told, everyone was getting on pretty well. Muslim cultural tradition dictated that the bride and groom should not see each other for a week before the wedding. They had taken turns in escorting the parents around the city, while studiously avoiding each other. Malek had taken the mothers to various attractions. They'd seen the Prophet Mohammed's shoes. About a size eight guessed Malek. Mrs Shirazi disagreed. She said they were a forty. Mrs Khalil chimed in with a guess of seven-and-a-half. No agreement was reached. But all of that didn't matter any more.

On the day of the wedding everyone got up early. The guests started to arrive. Wine was served. Qawwali music played in the background. They'd chosen a gorgeous Bollywood ballad for Neeka as she walked through the garden to where Malek waited for her: the song 'Dheeme, Dheeme', from the film *Zubeidaa*, with lyrics that spoke of softly-sung love. Malek stood inside the gazebo, watching as Neeka floated towards him. The bridesmaids were noticed by both the fathers, and the mothers noticed the fathers noticing. Ribs were poked. For Malek though it was all about Neeka. The song made her look even more resplendent and there was a smile on her face that he hadn't seen in a while. Her blue eyes sparkled with a scintillating expression. The wedding ceremony began with the imam explaining what was about to occur.

By the time Malek kissed the bride there wasn't a dry eye in the house. Apart from two pairs that watched from the outer rim of the circle. Neither belonged to an invited guest.

Postlude

The Devil sat with Gabriel. Both observed the wedding in quiet contemplation and stared as love was bonded into companionship.

It was Lucifer who sighed softly and said, 'Our wager is concluded. Malek has regained his soul and my angel has failed in her mission to capture it. Hell will not come for him when it is time. We had him for a while there in Babylon and beyond. But his faith in God was never shaken. Although I have to say, dear Gabriel, he still doesn't love God, he just believes.'

'Nowadays, I'll take belief if it means we win. The wager has indeed been concluded. Perhaps now would be a good time to settle accounts?' replied Gabriel.

'I wonder if our little experiment cannot be extended,' said Lucifer. 'Perhaps, Gabriel, we can keep competing. After all, in the eyes of God, they are bound in holy matrimony. I propose double or nothing. If by revealing a little of our powers, we can increase belief or deny belief in God, then will we have two souls as the prize? Two souls who are now joined as one?'

'Well, to be clear, Lucifer, the bet is as follows. You drive both souls mad and to the brink of death. When there is a firm denial of God, you have won. If they survive with faith in God intact, I win. In fact, I will throw in Justin as well. Make it three souls.'

'The terms are acceptable, Gabriel. What about a time-line? Let's make it final without the chance to extend. How about we inform Death that he can collect on his prize a year from now?'

Gabriel thought for a moment. 'A year seems reasonable. If they deny God, then let Azrael, Malak Al Mawt, come in the form of a terrifying person. If they love God, then let him come in the form of a beautiful person.'

'You and that love for God. It must get so boring being that smug.'

'Only God can decide whether it's heaven or hell.'

'God doesn't decide who goes to heaven or hell. We have a say also. And they say I am the Devil. Gabriel, you love to test people's faith, don't you?'

'And you, my dear boy, love to destroy faith.'

'I know, but these cupcakes are so delicious and you cannot get them in hell. Sport with you is my only chance to indulge. A jumbo box for this new bet?'

Gabriel ran his hand over the box. The logo on it said 'Heavenly Cupcakes'. He smiled. 'The things angels and demons do for cupcakes.' He opened the box and offered it to Lucifer. 'I presume you want the Devil's Food cupcake?'

'You know me so well. Thank you. Oh, and by the way, Gabriel. We have a surprise for you this November.'

'What now, Lucifer?'

'The election next week. Donald Trump. He wins. Forty-fifth president of the United States. You're welcome.'

Gabriel shuddered. 'I guess Malek, Neeka and Justin aren't retiring after all. Well, at least not for a year, until death comes for them all.'

Before you go

The book you are holding in your hand is the result of my dream to be an author. I hope you enjoyed reading it as much as I enjoyed writing it. As you suspected, it takes weeks, months or years to write a book. It exists today through dedication, passion and love. Reviews help persuade readers to give this book a shot. You are helping the community discover and support new writing. It will take *less than a minute* and can be *just a line* to say what you liked or didn't. Please leave me a review wherever you bought this book from. A big thank you.

Imran Khan

About the Author

Having kickstarted his career in the heady world of 1990s independent magazine publishing with work on *Dazed and Confused*, and launching seminal style title *2nd Generation*, Imran Khan jumped into the mainstream with BBC London, hosting radio shows on popular culture, arts and news as the millennium approached. In 2001 he produced a series of short documentaries for *BBC Newsnight*. His work was noticed in the aftermath of the September 11th attacks and Channel 4 commissioned the award-winning film *The Hidden Jihad*, which he wrote and presented. Imran subsequently moved full-time into TV news, working as a BBC producer and correspondent reporting from Lebanon, London and Qatar, with freelance stints in Afghanistan and Iraq.

He became a correspondent for Al Jazeera English in 2005 and is known for his extensive reporting from Pakistan, Iran, Iraq, Israel, Palestine and Libya, Ukraine, as well as covering the Arab Spring and the conflict in Syria. He continues to work as a correspondent for Al Jazeera English, dividing his time between the Middle East, South Asia and London.

instagram.com/imranism

Acknowledgments

No one writes a book in isolation. Well, that's not strictly true. You write in isolation but you put a book together with the help of others. To that end, there are a few people I want to thank.

To Alistair Crighton and Thalia Suzuma for initial advice and encouragement. To Azi Najafi, Nick Morley and Nadene Ghouri for initial thoughts. To Debi Alper and Mary Chesshyre for their clarity of thought and notes. To Stephanie L. Bretherton and Breakthrough for believing in this book. Honourable mentions for helping inspire and giving advice go out, in no particular order, to Inaya Khan, Eena Khan, Maz Zaman, Carlos Van Meek, Serene Qaddumi, Sarah Mroueh, Uzair, Mohammed, Bhav Panchal, Rima Davoudi, Bianca Brigitte Bonomi, Dana Al Fardan, Rina Saleh, Sam Shaaban, Carina Studholme, Damien Lay, Alex Gat, Dorothy Parvaz, Megan McDonald, Rebecca Ritters, Ayeh Naraghi, Dima Shaibani, Brent McNair, Vittoria Federici, Sofia Barbarani, Sarita Khajuria, Rosie Garthwaite, Jane Dutton, Hoda Abdel Hamid, Stefanie Dekker, Arwa Damon, Jamil Bassil, Raed Khattar, Saad Abedine, Charlotte Lysa, Justin Okines, Mimi Daher, Rania Zabaneh, Arsalan BD, Sia BD, Farhana Mir, Claire Brownsell, Soraya Lennie, Adrian Finighan, Phill Jupitus and Fatemeh Shams. To the OGs, Alex Studholme, Andrew Leber, Dane Wisher, Fraus Masri, James Brownsell, Matt

Wolfgram, Rahul Radhakrishnan, Sam Bollier, Sam Hasler, Taylor Bossung for the distractions. Thanks to Patrick Kincaid and Ivy Ngeow.

To the Breakthrough Book collective for more support, to the generosity of Dick Davies for allowing me to use an excerpt of a beautifully translated Persian poem from his book *Faces of Love*. You should read his book. It's amazing. To anyone who ever spent any time on the road with me in a professional capacity. To my Al Jazeera managers, editors and co-workers past and present. To every person I ever met on my travels. Each one of you has left a mark. Some good, some bad. To my friends and colleagues who have fallen in the line of journalistic duty, especially Yasser Faisal Al Joumaili. None of you will be forgotten. To everyone who reports from the front lines and streets of the world. Stay safe and keep your faith, whatever that may be. To my daughters Mia and Ava. I love you. To my parents, Suraya and Allah-dad, and my brother and sister, Semera and If, thanks for always being there.

Printed in Great Britain
by Amazon

28620658R00179